SONG OF THE BONES

A CHANTALENE MYSTERY

ALSO BY
MARCIA PRESTON

THE SPIDERLING

THE WIND COMES SWEEPING

TRUDY'S PROMISE

THE PIANO MAN

THE BUTTERFLY HOUSE

SONG OF THE BONES

PERHAPS SHE'LL DIE

SONG OF THE BONES

A CHANTALENE MYSTERY

MARY HIGGINS CLARK AWARD WINNER

MARCIA PRESTON

ROGUE RIVER

ROGUE RIVER

An Imprint of Roan & Weatherford Publishing Associates, LLC
Bentonville, Arkansas
www.roanweatherford.com

Copyright © 2023 by Marcia Preston

We are a strong supporter of copyright. Copyright represents creativity, diversity, and free speech, and provides the very foundation from which culture is built. We appreciate you buying the authorized edition of this book and for complying with applicable copyright laws by not reproducing, scanning, or distributing any part of it in any form without permission. Thank you for supporting our writers and allowing us to continue publishing their books.

Library of Congress Cataloging-in-Publication Data
Names: Preston, Marcia, author.
Title: Song of the Bones/Marcia Preston | Chantalene #2
Description: Second Edition. | Bentonville: Rogue River, 2023.
Identifiers: ISBN: 978-1-63373-751-8 (hardcover) |
ISBN: 978-1-63373-752-5 (trade paperback) | ISBN: 978-1-63373-753-2 (eBook)
Subjects: | BISAC: FICTION/Mystery & Detective/Women Sleuths | FICTION/Women
FICTION/Mystery & Detective/Traditional | FICTION/Thrillers/Crime

Rogue River trade paperback edition June, 2023

Cover & Interior Design by Casey W. Cowan
Editing by Anthony Wood & Amy Cowan

This book is a work of fiction. Any references to historical events, real people, or real places are used fictitiously. Other names, characters, places, and events are products of the author's imagination, and any resemblance to actual events or places or person, living or dead, is entirely coincidental.

ACKNOWLEDGMENTS

I AM INDEBTED to Oghma Creative Media for republishing this book and to my Oklahoma roots for a spooky upbringing.

ONE

LIDDY CAME TO him in the night, appearing at the foot of his bed, just as before. The old man didn't believe in ghosts or gauzy apparitions, but he did believe in the spirit world. Liddy wasn't a being of light or some wind-carved shape in the clouds. She was real. He curved his hand around her arm—not to make her stay, but to remember the feel of her, young and firm, her skin cool as cistern water.

It was spring, and the smell of wild honeysuckle floated through the open window. Or maybe that was Liddy's scent now. She always had smelled like flowers. But beneath the floral aroma, he scented trouble.

The weight of her gaze had awakened him, and he wondered how long she'd been there, watching him sleep. She retreated to the foot of his bed without speaking. He sat up in the bed facing her, and waited. Shadows veiled her eyes, but her skin glowed white as candle flame. He could feel her anger like a dark wing-beat in the room. And still she said nothing.

So he began to talk, his voice a low sing-song in the darkness, the way he used to tell her stories as they lay quietly apart before sleep. He had told her stories about the war, and about *Apokni,* the grandmother who raised him. Stories more real to him than yesterday. But Liddy had heard them all before. This time, because he knew how Liddy loved wild things, he told her about the foxes.

THE FIRST TIME he'd heard the sharp, strangled yap, it woke him from his shallow sleep. He'd lain awake a long time in the darkness, listening, his heart thudding slowly in its brittle cage. *What the hell was that?* The noise sounded more like a startled water-bird than a canine.

The next day as he walked at the edge of the pasture, he found scat loaded with blackberry seeds. He poked it with his walking stick and bent closer. Could be coyote, but it didn't look quite the same. He thought of the strange noise in the night. Something new had come to live on the creek.

The old man waited.

It was several days before he met the fox by accident, just after sundown on the path coming back from the pond. It turned to stare at him, haunches facing forward on the path, the lithe body curved back like a horseshoe so that it looked at him over the lowered brush of its tail. The nocturnal eyes glowed hollow in the fading light, neither startled nor afraid. Like Liddy's eyes.

He stood still, and for a moment they watched each other. Perhaps the fox coveted the three small perch that hung from his stringer. Finally it turned and melted into the tall grass with scarcely a rustle.

The next morning he saw the fox in the abandoned orchard north of the house. He watched it through the bent blinds of his bedroom window. It was a gray fox, the old man decided, though a vivid, red-fox color spilled between the peaked ears and streaked along the backbone to the black tip of its brushy tail. He had a horse that reddish color once, like chestnut but with more fire.

Then there were two of them. The second was smaller, a she-fox. Foxes were rare here. Maybe they'd been forced from their usual territory, to live here in isolation. That night he hid motionless in the brush and tracked them with his ears. In the morning he followed them to a den carved beneath a shale outcropping along the creek bank.

There are kits, Liddy, three of them. With thin tails and oversized, comical ears. Come back at first light, and I'll show you.

That's when Liddy spoke to him, her voice hollow in the darkness.

Silly old man. I didn't come back to look at foxes.

What did you come for, then?

She didn't answer. The dark wings beat a wind in the room.

Why did you come? I can't undo what's been done.

He wanted to make her say it but she wouldn't. She stood there in silence. As always, it was a test of wills between them.

He sat cross-legged in the bed, waiting for her to speak or go away. He would not beg. His knees grew stiff and his feet full of needles. Slowly his eyelids began to droop, and his mind wandered. When he caught himself and jerked his eyes open, she was gone.

The old man's chest filled with sadness.

Liddy girl, there are other things in this world besides money.

Her answer was a live thing in the darkness. *Silly old man. I didn't come back for the money.*

That was the first sign. He didn't sleep again.

AT DAYLIGHT THE old man walked the path to the pond, his fishing pole balanced on his shoulder, stringer hanging from a rear pocket. He didn't feel well. The sickness hadn't affected his body, still strong from chopping wood and other daily chores. This weakness invaded his spirit, like a warning.

And now this. At his feet lay the carcass of a baby fox.

He laid the pole in the grass and squatted down to examine it. It was the smallest fox, the runt of the litter. He saw no marks on it, no apparent reason for its death. Sometimes the smallest of a wild litter didn't survive because it couldn't compete for food. But this little fox didn't look starved. It looked perfectly healthy.

The old man grasped one paw in his fingers and carefully turned the fox over. The body was stiff and released a swarm of flies, their bodies iridescent in the sunlight. Brown ants foamed around the closed eyes. He found no bullet hole, no teeth marks, no blood. Nothing of this earth that would have caused the animal's death. The darkness that had inhabited him for days deepened into sorrow.

This was the second sign.

Apokni believed that an unexpected death, especially of something young, required penance. He knew what he must do. Removing the stringer from his pocket, he hooked the end meant for fish onto the tail of the little fox and dragged it home.

At dusk he laid the wood for his fire on a patch of bare ground near the old cistern in front of the cabin. At the center he placed cottonwood logs from a deadfall by the creek. Green wood made too much smoke. He covered the logs with smaller limbs, keeping the brush pile low.

With his Bowie knife, the old man cut four small branches the same length, each with a *Y* at one end. He sharpened the other ends into a point and rammed them upright through the brush in the shape of a rectangle. He placed four straight sticks in the vees of these supports to make a base for the platform. Smaller sticks placed side by side across the base formed its bed. He crouched beside the brush pile and examined his work.

When he was satisfied, he put on his gloves and laid the carcass of the small fox on the platform, careful not to disturb the balance. From the cabin, he retrieved an article of Liddy's clothing, something white she'd worn next to her skin, and from the shed he brought a garden rake and a can of gasoline. He doused the wood with gasoline and stood well back to strike his match and toss it onto the pyre.

The first match fell short and died in the dirt. The second hit its mark. Flames exploded in a whispered rush, throwing heat against his face.

It was fully dark now. He watched the smallest twigs at the edge of the fire ignite and shrivel. Flames snaked up to the larger branches. The fire breathed in and expanded, paling as its heat grew more intense. Tongues the color of sunlight licked the brushy tail of the fox.

Deep within the old man's chest, from a memory older than his years, arose the ancient chant of his grandmother. The night drew in around him and the moon rose. The old man stood beside the fire, singing, his voice nasal and clear.

He sang and his eyes saw a different fire, one they had seen before the cells of memory developed in his infant brain, part of his origin story. A coarse blanket wrapped him snugly on a cradle board; shadows flickered against his face as his mother and grandmother tended the fire. He heard his mother's wail. Saw the tiny swaddled form of his twin above the flames, divided in the womb but forever joined.

The old man's voice turned to gravel and faded away. He sat on the ground then and took a small seed pod from a tiny cloth bag in his pocket. He chewed the button and watched the largest of the logs turn pewter at the edges and glow red-orange within. He thought of the mother who was lost to him, first her mind, then her body. He had no memory of her face, only the long, dark hair.

He saw the shack on the reservation where he and his grandmother lived, her grave where he'd hidden pouches of silver coins stolen from his menial job where he was treated badly. Money so his grandmother would be wealthy in the spirit world. Pouch after pouch of it, until someone stole it from her.

The old man floated. He sang again, a song of loss beneath the moon.

Other memories came out of sequence, disorderly as life itself. He remembered Naomi, her waterfall hair and earthy smell, the only woman besides *Apokni* he'd ever loved. He saw the fire in her eyes the day she left him. Took her young daughter and left. Saw his fingers crushing the neck of Naomi's beloved white bird before that, and before that, his burning rage when he discovered she'd been with someone else.

Saw the strange, knowing eyes of the little girl when she turned to look at him as her mother took her away. And those same gold eyes a decade later, their innocence gone. Eyes that aroused his lust, haunted his nights, and now his old age. Liddy was his curse, his obsession. He sang again, his voice brittle as wasted passion.

By midnight the flames had died away. Nothing but ashes and bones remained of the platform and the kit fox. The cottonwood logs at the center of the fire collapsed and opened, brilliant red flowers edged in silver. They pulsed and breathed.

It was time.

He rose smoothly, his joints lubricated by the chewed weed. With the garden rake he spread the coals flat and smooth, forming a path. Then he tossed the rake aside and bent to fold up his pants legs, over and over until they reached his knees. His feet were bare, his knotted bones like pale, burled wood in the moonlight.

The old man straightened. He stood at one end of the glistening path and lifted his face to the stars. His head felt light, his spirit thirsty. He raised his arms and waited for the call. Then he stepped out onto the coals.

He walked with a measured step, without haste, looking straight ahead and not at his feet. He felt the lumps beneath his soles but not the pain. His chest expanded with hot air, swelling until he thought his bones would split open. Then he tipped his head back and opened his mouth.

He exhaled deeply and his spirit poured out, blooming umbrella-like above his body. He was brilliant and shining, alive like the coals but brighter, illuminating the dark all around. Beneath him, he watched his body close its eyes and keep its feet moving. The song of his grandmother rang in the air.

The vision came to him as a recent memory—a young woman riding a horse along the pasture ridge, a black-and-white dog ranging ahead, the trio outlined against the horizon. At first glimpse he had thought, *it's Liddy,* and it stopped his breath.

Everything about her was Liddy, the long thigh bones, the erect carriage—everything but the hair. This girl's hair was petroleum-black, and even from that distance he could tell it was curly. Liddy's was straight and tawny. He had wanted to see the girl's eyes, wondered if they were Liddy's, too.

Now he understood the vision, and the knowledge electrified him. *This was Liddy's alternate form, the shape she had taken to exact revenge.*

Then it was over. His spirit was sucked into his body like an inhaled draft of wind.

The old man stepped off the coals onto the cool earth. His knees trembled and thirst parched his throat.

In the cabin, he opened a cold beer and rubbed the soles of his feet with shortening. He seldom drank beer, but tonight he drank two.

Forewarned was forearmed. He had seen the black-haired girl before, knew where she lived alone in a small white farmhouse. There was no hurry. Hunting was in his blood. And a true hunter loves the hunt more than the kill.

TWO

"I DON'T BELIEVE in divorce," Thelma Patterson said. "I want him dead." Her knitting needles never missed a stitch in the intricate pattern of pastel yarn that draped her round lap.

Chantalene grinned at Thelma across the cluttered desktop. Had to admire a woman who knew what she wanted.

"I assume you mean *declared legally dead,*" Drew corrected, in lawyerly fashion. He had perched on the front edge of the desk, giving Chantalene a pleasant view of his Levied rear end. Thelma sat in the single chair reserved for clients in the tiny office Chantalene and Drew shared.

"Whatever." Thelma's brown eyes followed the movement of her needles. "Just so we get his name removed from the deed to my farm. If I hadn't been distraught after my father's death, I'd never have set it up as joint tenancy, anyway."

Thelma glanced up then, the busy hands relaxing for a moment. "Well, that's not true," she admitted, and sighed. Her gaze drifted past Drew and Chantalene and seemed to settle on some point in her memory. "I put both our names on the deed to bind Billy Ray to me. He was nine years younger, and I knew all along he married me for money. But I didn't care. I was twenty-nine and figured if I didn't marry Billy Ray, I'd be alone all my life. I was looking for security, same as he was. Just a different kind."

But neither of them got it. After three years of marriage, Billy Ray had disappeared without a trace—even without a trace of Thelma's money. Chantalene kept this thought to herself, because she wouldn't hurt Thelma's feelings for all the Egg McMuffins at McDonald's. Thelma was like a surrogate aunt, especially since Chantalene had no real aunts, only a great-grandmother in Arkansas that she'd met once when she was eight years old. In fact, Thelma had been her only real friend in Tetumka since she was orphaned at age twelve.

But Thelma also made a career of knowing everybody else's business—which usually didn't amount to much in the tiny burg of Tetumka. Chantalene figured turnabout was fair play, and she was delighted to be meddling in Thelma's failed romance. It alleviated the boredom of posting local farmers' tax returns on the computer, which constituted the bulk of Drew's law practice.

Thelma's fingers resumed their rhythmic pattern and her smile brightened again. "Imagine thinking I needed a husband in order to be happy." She winked at Chantalene. "That was back in the dark ages. Nowadays, we know better, don't we?"

"Damn straight," Chantalene said.

She caught Drew's slight blush at this exchange—and so did Thelma. Chantalene hadn't told Thelma the major issue that stood between herself and Drew. She didn't have to. Thelma knew. Just as Chantalene knew without Thelma's telling her that the legal issue was only part of the reason Thelma had hired them to find Billy Ray Patterson. For nearly thirty years, Thelma had wondered what happened to the younger man she'd married. And so did Chantalene.

"If you want us to pursue the search, I'll need more information about Billy Ray," Drew was saying. "We traced down all the Pattersons in Tulsa but couldn't find one who's related."

"I'm not surprised," Thelma said. "Who knows where his family really lived? He used to take off sometimes, and he *said* he went to Tulsa to see his sister. But he made excuses to keep me from going with him, and he wouldn't bring his sister to visit us. If I pressed too hard, he got angry, so I let it slide. For some reason, Billy Ray didn't want me to meet his family."

Thelma's head bobbed over the clacking needles. Chantalene imagined her smooth, rosy face as a thirty-year-old newlywed, trying hard to hang onto a doomed marriage.

"Maybe he was ashamed of them," Drew said.

"Maybe so. Or ashamed of me." Thelma lifted penciled eyebrows behind her glasses. "I know he hated his father, who ran off and left his mom with three kids when he was small, someplace in Texas. He told me he had a brother close to his age and an older sister. His mother left them alone a lot. I got the impression she was a drinker. He'd lost contact with her."

Thelma finished a row of stitches and deftly switched the blanket to the opposite side. She knitted for every newborn within a fifty mile radius of Tetumka. Chantalene wondered whose child would be the lucky recipient of the intricate, pastel afghan.

"Childhood memories seemed painful for Billy Ray, so I didn't push him to talk about it," Thelma said, inserting a bone needle and looping a strand of yarn over it. "Every time he left, he'd promise to be back in a few days, and he was. But I always worried that one day he wouldn't come back. And finally he didn't. After he'd been gone a couple of weeks, I knew I'd never see him again."

Her voice was matter-of-fact, but Chantalene sensed old pain behind the words. "Did you look for him then?"

"I drove to Tulsa and hunted up every Patterson I could find," Thelma said. "Tulsa wasn't so big back then, but I had the same luck you did. His sister had married and I didn't know her last name. All I knew was that he called her Sunny. I took a picture of Billy Ray to the Tulsa police and reported him missing, but I don't think they took it seriously. They never found anybody who'd seen him, or his pickup."

"Maybe you should consider hiring a private detective," Drew said. "I could find one for you out of Tulsa."

Thelma shook her head. "Don't like working with people I don't know."

Drew shrugged. "We managed to learn that the Social Security Administration has no record of taxes paid on Billy Ray's number since he's been gone, but no notice that he's deceased, either. Without something else to go on, I'm stumped."

"If he hasn't worked and paid taxes in twenty-eight years, he probably is dead, don't you think?" Chantalene asked.

"Not necessarily. He may be indigent, though if he is, he hasn't applied for benefits or that would show up on his government record. Or he might have an illegal source of income which he doesn't report."

That thought struck them silent for a moment.

"What do you know about Billy Ray's brother?" Drew asked.

Thelma shook her head. "Never met him either, but I think he's dead. Shortly after Billy Ray left, I got a call from the New Mexico State Police. They'd had a fatality on the highway out there, and both the car and driver burned to cinders. But the driver's wallet was somehow thrown clear, and they found my phone number scribbled in it. The officer asked me if I knew a Donnie Patterson with an address in Texas—I can't remember the town. It scared me because at first I thought he meant it was Billy Ray. When he read me the name and address again, I said I didn't know him. I was so flustered I couldn't think to ask questions. Later, I figured it must have been Billy Ray's brother, and that's why he had our phone number."

"Or maybe it was Billy Ray, with an alias," Chantalene said, her interest rising. "Would the New Mexico State Police keep a record of that address for this many years?"

"I doubt it," Drew said. "Especially if they found his family in Texas and closed the case."

Still, it wouldn't hurt to check. Chantalene made herself a note.

"I don't think the court will declare him legally dead without more information," Drew said to Thelma. "But if you're willing to give up knowing exactly what happened to Billy Ray, we could file a petition asking to remove his name from your property on the basis of desertion. I think the court would be sympathetic."

Thelma pursed her lips a moment, her fingers still working. "All right, let's do it. There's an oil company interested in leasing my land for exploration, and if I keep putting them off, I stand to lose a lot of money." Her eyes betrayed the joy of dispensing good gossip, even if she herself was the subject.

"Wow, that's good news," Drew said. "There hasn't been any oil activity around here since the late seventies." He smiled. "We can't let you miss a chance to become Tetumka's only wealthy dowager. We'll get the papers drawn up for your signature right away."

Thelma jabbed the points of her knitting needles into a ball of yarn and gently folded the blanket into her canvas bag. "Just give a holler when you're ready."

And that was literal, because Thelma was the town's postmaster and the post office was right next door.

Thelma glanced at the clock imbedded in a steer skull that hung on the office wall, one of Drew's estate-sale purchases. "I'd better get back to work." She carried her tote bag toward the door and Drew hopped off the desk and opened it for her.

"How's your wheat crop looking?" Thelma asked him.

"Not bad. We could use some rain."

"It's almost April, then you'll have more rain than you want."

Chantalene waved to Thelma and Drew closed the door. "Speaking of April," he said, "we've got three weeks to finish all these tax returns before the deadline."

"No sweat," Chantalene said, "unless you take on another last minute client like Grant Selby."

"You can't build a client list by turning people down."

She knew he'd felt sorry for Grant when the farmer came in last week with an egg crate full of crumpled receipts and panic on his whiskered face.

Drew pulled a yellow legal pad from his brief case and handed it to her. "I plowed through all his records last night and distilled it down to this. Would you have time to get it on the computer today?"

"Right after I contact the New Mexico State Police."

"Don't bother. I feel sure the court will let Thelma change the deeds without proving Billy Ray's death."

"Maybe, but then Thelma will never know why her husband deserted her."

Drew bunched his eyebrows. "You mean *you'll* never get to know. I'll write up the petition tonight and type it on the computer this weekend."

Chantalene sighed. "We need another desk in here. And a modem to connect with my computer at home...."

He waved away the idea. "Too much technology. And there's no room in here for another desk. When you're at home you're supposed to be studying for your classes, anyway, not typing taxes."

She made a face. "I'm a slave around here. All I do is process data."

"I never said the tax business was exciting."

"At least let me go to court with you when you present Thelma's petition."

"No problem."

"Stop saying that! It drives me nuts."

"No problem." He gave her a toothy smile and gathered folders from the desk to stash in his briefcase. "Missus Sherwood is supposed to come by and pick up their tax return today. Be sure to collect our fee."

"Where are *you* going?"

"I've got to pick up fence posts in El Rio. And get a haircut. Want me to bring you anything?"

She picked up the yellow pad with Drew's ballpoint scratchings indenting the pages. "Bring me some excitement. Nothing interesting ever happens around here." She huffed a breath that blew a corkscrew of black hair off her forehead.

Chantalene stood on the crumbled sidewalk in front of their office while Drew climbed into his red pickup and drove away. Half a century ago, in Tetumka's more prosperous history, their office had been a creamery. Her eyes scanned the other two establishments that now made up the main drag—the post office, and the general store. She wasn't given to sighing but she sighed now, awash in that left-behind feeling she always got when Drew went to town without her. If you could call El Rio a real town. It was the county seat, but it was still rural Oklahoma.

God, would she ever get to live somewhere *exciting*? She kicked a tickle-weed off the dusty curb and went back inside.

Gandalf the computer purred from the desk like a gray plastic cat. The afternoon had grown warm and so had the office. She pulled her hair up into a frizzy pony tail, fastened it with a rubber band and kicked off her shoes. Cross-legged on the chair, she tucked her flowered skirt over her knees and began typing, nagging at herself to sit up straight.

A few minutes later she was slumped over the keyboard, totally engrossed in Grant Selby's itemized deductions—the man had lost 150 chickens in a hailstorm last spring—didn't the stupid things know enough to run for shelter?—when the office door swung open.

Chantalene swiveled her chair away from the monitor and faced a tall, middle-aged stranger with an athletic build and electric-blue eyes. A stunningly good-looking man.

He removed a cowboy hat from salt-and-pepper hair. "Howdy, ma'am." A smile stretched beneath his bushy moustache and etched deep creases in his cheeks.

She returned the smile. *Did I say nothing interesting ever happens around here?* "May I help you?"

"I'll bet you can." His deep voice held a hint of mischief.

She saw his eyes take in her disheveled black hair, the red and black skirt that had slipped up to expose the points of her knees.

"Heard you been lookin' for me," he said. "I'm Billy Ray Patterson."

THREE

"YOU'RE JOKING," CHANTALENE said.

"No, I'm Billy Ray Patterson."

Chantalene stood up from the desk. It just seemed like the kind of thing she shouldn't hear sitting down. "Where the hell have you been?"

The stranger smiled, his tanned face crinkling around blue eyes. Sharp, observant eyes that contradicted his Texas drawl. "Not one to shy around the question, are you?"

"No," she said, "I'm not."

"Mind if I sit down first? The trucker I hitched with let me off on the main highway. These boots weren't designed for walkin' that far."

Indeed, they were the high-heeled kind cowboys wore to keep their feet in the stirrups. His plaid shirt looked wilted, and she was pretty sure the faded jeans would maintain their bow-legged shape even after he took them off. Chantalene gestured toward the lone chair, wondering ironically if its wooden seat retained the body heat of the stranger's abandoned wife, who'd sat there half an hour ago.

If, in fact, this *was* Billy Ray Patterson.

"Do you have identification?" she asked.

He dropped a tattered duffle bag behind the chair and pulled a leather wallet, curved as a crescent moon, from the hip pocket of his jeans. He extracted a driver's license and handed it to Chantalene before folding his lanky frame into the chair.

The license was from Wyoming. The name said Billy Ray Patterson, all right, and the photo looked like him, without the traces of gray in his hair. If the birth date was accurate, he'd be about fifty now, the right age for Billy Ray.

"This expired five years ago," she noted.

He nodded. "Yup. But I was the same fellow back then."

"Or it's a forgery," she said, frowning. "Phony drivers' licenses aren't hard to get."

"I wouldn't know."

Chantalene sat down. They looked at each other.

What should she do now? She'd never thought about what would happen if they actually found Thelma's husband. Why was Drew never around when she needed him?

The stranger hung his cowboy hat over a bent knee. "Is it Thelma who's lookin' for me? Is she all right?" His voice sounded gentle, concerned.

"She's fine," Chantalene said. "In fact she works right next door in the post office." What if Thelma popped in? The shock could give her a coronary.

The stranger's eyes followed her nervous glance toward the door and he stiffened in the chair. "Next door?"

"Yes. But I don't think it's a good idea to surprise her."

"No, ma'am," he said quickly. "I don't either."

They regarded each other a moment in silence. "You have me at a disadvantage," he said.

"I beg your pardon?"

"You know my name, but I don't know yours."

"Oh. Chantalene Morrell. If you don't know who I am, how did you know we'd been looking for you?"

He inclined his head toward the entrance. "Name on the door said Drew Sander. Somebody in Tulsa told me a fellow by that name was making inquiries. I assume you work for him."

"I work with him. So you *do* have relatives in Tulsa."

He nodded. "Yes, ma'am. My sister's family. I'm afraid they're not exactly talkative folks, though."

Apparently he wasn't either. Chantalene kept quiet and waited, a tactic she'd learned from Drew. Most people were uncomfortable with silence, he'd told her, and they'd start talking to fill up the empty spaces.

But the cowboy seemed accustomed to silence. He picked up his hat and began turning it round and round, shaping the brim. The blue eyes watched her with interest and patience.

Sure enough, in a moment, she felt uncomfortable. "What's your sister's name?" she asked. "We couldn't find her."

"Sunny Ray Diehl," he said.

He spelled the last name and she wrote it down, then fell back on good manners. "Would you like something to drink? I have hot tea in my Thermos."

"I'd appreciate something cold if you've got it. It's warmin' up out there."

She fished an orange soda from a small cooler Drew kept behind the desk. Yesterday's ice had melted but the water was still cold. She dried off the can with a paper towel and handed it to him.

The cowboy's hands were work-roughened and carried the small scars of an outdoor life. She'd always believed you could tell a lot from people's hands. He wore no rings.

He drained the can in one draft. "That hits the spot. I'm obliged." As if to prove it, he began to talk.

"I've been cowboying the last ten years or so. Wyoming and Montana. Lately out in the Great Basin." He smiled. "Man doesn't need a current license to drive cattle and horses."

Chantalene picked up her pen again. "You can supply names and addresses of your employers, then?"

"Yes, ma'am. But you'll have to promise me something. Ask them whatever you want about me, but don't get 'em in trouble with Uncle Sam. See, they paid me in cash or livestock, at my request, so it couldn't be traced. If they got nervous about it, I moved on to the next ranch."

"Who did you think was looking for you? Surely you weren't worried about Thelma finding you after all these years."

He narrowed his eyes at her, as if assessing. "There's no simple way to explain it," he said finally. "Let's just say that I've spent my last twenty years putting distance between me and my first thirty." He paused. "I did some pretty crummy things back when I was young, Miss. . . Morrell, is it? Like the mushroom?"

"Unfortunately." She'd never been happy about sharing her name with a fungus, even with the addition of a couple extra letters. Luckily, not many folks knew what a morel was.

"Crummy things like abandoning your wife?"

He nodded, examining the empty soft drink can in his hands. "Like abandoning Thelma. And worse. Spent some time in a California prison."

Her neck stiffened. "Which one?"

"San Juan, down south in the desert."

"What did you do to get there?" She warned herself not to push too hard lest he rise from the chair and disappear again before she could unravel the mystery—or figure out how to tell Thelma. But her curiosity was hard to quell.

The alleged Billy Ray looked at her with the beginning of a frown pinching his eyebrows. The smile was gone, and without it his face hardened. "Ask the warden. I'm not lookin' to relive all that. I've stayed out of trouble and haven't hurt anybody ever since I got out."

A shiver ran down Chantalene's back. She wondered whether he meant hurt anybody the way he'd hurt Thelma, or something more physical. She was still debating whether or not to ask, when she saw a shadow pass the window and stop at the office door.

Oh no. Was it Thelma?

She caught her breath as the door opened, then released it when she saw the grizzled face of Grant Selby.

The farmer hesitated before stepping inside. "Morning, Chantalene." He glanced at the stranger, nodding an apology. "Sorry to interrupt."

"Come on in, Grant," Chantalene said. Nobody in Tetumka called each other *Mr.* or *Mrs.* "You didn't find more tax receipts, did you?"

Selby hovered in the doorway, blushing. "No, ma'am. Just stopped by while I was in town to see if y'all needed anything else." A wispy white feather clung to the knee of his overalls. She wondered whether the chicken who donated it was dead or alive.

"No. As a matter of fact, I was just posting Drew's figures to the computer. We'll have a preliminary return ready to go over with you tomorrow."

Selby raised unruly eyebrows, elevating the bill of his ball cap at least an inch. "You guys work fast," he said. "Sure takes a load off my mind. I'll stop by tomorrow, then, and settle up."

He glanced at the stranger again, about to bid them good-bye, but instead he squinted and dropped his hand from the doorknob. "Well, I'll be a red-legged rooster. Billy Ray Patterson!" He fairly shouted the name.

The cowboy got to his feet. "Yes, sir." Confusion was plain on his face.

"Grant Selby," the farmer explained, sticking out a stubby hand in greeting. "Just down the road a piece from Thelma's place."

"Mister Selby! Sorry I didn't recognize you."

Grant brushed his hand across a six-inch beard. "It's been a long time, and I didn't have all this fur on my face back then. But I swear, you look just the same. Plus a few years, of course." Grant was grinning, clearly amused to see his erstwhile neighbor. "What brings you back to town?" Then, quickly, "Sorry. That's none of my business."

"It's all right," Patterson drawled, smiling now. "I came to see Thelma. Mend some fences, I guess."

Grant chuckled and bobbed his head so hard Chantalene thought his cap might fly off. "Hang onto your socks!" he said, and laughed again. Chantalene had never heard Grant Selby laugh this much in all the years she'd known him.

"I gotta go," Grant said. "Good to see you, Billy Ray. And good luck."

"Thanks."

Selby closed the door. The cowboy looked at her and shrugged.

"Okay, you *are* Billy Ray Patterson," she conceded, keeping her voice neutral. "You came back to see what you'd inherited, didn't you? You thought Thelma had died and we were looking for you because your name showed up on her estate."

He stared at his hands, the color in his weathered face deepening. "Yes, ma'am." Then he met her eyes. "But I'm glad I was wrong."

If he wasn't sincere, he was an awfully good liar. Either was possible. "I guess you'll be anxious to see her then."

He nodded. "Anxious is exactly the word. But not right now… I'd like to clean up some. I don't suppose you know of a place I could get a shower."

"We're fresh out of motels around here." She thought of taking him to her house, rejected that idea, and decided on Drew's. That's what Drew got for going off to El Rio without her.

"I have to wait for another client, but then I'll take you out to Drew Sander's house. He'll want to talk to you anyway, and you can clean up there. He should be back from El Rio in an hour or two."

"I'd be beholden."

"In the meantime, if Thelma walks in, you're on your own."

His smile was rueful. "Fair enough."

Chantalene turned away and began posting the Selby's tax figures onto the computer. Billy Ray was polite enough not to watch her work. From the corner of her eye she could see him thumbing through the only magazine in the office, an old issue of *Farmer Stockman*.

What had this mild-mannered cowboy done to wind up in San Juan prison?

She was so interested in him that she had to double check every figure she entered to avoid mistakes. She could hardly wait to see how Thelma would react. She pictured Thelma next door behind the service window that faced a small lobby cramped with post boxes and ancient posters of the missing and wanted. Thelma was jovial and compassionate by nature, but Chantalene also had seen flashes of her righteous indignation, and this guy had left her without so much as good-bye.

Half an hour later, Patsy Sherwood arrived to pick up their completed tax returns. Mrs. Sherwood cast a quizzical glance toward Billy Ray, whom Chantalene didn't introduce for fear Patsy would go straight next door and talk to Thelma. At first Chantalene wondered why Patsy didn't recognize him, then remembered the Sherwoods had moved here a mere ten or fifteen years ago. Billy Ray was long gone by then.

It was past four o'clock by the time Patsy left. Chantalene switched off the computer and gathered her Thermos and book bag. "I'm parked in the alley behind the building," she told her visitor, "right beside Thelma. Let me step out and be sure we won't bump into her before you come out."

"Good idea," he said.

When she was satisfied the coast was clear, she motioned Billy Ray out the back door and locked it. They hurried into the alley like two thieves and crawled into the silver Volvo. Drew called it her car, but in fact it was his, on sort of permanent loan. Chantalene took the back way out of town so that Thelma's curious eyes wouldn't spot her passenger.

On the four-mile drive through the countryside, Billy Ray scanned the fields and farms. "Monkey Jenks still live around here?"

"Yes, a few miles west. Do things look the way you remember?"

"Pretty much. But my directions are a mite fuzzy."

"Thelma's place is a mile east," she said, pointing, "and about two miles on north."

"That seems right." His voice sounded far away. "It's been a long time."

Before she was born. For a moment she managed to glimpse the flat wheat fields and hilly pasture land through the eyes of a stranger, but she blinked and the moment was lost. She'd lived here all her life, and the landscape was as familiar as her own bed. She tried to picture the high prairie country of Wyoming and Nevada. How did it smell, how did it feel? Someday she'd love to know.

She imagined what this uncombed cowboy must have looked like in his twenties. No wonder Thelma fell for him. The image made her smile. She liked thinking that Thelma had experienced at least one passionate love affair in her life.

He caught her glancing at him and smiled back as if he'd read her mind. She felt amazingly comfortable with him, considering his clouded history and the fact she'd met him only hours ago. Maybe it was a kinship of outsiders— two born wanderers among the rooted farm folks.

She centered her breathing and waited. In a moment she perceived a vivid outline of light around him, like the halo around a summer moon. The ability was a gift she'd inherited from her gypsy mother—that and prescient dreams, and raging black hair. Her breathing quickened. She'd never met anyone with such a variegated aura. Over the years, she'd learned two things about auras. The first was not to discuss her perception with the superstitious locals, who perceived any unusual talent as either wicked or insane. The second was to trust what her instincts told her about a person when she had such an experience.

The aura around Billy Ray Patterson was... confusing. She tried to sort through the tangle and identify the sensations. The closest she could come was agitation, an impression that contradicted the placid exterior of the man sitting beside her. That probably meant the fellow wasn't exactly what he seemed.

But then, who was?

A late March sun warmed the afternoon and scented it with spring. Chantalene parked in front of the two-story farmhouse Drew was gradually restoring to a grandeur it had never known.

"Nice house," Billy Ray said.

"You may remember Matt and Rose Sander, Drew's parents. Of course, the house was all white frame then, without the brick facing."

"The Sander place. Sure." He nodded as if remembering.

Drew wasn't back yet. They got out and Chantalene used her key to the front door. Billy Ray stood on the front porch holding his duffle until she invited him inside.

"Drew's bathroom is right down the hall," she said. "Clean towels in the cabinet above the commode."

"I'm much obliged."

He removed his hat and disappeared into the bathroom. When she heard him lock the door, whatever doubts she might have had about being alone with him melted away.

Chantalene pulled off her sandals and went into Drew's kitchen to survey the supper possibilities. Perhaps they could invite Thelma, too. Given the circumstances, both halves of the estranged couple might be more comfortable meeting again in the company of others.

In the refrigerator, she found a cut of raw red meat still in its grocery store wrapper. She poked it with a finger and decided it was pot roast. Yuk. But neither Drew nor Thelma were vegetarians like her, and she'd bet money the cowboy liked beef. She seasoned the roast with garlic and celery salt and put it in the oven.

She had started to peel potatoes when she heard Drew's pickup in the driveway. A little thrill passed over her, partly because she had big news for him, and mostly because his arrival always affected her that way. She dried her hands and went out to meet him, smiling.

Drew stepped down from the red truck and grinned, his eyes pleased and hopeful, blond hair tousled in an appealing way that suited his open face. Right now that face was a billboard. As soon as he'd spotted the Volvo in the driveway, he expected she would stay overnight. He wanted her to stay every night. She enjoyed those occasions as much as he did, but she wasn't willing to make it permanent. Not yet, anyway. That wouldn't be fair to either of them, given the wanderlust she'd never had an opportunity to satisfy. At thirty-five, Drew was nine years older and he'd spent nearly a decade in New York, while she'd rarely been out of southeastern Oklahoma. She assured him often that her restlessness was geographical, not sexual, but Drew viewed the distinction skeptically.

He left the pickup door open and kissed her hello. For one lovely moment she forgot all about the stranger in the bathroom, but she pulled back before it was too late.

"Hold on, we're not alone."

He frowned. "What?"

"I've brought someone you'll want to meet. He walked into the office right after you left today."

"He?"

"Um-hum. Billy Ray Patterson."

Drew's arms dropped from her waist and his eyes widened. "No shit?"

She giggled. "Apparently not. Grant Selby recognized him when he stopped by the office this afternoon."

"I'll be damned. I really didn't think the guy was still alive."

"Neither did Thelma. He says he's been cowboying out west, all over the Great Basin area."

Drew pushed the pickup door shut and they moved toward the house together, walking slowly and keeping their voices low. "Does Thelma know?"

"Not yet. He hitch-hiked from God-knows-where and wanted to clean up before he saw her. I didn't know what else to do so I brought him here. One of us better talk to Thelma quickly, though, before Grant or his wife does."

"Good point. I'll give her a call."

"I thought we could invite them both for dinner this evening. Thelma may want her attorney present—and I wouldn't miss this reunion for anything."

They shared a mischievous grin. "It could be a hum-dinger," he said.

Her smile faded. "Will this keep Thelma from purging his name from her property deeds?"

Drew shrugged. "He still deserted her. But he could definitely complicate things."

They entered the house just as the subject of their conversation came out of the bathroom. For a split second, all three of them stood speechless.

The man standing before them scarcely resembled the soiled drifter who'd appeared in the office a few hours ago. In a clean denim shirt and jeans, his damp hair combed into waves and his creased cheeks freshly shaven, the cowboy errant looked little short of stunning.

"Wow," Chantalene said. "You clean up just fine." She stood up straighter and brushed the hair from her forehead. Drew's posture stiffened as her smile widened.

Billy Ray didn't bother to blush. "I sure feel better." He stepped forward and stuck out his hand to Drew. His rolled-back sleeves revealed powerful, tanned forearms and a gold watch. "Billy Ray Patterson."

"This is Drew Sander," Chantalene said.

"Obviously," Drew said.

The smile never left his face, but Chantalene noticed his extra-firm handshake. *My god, he's actually jealous.* A mean little smile pulled at her mouth, and Drew caught the smirk.

"You have a nice home here," Billy Ray said. "I appreciate the hospitality."

"No problem."

For an awkward beat, they assessed one another and nobody said a thing.

"How about a beer?" Chantalene suggested. "You guys can talk things over while I finish peeling potatoes."

"I'll do that," Drew said, his eyes still on Billy Ray. "Why don't you drive over and talk to Thelma in person. See if she'll join us for dinner."

Hard-ass. But she smiled, too sweetly. "No problem."

Without retrieving her shoes, she walked out the front door, leaving the two of them faced off in the living room. Men. Only a thin veneer of civility separated even the best of them from wolves vying for dominance in their territory. Still, Drew was sometimes so good, it was fun to catch him acting like an idiot.

And he was probably right about warning Thelma in person. This was going to be quite a shock. She could hardly wait to see Thelma's face when she learned Billy Ray was back.

FOUR

A SLEEK BLACK sedan sat nosed-in beside Thelma Patterson's front gate, dwarfing Thelma's little red Dodge. Chantalene frowned. Who besides a funeral director would drive a black Caddy? The IRS? The Mafia? Nobody in Tetumka, that was for sure.

Whoever it was, Chantalene would have to out-wait him to talk to Thelma alone. She let herself through the gate and climbed the steps to the wide and shady front porch. An empty swing creaked pleasantly on its chain, occupied by the invisible spirit of a March wind that tinkled an array of chimes suspended under the eaves.

The wooden frame of the screened door rattled under Chantalene's knock. She admired Thelma's white farmhouse, which had aged with more grace than the twentieth century though it wasn't much younger. The condition of the old homestead was a credit to the skills of its mistress. Thelma tended not only to the painting and decorating, but also to the plumbing, wiring, and general repairs. If anything, the house was over-loved. Shrubbery crowded around the exterior, and inside, the rooms were plump with flowered chintz.

Chantalene pictured Thelma growing up here, an only child. Her mother had died when Thelma was young, and Alzheimer's began its insidious work on Samuel Mills while his daughter was still in her teens. At an age when most kids were playing basketball or leading cheers, Thelma had shouldered adult responsibilities. When Samuel died, she inherited the house and a section of farmland, and later bought an adjoining farm to bring her holdings to nearly a thousand acres. Thelma had run the farm with the help of hired hands until she took the postmaster job. Nowadays she rented the fields to a neighboring rancher, which paid the land taxes and ensured her a comfortable living.

Thelma's smile appeared from the shadows behind the screen as she opened the carved front door. "Chantalene! Come in!" She wore the same flowered dress she'd had on that morning. Her guest must have arrived before she had time to change.

"Hi, Thelma. Sorry to bother you while you have company, but something's come up I need to talk to you about."

"It's only the man from the oil company," Thelma said, adding in a stage whisper, "He'll be gone in a minute and we'll have some tea." She held open the screen and chuckled as Chantalene stepped inside. "Leave it to you to go barefoot in March!"

On one end of Thelma's overstuffed sofa in the living room, a man Chantalene judged to be about forty sat forward, arms propped on his spread knees. His military-style haircut made his hair appear colorless and emphasized his angular face.

"This is Mister Hill, with Ballenger Energy Corporation," Thelma said. "My neighbor, Chantalene Morrell."

The man stood and smiled, assessing her with small hazel eyes. "Miss Morrell." His suit didn't look quite as new as the Caddy. Oil companies in the region had seen better days.

"Sorry to interrupt," she said.

"I was just leaving." He flashed Thelma a smile that seemed to be his idea of flirting. "It was a pleasure to see you again, Missus Patterson. I'll check with you in a few days, but meanwhile," he pulled a business card from his jacket pocket and handed it to Thelma, "here's the number for my mobile phone. If you've made a decision—or hear from Mister Patterson—will you give me a call?"

"Why, of course!" Thelma's smile was so sunny Chantalene knew she had no intention of calling. She squelched a smile until Mr. Hill's serge backside had disappeared out the front door.

Thelma peeked out the window, watching to see that the city fellow didn't ding her prized red buggy. "He practically parked on top of it," she complained, then dropped the curtain and motioned Chantalene to the kitchen.

"They're driving me crazy about that lease. That's his third visit!"

Chantalene detected the mischief in Thelma's smile. She was clearly enjoying the oil company's attention.

"Now," Thelma said, "come to the kitchen and I'll make us something to drink. Iced tea or hot?"

"Iced, please. No sugar."

Despite her evident curiosity about the unexpected visit, Thelma herded Chantalene to the well-oiled table in her kitchen and attended to hostess duties. First things first, her demeanor said, the better to enjoy whatever newsy tidbit might come next. She clinked ice into two tumblers and poured fresh sun tea from a gallon jar.

"You may want to add a little Jack Daniels to yours," Chantalene teased. "I have some pretty big news for you."

Thelma stopped in mid-motion, an iced tea spoon in one hand and a glass in the other. She turned to face Chantalene and lost her habitual smile.

"You've found Billy Ray," Thelma said, deflating Chantalene's big surprise.

"Yes. Rather, he found us."

Thelma set the glasses on the table, forgetting the lemon, and sank into a chair. Her eyes tightened at the corners. Chantalene was reminded of the panic she'd seen on Billy Ray's face that afternoon when he'd thought Thelma might walk into the office.

"He's alive, then," Thelma said, and her chin trembled ever so slightly.

"Oh, yes. And looking quite well."

"You've seen him?"

Chantalene leaned forward and put her hand over Thelma's, an out-of-character gesture that served as a warning. "I just left him, Thelma. Billy Ray is at Drew's house right now."

Thelma's round body shrank in the chair. "He's here?"

Chantalene nodded. "And he wants to see you."

She didn't add the motive Billy Ray had admitted to her. Thelma was a sharp cookie; she'd figure that out soon enough.

Thelma's gaze drifted to the kitchen wall, watching some memory play out that only she could see. A range of emotions passed over her face, and Chantalene kept quiet and waited for Thelma to come back.

"When?" Thelma said.

"Tonight, for dinner at Drew's house, if you're willing." A spark of curiosity returned to Thelma's eyes, and Chantalene smiled. "You neglected to tell me Billy Ray was a hunk."

Thelma blushed, then chuckled. "Hunk wouldn't cover it. He was the most beautiful man you've ever seen."

"He still is."

Thelma turned the foggy tea glass in her hands without drinking. Her tone was tinged with nostalgia. "I don't think I want to see him. I'd rather remember the way we used to be."

"Don't worry. He's aged well."

Thelma's smile was half-hearted. "He would. But I'm twenty pounds fatter and every crow in the county has left tracks on my face."

"Nonsense. You look terrific."

Thelma wagged her head, and her eyes drifted away again. "All I've done in twenty-eight years is knit for other people's babies."

An image illuminated in Chantalene's mind like a photo—a young Thelma, dazzled by love and filled with dreams of children and grandchildren. The unexpected truth of it caught in her chest. Thelma's dreams had disappeared like a wisp of smoke, without reason or explanation. More than most people, Chantalene understood that feeling. Her own mother had disappeared, leaving a twelve-year-old girl to wonder why she'd been abandoned. And when it happened—she'd almost forgotten—Thelma Patterson had brought her a handmade doll in a crocheted dress. At the time Chantalene had felt too old for dolls and put the toy away. Only now did she understand the poignancy of that gift.

She looked at Thelma with softer eyes, remembering her own search for her missing mother. Thelma never knew why she was abandoned. Now that the answer was within her reach, perhaps she was afraid to know.

"You never told me how you met Billy Ray," Chantalene said.

A wistful smile curved one side of Thelma's mouth. "He was a hired hand with the combine crew that cut our wheat every spring. They'd start in Texas and follow the harvest north. Dad used the same outfit every year since I was old enough to remember, a family business run by a man named Weaver."

Talking always agreed with Thelma, and the color returned to her face. Chantalene kept quiet and listened.

"After Dad got sick, I gradually took over the farm, doing the things I'd helped him do for years. When harvest time came close, I didn't have to worry about hiring cutters. I knew it wouldn't be long before I'd see a procession of red combines in the distance, rolling down those shale roads toward the farm. It was funny how Dad remembered old man Weaver after he couldn't remember anything else."

Thelma took a deep breath. "One year Billy Ray came with them. He was tall and slim, with black curly hair and eyes so blue it hurt to look at them. Full of fun, always laughing. And only nineteen, although I didn't know that until later."

The pleasure in Thelma's voice made Chantalene smile. She'd give a year's tomato crop to have seen the wandering cowboy at nineteen.

"I was twenty-eight," Thelma said, "an old maid by country standards. In high school, I wore glasses and made straight As. Had plenty of girlfriends—probably because I wasn't any competition with the boys—but I never had a date. Not one.

"From the first day I met Billy Ray, he treated me with respect. He was so polite, but not condescending like so many men were toward women who worked in those days. Billy Ray seemed impressed that I was running the farm by myself. Dad was too sick by then to work in the fields. Most of the time he stayed in the house and watched TV. Billy Ray talked to me like a real person, the way he'd have talked to a man who was running a farm. Yet every time I looked at him, there was something in his eyes. He saw me as a woman, too." Thelma smiled. "And Lord, he was handsome. He fairly took my breath away."

"You got married that same summer?"

"No. We spent only a few minutes alone, actually. When I'd bring lunch to the field, he'd time his break so the others would be finished and back at work. Once I rode in the truck with him to take a load to the grain elevator. It was the most exciting thing that had ever happened to me. Then the cutting here was finished, and he went north with the crew."

Thelma's eyes grew misty. "But he wrote to me. From every stop they made. He hadn't promised to write, and I can still remember my sense of wonder when that first letter appeared in the mailbox.

"Billy Ray wasn't educated, but he was gifted with words. He made me see the rolling hills, golden with wheat ready to be harvested, and feel the summer heat on his back. I felt the lonesomeness of being on the road, and his restlessness to keep moving."

She sighed. "I fell in love with his letters. It was safe, you see, because I couldn't write back. By the time his letters arrived, he had moved on to the next town, or state. Towards the end of the summer, he began to write about coming to see me when harvest was over, but I never believed it. It was just a lovely part of the fantasy."

"But he *did* come back," Chantalene prompted.

Thelma nodded. "He showed up at the farm one October afternoon. I was coming in from the barn where I'd been bucket-feeding a calf, and I looked a mess. When I saw who it was, my mouth fell open and I couldn't say a word. He sauntered up to me, all grinning and gorgeous, and said, 'You didn't believe I'd come, did you?' He put one hand under my chin and kissed me, right there in front of the chickens."

Thelma laughed and lifted her glasses to blot her eyes. Chantalene wiped her own nose with her paper napkin.

"He stayed a week," Thelma said, "and the next week we drove to El Rio and got married at the courthouse. He went back to Tulsa—or somewhere—to get his clothes, and he moved in.

"I don't know if Dad ever understood we were married. Who knows what he thought in that poor scrambled mind. But he liked Billy Ray, and Billy was good to him. Dad died that same winter, and when we settled the estate, I put both our names on all the property. I had no illusions about what attracted Billy Ray to me, but I was willing to settle for that if he was."

Chantalene frowned. "Maybe you did have illusions. What if he really loved you, and you're selling him short?"

"He left, didn't he?" She shrugged, as if that act were self-explanatory. "Even the title to the land wasn't enough to tie him to a plain woman."

"Maybe. Or maybe he left for some reason that had nothing to do with you. Wouldn't you like to see Billy Ray and give him a chance to explain?"

"Achieve closure, like they say on TV?" Thelma's smile twisted to one side.

"Something like that. Or just out of curiosity."

"Sure I would. That's the real reason I asked Drew to look for him. But I expected to learn he was dead, or maybe happily married to somebody else. Once I had a dream about seeing his children, being kind of a godmother to them." She swallowed. "Isn't that sick?"

Thelma met her eyes, and Chantalene saw years of sadness there. "I wanted to know what he'd done with his life, but I never wanted to face him again. It took a long time for that wound to scar over."

"I understand," Chantalene said. "It's your decision. You certainly don't owe him anything."

She stood up. "I imagine Billy Ray will spend the night. If you change your mind, come over any time this evening. Otherwise, I'll call you tomorrow."

When Chantalene left, Thelma was sitting in the kitchen, an old scrapbook on the table in front of her. Closed.

FIVE

DREW HEARD CHANTALENE'S car scatter gravel in his driveway as she drove off to see Thelma. Alone with the too-handsome cowboy, he felt the heat of embarrassment on his face. He had just behaved like a hormonal teenager, and nobody was more surprised about it than he was. It was the first time in their eighteen-month relationship he'd had occasion to see Chantalene react to any man except the aging farmers she'd known all her life. His neck hair had raised like a dog's, and he felt ridiculous. But geez! She had looked at Billy Ray Patterson as if he were an ice cream cone.

The cowboy watched him with amused interest. This fellow didn't miss much. Drew would have to remember that. "I think I promised to peel potatoes," he said. "Come to the kitchen and I'll get us a beer."

Billy Ray Patterson followed him into the big country kitchen where Drew's mother and grandmother had once cooked meals for harvest crews. Neither of them would recognize it now with its modern appliances, but the ambiance was still there, at least for Drew. It was his favorite room in the house, and he was gradually teaching himself to cook.

Patterson took a seat at the wooden table and Drew opened the refrigerator. "Bud Lite or Michelob?"

"I appreciate the offer," Patterson drawled, "but I quit drinkin' some years back. It finally came clear to me there was a connection between alcohol and most of my troubles."

"Hmm. That's too bad." Drew popped open a blue and silver can. "How about iced tea?"

"That sounds great."

Billy Ray added three spoons of sugar to the tall glass Drew gave him, and commenced stirring. He slumped back in a kitchen chair, remarkably at ease for a man who was about to re-meet the wife he'd once deserted. He stretched out long legs that ended in a pair of well-worn boots. Justins, Drew guessed.

Chantalene had laid six potatoes on the cutting board along with the paring knife. Drew washed his hands and started peeling. "Chantalene says you've been working cattle in the Great Basin area for the past few years."

"Yessir. And Wyoming, and before that in California. I been astraddle a horse most of the last decade." His speech clopped along at a pace even slower than that of the farmers Drew dealt with every day. It was something he'd had to readjust to after living in New York for so long.

"I didn't know any ranches still used cowboys and horses to work cattle," Drew said. "Around here the ranchers use those four-wheelers."

"Yeah, lots of those up north, too. But there's still some high country ranges where those things aren't practical. And besides that, some guys just hate the racket."

Drew smiled. "Me, too. There's something fundamentally wrong with engine noise in wild places."

Billy Ray nodded. "There sure is. Noise pollution is almost as bad as water pollution, in my book." He drank his tea.

Drew chunked a peeled spud onto the chopping board and started another. When Patterson spoke again, Drew heard a change in his voice, some guard temporarily dropped.

"If you like unspoiled country, you ought to see some of the ranches out there," he said. "Wide, flat pastures run right up to the base of these blue-gray mountains. Always a little snow on the peaks, even in summer. When the low pastures get hot and dry, they herd the cattle up onto the high ranges, and up there it looks like spring again—lush grass and wildflowers."

"It sounds beautiful."

"It sure is. You can sit your horse on one of those buttes and see across the valley for miles and miles. Not a sound except for wind and birdsong. Once I sat at eye level with a hawk that was circling for prey." He paused again to sip his tea. "It's lonesome, too."

"That why you came back? The lonesomeness?"

The cowboy shrugged. "Naw. I liked it. Bein' lonesome gets addictive."

Drew squinted at him, surprised at the insight.

"Now that I'm here," Patterson said, "I'd really like to see Thelma. But I admit that when I got wind a lawyer was lookin' for me, I thought maybe something happened to her and I'd inherited the farm. I'm not proud of thinkin' that, but there it is. I guess the idea of working a piece of land that's my own instead of somebody else's sort of appeals to me these days."

"I know what you mean," Drew said. "I gave up a good salary in New York to come back and work the family farm, even though I knew you couldn't make a decent living from it now." He took the roast from the oven and dumped chunks of potato and mini carrots into the tinfoil wrapper holding the beef. The fragrance of roast beef floated through the kitchen.

"Man, that smells good," the cowboy said.

Drew had to agree. His stomach growled as he re-sealed the foil and slid the dish back in the oven.

"So how's the farming?" Patterson asked.

Drew smiled. "Not as pure and noble as I remembered. Of course, there were other reasons I came back, too, like a marriage gone sour."

"That's too bad. I've had some hard experiences, but not that particular one."

"Is that right?" Drew brought his nearly-empty beer to the table and took a seat. "Then why did you take off and leave Thelma?"

Billy Ray looked at him. "I walked right into that one, didn't I?"

Drew met his eyes. "I'm Thelma's lawyer, and her friend. You should be aware that I'll do what I can to protect her interests."

The cowboy nodded. "I'm glad to know she's got that kind of loyalty."

Drew kept quiet and waited.

"I know I owe Thelma an explanation," Patterson said, "and maybe I owe you one, too, since I've shown up. But it's a long story with a lot of family history in it."

"In that case I'll have another beer."

Drew refilled Billy Ray's tea glass and opened another Bud. He sat down again, looked at the cowboy and waited.

Patterson took a deep breath. "The summer I met Thelma, I was a jingle-brained kid working for a traveling harvest crew. I never told her I'd signed on in order to escape the consequences of a minor scrape with the law."

"How minor?"

The cowboy sighed. "I was waitin' in the car when a couple buddies of mine decided to knock over a liquor store. Luckily I wasn't old enough to go in with them. I swear I didn't know about it ahead of time, but somebody recognized me and I decided to make myself scarce until the whole thing blew over."

"You couldn't have convinced the police you were innocent?"

"Not likely. That's where the history comes in."

The cowboy rubbed the sweat off his tea glass with calloused thumbs. "I had a brother, named Donnie Ray, just a year younger'n me. We grew up like twins in a little town called Cut and Shoot, Texas. Honest to God," he added, when Drew frowned. "Our daddy was a roughneck on the oil rigs and gone for months at a time. Mama spent a lot of time quenching her loneliness at the local honky-tonks, so we didn't have much supervision. Finally he didn't come back at all, and after that Mama kept us movin'. If it wasn't for our sister Sunny, Donnie and I would have ended up wards of the state. Sunny was six years older, from our mom's first marriage. She did the best she could with us, but at eighteen, she got pregnant and moved to Tulsa. Her marriage didn't last, but she had a job there and stayed on, so Donnie and I were pretty much on our own."

He stopped for a slug of iced tea. "Somehow we lived through being teenagers, but we spent a lot of time in trouble of one sort or another. Nothin' serious—we skipped school, shoplifted beer, stuff like that. We also played poker with a group of older guys and usually won. That kept us in pocket money."

"So that's why the local law wouldn't have believed you weren't in on the liquor store robbery," Drew said.

"Right. We got by with a lot because the other kids covered for us. We were sort of like Tom Sawyer and Huck Finn to them, I reckon. We always took up for the underdog in a fight, and our knuckles stayed bruised most of the time." Suddenly he looked embarrassed. "I haven't talked this much in twenty years. I reckon you've had enough."

Drew shook his head. "We have time. It may take Thelma a while to overcome her shock when Chantalene tells her you're here."

"I reckon so. She must have thought I was dead long ago."

"Hard to say what Thelma believed. Somebody called her from New Mexico once and said a fellow named Donnie Ray Patterson was killed in a wreck. She didn't even know your brother's name."

Drew saw a look of old pain flicker across the cowboy's face. "Donnie Ray and I were close."

"That's where you went when you told Thelma you were going to visit your sister? To touch base with Donnie?"

"Pretty much. I really did visit Sunny sometimes, but mostly I hung out in the bars with Donnie Ray, hustlin' pool and drinkin'. One of those times we met up with this fellow named Songdog Jones. That's where our real trouble started."

"Songdog, like a coyote?"

"Yeah. His real name was Oswald, but everybody called him Songdog. He was a lot older, kind of dark and quiet, with a wicked sense of humor. We were real fascinated with him.

"Old Songdog spent a lot of time at a high-stakes bingo parlor hidden away in the hills on Indian land. We bugged him to take us along. This was the '70s, and other forms of gambling were illegal so lots of people went there, Indian or not. The place was owned by the tribe, but it was managed by white guys. Some real slick Willies." He said the phrase with distaste and studied the scuffed tips of his boots a moment before going on.

"Songdog claimed the management was skimming off hundreds of dollars every week and cheating the tribe. He said it was money that should have been going to the Indian kids for schools and medical care. That didn't set well with us, especially with Donnie Ray. He always had a soft spot for little kids. So we sat at the tables a few nights and watched the fellows that ran the place real close. We figured out where they kept the till.

"One night the three of us had a few beers and decided the only right thing to do was to cheat the cheaters and steal the money. Songdog said the management couldn't report it to the police, because it was stolen in the first place. We agreed we'd give half of it back to the Choctaw tribe and split the other half among us for our trouble."

"The Robin Hoods of the West," Drew said.

"Like I said, most of my bad decisions I made while I was drinkin'." He shoved his tea glass back on the table as if even that might damage his judgment.

"So you burglarized the place?"

He nodded. "Broke in after hours. There wasn't even an alarm. That was the easy part. What we hadn't counted on was the size of the haul, which turned out to be a whole lot more'n old Songdog thought." He glanced at Drew. "Just over a quarter of a million dollars."

Drew whistled through his teeth. "I had no idea that bingo was such big business."

"Me, neither. That was a mountain of money in those days. We figured they'd either been saving it up for a long time, or the place was a front for some other kind of business. Sure enough, it turned out the operation was controlled by a rich family down in Dallas with some heavy political connections. Rumor had it they were mobbed up, too. The family didn't take kindly to some two-bit hoodlums ripping them off."

Drew shook his head. "Buzzard luck."

"One of Songdog's buddies warned us that the family had sent some muscle after us, and these guys weren't playin'. We had two choices—run like hell or get planted with the cactus out in Big Bend somewhere. That night Donnie and Songdog stashed the loot, thinking that'd be our life insurance in case they found us, while I played in a pool tournament to win us some road money."

He lowered his eyes and swirled the ice cubes left in his glass. "I hated to run off without tellin' Thelma, but I figured the less she knew about it, the better. Honest to God, I was trying to protect her. I didn't want those thugs to track down my other life and cause Thelma any harm.

"So we took off in the middle of the night, headed west. At a truck stop in El Paso, Songdog ran across some gal he used to know and that's where we parted company. Donnie and I high-tailed it north across New Mexico, nervous as cottontails in short grass. We didn't have any notion where to go. We took turns driving and sleeping but about 5 a.m. one morning we were both asleep when the pickup collided with one of those concrete abutments beside an overpass. I was thrown out and when I came to, the truck was in flames." The cowboy's Adam's apple worked up and down in his throat. "There was nothin' I could do."

He paused a long time before he went on. "I lit out on foot with nothing but my watch, about a hundred dollars, and the clothes on my back. I blamed myself for Donnie's death. Still do. I shoulda stayed awake."

"That's rough," Drew said.

"Anyhow, I hitchhiked clear to California. Got to drinking and doing stupid things, trying to get myself killed too, I guess. Finally got into a bar fight that landed me some prison time."

Drew frowned. "Prison time for a bar fight?"

"It was my third assault charge. Prison was the best thing that coulda happened to me. I sobered up by necessity, and I had lots of time to examine what kind of man I was. I didn't much like what I saw. I swore if I ever got out, I'd make a different kind of life, for Donnie Ray as well as for me."

He drained the ice-melt from his glass. "Took every re-hab class they had in the prison, and I read a lot. Soon as I got out, I signed on as a ranch hand with an outfit that didn't do background checks, and I learned to cowboy. I liked being outdoors. It was a solitary kind of life and it suited me. When that job ran out I drifted north and got on with another ranch, and I been doing that ever since."

"But you stayed in touch with Sunny, and she told you we'd been looking for you."

He nodded. "I got to thinkin' that one of these days I'll be too old to cowboy and need someplace to settle."

The sound of a car in the driveway drifted through the kitchen window. "Sounds like the ladies are here," Drew said.

Billy Ray's jaw tensed. "It's times like this I miss drinkin'."

Drew stood up and headed for the living room. "So what happened to the stolen money?"

The cowboy rose to follow. "I got no idea. I didn't want it after Donnie Ray died. I figured old Songdog'd probably circle back and get it, but I heard he died of a heart attack not long after he took up with that young thing down in El Paso."

"A younger woman can be a dangerous thing," Drew allowed.

A smile played at one corner of Billy Ray Patterson's mouth. "I'll have to take your word for that."

SIX

DREW'S HOUSE SMELLED like carnivore heaven when Chantalene returned from Thelma's. She might not eat meat, but she loved the smell of it cooking. Drew and Billy Ray Patterson, lounging amiably in the living room, looked at her expectantly when she walked in.

"You're alone?" Drew asked. "How did it go with Thelma?"

She passed up the empty armchair and sank onto Drew's new area rug, wrapping her arms around her knees. "Not great." She glanced at Billy Ray and saw anxiety etched on his face. "Thelma's not coming."

Billy Ray released his breath.

"She doesn't want to see you," she said gently. "She only wanted to find out what had become of you."

He nodded. "Can't say I blame her."

"Maybe she'll change her mind," Drew said. "I've known Thelma to do that sometimes."

"Right," Billy Ray said, but he didn't smile.

The aroma of the roast and potatoes drifted into the silence. Chantalene's stomach growled. "When will the roast be done?"

Drew checked his watch. "Probably by the time we get the junk cleared off so we can set the table."

They scooped up armloads of books and tax forms from the big round dining table Drew used for a desk, stacking everything on a nearby bookcase. Billy Ray followed them to the kitchen, willing to help but obviously out of his element.

Chantalene smiled at him. "Here. Pour us some tea, will you?" She put out tall glasses and the cowboy set about filling them with ice.

Drew transferred the roast and vegetables to a platter while Chantalene tossed a salad. He set a fourth place at the table and she flashed him a look.

"She might come," he said. Always the optimist.

When they were seated, Billy Ray touched his cloth napkin uncertainly but followed suit when Chantalene placed hers in her lap. Drew cut the roast and dished up generous portions for himself and their guest while she mounded potatoes and carrots on her plate and covered them au jus.

Among Drew's numerous gifts was his ability to draw intelligent conversation from any living being. He was interested in all people and all subjects with a genuineness that put others at ease. Chantalene munched her salad and watched him work. Soon Billy Ray was relating a story about bringing range cattle down from the high country before the first winter snows.

A blustery March wind assailed the house with appropriate sound effects. The cowboy was a good storyteller, with an eye for detail and an understated sense of humor. He talked about the wild mustangs that roamed free in remote parts of Wyoming, and she felt the loneliness of hitch-hiking back to Oklahoma after his last wrangling job in Utah had run out. Listening to him, she thought of the letters Thelma had described. She could have listened to his soft drawl for hours.

Throughout the meal, the empty place at the table lay like a reminder of someone deceased. Twice Chantalene caught Billy Ray glancing toward the empty chair, then at the door. Was it dread or longing that kept him waiting for his estranged wife?

"Too bad we don't have dessert," Drew said, when they'd all cleaned their plates and pushed back from the table.

"I couldn't eat another bite," Billy Ray insisted. "That was a terrific meal. I'm mighty obliged."

He might be rough around the edges, but you couldn't fault him for politeness. Chantalene lingered with their guest while Drew carried plates to the kitchen and made coffee.

With Drew gone, silence settled over the table. Then they both spoke at once. "You first," he said.

"I was going to ask what your plans are now if Thelma won't see you."

His tanned face creased into a thoughtful expression. "Drew was kind enough to say I could bunk over tonight. Then I'll be moving on, I reckon. Look for work somewhere." His voice was low but not regretful. "What about you?"

The question caught her off guard. "Me?"

"I get the feeling you'd rather not stay in Tetumka forever," he said.

His blue eyes had sharpened, a distinct contrast to their wistful expression a few minutes before. Was her wanderlust that obvious? She was still deciding how—or whether—to answer that question when someone rapped on the front door.

The two of them froze as if caught in some forbidden act.

Drew came in from the kitchen and opened the door, which was clearly visible from the dining room table. "Thelma!" he said, his voice exuberant. "I'm glad you came." He stepped aside.

Thelma Patterson hesitated in the doorway, a silk scarf loosely protecting her short curls from the wind that rippled her skirt. Despite her plump figure and wire-rimmed glasses, Thelma made a dramatic impression, poised on the threshold of her past. The conflicted emotions that lay open on Thelma's face hurt Chantalene's heart. She held her breath.

Billy Ray's face was not so easy to read. He stood up, his eyes riveted on the woman framed by the open door. "Thelma?"

He crossed the room like a calf at the end of a rope and stopped within arm's reach of Thelma.

"You look different," Thelma said, as if that surprised her.

Billy Ray's eyes hadn't left her face. "You look just the same."

His voice was deep and soft, the same tone in which he'd described a sunset over the Tetons. A lump rose in Chantalene's throat.

Thelma's smile was sad. "And you still know just the right lie, don't you?"

"I never considered them lies if they made somebody happy." Billy Ray held out his hand to her. "Will you come in?"

Thelma looked at the palm extended toward her, then at his face again. Seconds elapsed with the scene frozen like a still photograph. Then Thelma took his hand and let him lead her into the living room.

Drew flashed Chantalene a triumphant smile. He came to the dining table where she stood shaking her head in amazement. "Let's do dishes and let them have some time alone," he said.

"And miss the fun?" she whispered. "Would Thelma do that for us?"

But Drew insisted. They carried the remaining dishes into the kitchen.

Luckily, Drew's kitchen had no door. Chantalene could hear snatches of conversation from the living room—until Drew turned on the tap full blast to fill the sink with sudsy water. She scowled at him. He threw a clump of soap bubbles which landed on her right breast.

"So sorry!" he exclaimed, and started toward her with the dish towel. "Let me get that for you."

"Forget it," she said, dodging. She wiped the bubbles from her blouse, deposited them in his ear, and felt a quick wish that they were alone in the house. The romantic scene she'd just witnessed had put her in the mood.

Drew washed and she dried, chatting idly to give Thelma and Billy Ray the illusion of privacy. It was impossible not to wonder what the two of them might be saying to each other, and Chantalene caught Drew listening, too, between the clatter of dishes. She heard the words "farm" and "daddy" from Thelma, but the cowboy's voice was a low rumble, meant for Thelma's ears only.

When the kitchen was spotless, Drew followed her into the living room. Thelma sat in one of the plaid chairs, her hands gripping the armrests. Billy Ray leaned forward on the sofa, his knees only inches from Thelma's, his gaze intent on her face. Neither one spoke when Drew and Chantalene joined them.

Oblivious to the tension, Drew plopped into the empty chair, leaving the vacant end of the sofa for Chantalene. "How's it going?" he said amiably.

Thelma sat speechless, a rare occurrence.

"Twenty-eight years needs a lot of explaining," the cowboy said.

Chantalene could take a hint, even if Drew couldn't. She rose from the sofa as if the seat were hot. "Why don't Drew and I take a drive." She looked at Thelma for confirmation. "Are you all right?"

Thelma's face looked flushed and rigid, but she nodded. "Put on your shoes, girl. You'll catch your death of cold."

Chantalene scooped up the sandals that lay where she'd left them that afternoon. You catch colds from germs, not from cold feet. But she smiled. "Yes, Mom." She extended her hands to Drew and pulled him up from the chair. "Come on. We can go by the office and look over the Selbys' taxes."

They shut the front door on their way out, leaving a heavy silence behind them.

ON THE SEAT of Drew's red pickup, with her bare feet curled under her, Chantalene realized Drew actually was driving towards the office. Sometimes the man was so literal.

She leaned against him and laid her hand on his thigh. "I was only making an excuse. Surely you can think of somewhere we can go besides downtown Tetumka."

Drew grinned at her with malice of forethought.

His truck had a nice, wide seat and an adjustable steering wheel. They parked on the service road to an abandoned oil well and helped the March wind rock the car.

Afterward, she made Drew repeat every word Billy Ray had told him while she was gone.

"He's lived an interesting life, I'll say that for him," she said.

"Weeks alone on a cattle range is interesting?"

She shrugged. "He's seen the whole western half of the country."

There it was again, that longing. Drew heard it, too, and looked away.

It was an hour and a half before they returned to Drew's house. Chantalene still carried her sandals, her hair falling loose and frizzy above her shoulders.

Apparently, things had gone well at home, too.

Billy Ray and Thelma met them at the door, and Billy had his battered duffle in his hand.

Thelma's eyes were red, but her face looked positively radiant. "We're going home."

"What?" Chantalene said. "What do you mean, *going home?*"

But Thelma and her man were already off the front porch and headed for

Thelma's car. He tossed his duffle in the back seat and opened the driver side door for Thelma, then went around to ride shotgun.

As they drove away, Billy Ray Patterson bid them good-bye with a tip of his cowboy hat and a smile. "Thanks for everything!"

Chantalene and Drew stood speechless on the front porch while Thelma's red tail lights disappeared into the blustery March night, leaving all their questions unanswered.

SEVEN

THE OLD MAN returned to his cabin at daylight. Two rangy chickens squawked from their makeshift nests beneath a bush beside the cabin. He reached beneath the foliage and removed two eggs, still warm, and carried them indoors to the rusty refrigerator.

In the bedroom, he emptied an item from his pocket and added it to the collection on top of the three-legged bureau—a red-handled hairbrush, a silver teaspoon with the floral pattern on the handle nearly worn away, a pencil embedded with teeth marks. The small, red-and-black scarf still carried the scent of her hair.

He arranged the items carefully to the north, south, east and west. In the center he placed a candle, unlit, and a yellowed paper that carried Liddy's picture. *Have you seen this girl?* Her eyes stared up at him, defiant.

He had seen her, all right. Even the fire ceremony where he'd burned the hair from her brush had not succeeded in driving her away.

His head felt strange and heavy, but he dreaded sleep. He put on his boots and took his fishing pole and walked toward the pond.

At a certain place on the path, he veered off toward a thicket of sand plums, across the creek and upwind from the foxes' den. Crouched motionless in the thicket, he could see the mouth of the den but the foxes could not see him. From here he had often watched the kits before their parents returned from hunting. In the beginning they were three, now only two. They played like kittens, crouching behind rocks with only the pointed ears showing, opaque and blood red in the early sunlight. He liked the way their dark eyes peered over the rocks while they bunched their bird-boned bodies, ready to pounce when a sibling walked by.

The foxes were the only thing that made the old man smile.

But today when he hunkered down in the thicket, the den was starkly quiet, the earth at its mouth undisturbed. The den was abandoned.

The empty hole gaped like the mouth of someone dead. The familiar darkness filled up the old man's chest. Living things sensed this darkness and fled from him. This was Liddy's legacy, her curse.

He rose from his hiding place—no need for quiet now—and continued to the pond, his steps heavy in the brush.

Sometimes when he sat by the pond with his line in the water, time spun out in circles. Past and present existed together. He was forever old and at the same time young. It happened sitting in his chair by the cabin window, too. Often he lost whole afternoons that way. He would come back to himself surrounded by darkness, but when he went to bed, he was swept up by visions instead of sleep.

He slept now. He was hungry and he dreamed of slow catfish and shiny perch that swam past the grasshopper impaled on his hook. He dreamed of fish sizzling in his skillet, the white meat flaky and warm on his tongue. And then he dreamed of Liddy.

He saw himself crouched outside the shape-shifter's house, watching. In his dream the night turned to daylight around him and he rose and walked straight to her house, the black and white dog asleep on the porch. But once he was inside, the house turned into his cabin, years ago when Liddy lived with him. She was drying her hair beside the open window, her head thrown forward in the sunlight. She brushed with long, slow strokes that pulled sparkles of light through her hair, and she was singing. Liddy had a fine, clear voice, a perfect ear for melody. Sometimes when she was sleeping he heard the singing of her bones.

LIDDY ONCE SANG at a beer joint in Texas. The local cowboys came to hear her country songs and fall in love with her. The owner made sure they didn't touch her but had no such rules for himself. She was only fifteen.

That's where he'd found her again. He wasn't so old back then.

He hadn't seen her since she was seven, the day Naomi took her and stormed out of the house. He hadn't even thought of Liddy; in fact, he'd done his best to forget Naomi and put those days behind him. For a while he worked construction, moving from one town to the next, and then he got a job as a grave digger for the county. The job kept him busy and he liked working alone, maneuvering the big backhoe among the gravestones, its noise blotting out everything else as it gouged into the raw earth. Once they'd given him the wrong plot number and he'd dug into an unmarked grave, the giant teeth of the backhoe scraping up one corner of the concrete vault from its resting place. It gave him a chill.

He hadn't recognized Liddy at first, but she knew him. She'd spotted him in the meager audience as she was singing a tune about lost love that he'd never heard before. He watched her and thought she looked familiar. And when the song was over she came back to the booth where he was sitting alone with his beer, graveyard mud drying into a dusty puddle around his boots on the concrete floor.

"Hi," she said, and sat down across from him. "Don't you know me?"

He looked at her, the translucent eyes fearless and far too knowing for her smooth young face. He saw Naomi there, and calculated quickly how long she'd been gone.

"Liddy," he said. "You're Liddy, aren't you."

She smiled and settled into the booth. "Buy me a drink?"

"You're too young."

She gave him one of those universal looks of teenage disdain. "They have Cokes here."

She turned and yelled at the barkeep. "Red. Can I get a Coke?" Red was a young fellow, not the owner, and he waved back. He set a bottle dripping ice water onto the bar, and Liddy went and got it.

"So how the hell have you been?" she said to him. Like some crony, some construction cowboy he used to work with.

"I'm okay. How about you?"

She cast her eyes toward the back room, where the boss was. "Not so hot."

"Where's Naomi?"

She shrugged. "Who the hell knows? She shacked up with some creep that wanted more than he was entitled to, and I split." She took a drink from the curved bottle. "Not that it's any better here."

The neck of his beer bottle felt cool to his fingers. He saw the dirt under his nails. "Why do you stay, then?"

She shrugged again. The jukebox started up Willie Nelson. "It's a living. Someplace to crash."

"So you're tough now, are you?" He smiled at her then, but he didn't like seeing her this way. She was just a kid. She ought to be in school, going to football games with her friends on Friday night. Not shacked up with the owner of a beer joint and singing to earn her meals.

She didn't answer him, just drank her soda.

"You can stay with me if you want," he said. "I have a little house outside of town."

She looked at him. "Yeah, right. How would I be better off?"

"I won't bother you. There's an extra bedroom. You could go back to school." He drank his beer. "Just an offer. Doesn't matter to me."

She glanced over her shoulder at some cowboy entering the bar, then toward the back room again. "Where is it? Your house."

The next night when he came home from work, she was sitting at his kitchen table, a brown grocery sack on the floor beside its chrome legs. All her worldly goods. She didn't say anything, just looked at him, nervous, like she thought he'd kick her out.

He took his boots off beside the door and walked in his stocking feet to the refrigerator, an appliance older than she was. He took out two colas and handed her one. "I'll show you your room."

She stayed with him three months but wouldn't go back to school. Who knows what she did in the daytime, when he was working. Then one night she came into his bedroom. He'd been in bed an hour but he wasn't asleep. It was summertime and he had only a sheet on the bed. She slipped in beside him not wearing anything, cool as water.

"What are you doing?" he asked, thinking, *no, this is not right*.

"What do you think I'm doing?" And then she touched him.

"Why?" Knowing he was lost now, nothing he could do.

"Because I don't have to," she said. "Because you've been good to me." Her skin was exquisite and smelled faintly like flowers.

Then one day when he came home from work she was gone.

THE OLD MAN awoke, surprised to find himself there in the grass. The sun hung low above the pasture, and his fishing pole was gone. He sat up.

In the middle of the pond, the cane pole floated like a disembodied limb. It was moving slightly, pulled at the tip by something unseen in the murky water. A big catfish had caught the hook and dragged the pole in. No way to get it unless he swam out there. He debated. That was his supper, but he hated the feel of that muddy slime beneath his feet.

He picked up his empty stringer and headed home. Sooner or later the pole would float back to the bank. Tonight he'd have noodle soup from a can.

When he passed the thicket he thought of the foxes again, gone, like Liddy.

Only Liddy didn't stay gone. She kept coming back to torment him.

The dreams had tired him. He didn't ask for much, just to live out his days alone and in peace. But she wouldn't allow that. He'd known from the beginning she was wrong, yet he hadn't resisted. He'd let her possess his mind and his body, and lead him to the blackest of sins.

Clearly, no ritual or fire ceremony was enough to exorcize this demon. If he didn't put an end to it, she would suck out his soul.

EIGHT

CHANTALENE HADN'T HEARD from Thelma all weekend, and when she arrived home from class at East Central U on Monday afternoon—a two-hour drive—the first thunderstorm of spring had temporarily knocked out the phone lines. There was no use driving to the office. She couldn't risk Gandalf's sensitive innards by booting up during an electrical storm. So she spent the evening studying for her mid-term test in British Lit, reading Chaucer aloud while lightning split the sky and the lights flickered. She felt wired, the Middle English rolling off her tongue like thunder.

She loved a good storm. Too bad Drew had gone to Oklahoma City to call on a tax client. They could have had some fun on a night like this. Then again, maybe not. He'd be too worried about hail damage to his wheat crop.

Bones wasn't any fun, either. Usually an outside dog, she was huddled in a black-and-white lump underneath the kitchen table. Bones hated thunder.

Neither tornado nor hail materialized from the clouds, and early the next morning Chantalene opened the front door to a world washed clean. Bones bounded off the porch steps like a freed prisoner and set about her morning rounds, sniffing out the smells of the night. Chantalene scooped oats into Whippoorwill's feed bin, and the gelding whickered gratefully. Then she stood on the bottom rung of the corral fence to survey her half-acre of asparagus plants in the adjoining field.

Delicious green arrows sprang up from the sandy soil, but the field was too muddy for picking. She'd have to cut them soon, though, or they'd be lost. Her potato patch, a wide brown swath of worked soil south of the asparagus, was already planted with Red Pontiacs. Before she'd started working with Drew, the truck garden was her only source of income. This year, with a salary to count on and less time to work the fields, she would cut down on labor-intensive crops like tomatoes and squash.

Her chores finished, she showered, turbaned her hair, and reached on the dresser for her hairbrush. It wasn't there. Not in the bathroom, either. Huh. How in the world did you lose something in a house this size?

And what was that slightly funky smell that hung in the house? Must be something the wind blew in.

She combed out the tangles and dressed in black jeans and an untucked red blouse to head for the office, negotiating the muddy driveway with one wheel on the grassy shoulder. In her roadside mailbox, two slightly-damp letters that had arrived the day before waited for her. One was from Gamma Rose. She smiled and tossed them on the seat to read later.

Three hours later, she hit the print command on Gandalf's keyboard and watched Monkey Jenks' 1040 form and Schedule C churn out from the printer, while she massaged a knot that burned between her shoulders. Monkey's income was down this year. When he lost Martha, he seemed to have lost his heart for farming. But then, it hadn't been a good year for any of the local farmers. Maybe the oil company who'd contacted Thelma would offer Monkey a lease contract, too.

She stretched and picked up her two letters from the desk. Gamma Rose, the Gypsy great-grandmother who had raised Chantalene's mother, had to be at least ninety now. As far as she knew, Gamma Rose was her only living relative. If Chantalene didn't go see her soon, it might be too late.

The other letter was from her advisor at ECU. Mrs. McBride had scribbled a note on the margin of a flyer about an intern program at a small western history museum near Santa Fe. "This could be a great opportunity," Miz Mac's hurried handwriting read. "You have enough hours to declare a major in history, which they require, and they furnish a small salary and furnished apartment for the year." Chantalene also had enough hours to declare a major in psychology, and a good start on criminal science. Miz Mac kept advising her to focus on one area instead of choosing classes like a kid in a cafeteria. But how could she settle on one field when there was so much she didn't know?

Chantalene read the flyer and pictured herself on her own, going to work each day in a place that might resemble Los Padres. It sounded like fun—until she thought of being away from Drew for an entire year. Of course, he could come for visits. Long, lost weekends when absence made the lust grow fonder.

She'd never been able to resist filling in blanks if she knew the answers. She picked up a pen and idly filled out the first page of the application while the Hewlett-Packard regurgitated its last page. When the printer hummed into silence, she stuck the flyer and application under the keyboard and gathered the tax forms into a file folder, ready for Monkey's signature.

The cooler behind the desk held nothing but yesterday's melted ice, so she pulled on her faux Birkenstocks and crossed Tetumka's unnamed main street toward the market, stepping over puddles of rain in the crumbled asphalt. Sunshine steamed down on her shoulders.

Three pickup trucks sat along the curb in front of the local grocery, a big crowd for a weekday. Beneath the whitewash on the sign out front, the faded outline of "Bond's Market" lingered like a ghost. The store was nameless, too, ever since the former owner died on the premises. Bad karma, but she was desperate for a cold drink. She pulled open the screened door and stepped inside.

The dim interior smelled dusty and the wooden floor creaked beneath her feet. She took an orange soda from the cooler along the side wall and pressed the cold can to her temples. In a back corner, four local joes played pitch at a card table, whiling away an afternoon when their farm work was caught up. Grant Selby was there, along with John Sherwood and the Hahnemann twins, whom she could never tell apart. One of them was supposed to be minding the register. Carrying her purchases to the counter where a "No Out-of-Town Checks" notice was printed in red crayon, Chantalene heard Grant telling a story his buddies found enormously amusing.

"I can't believe she took him back," one of the brothers said.

"Why not? Would you want to live out there by yourself the rest of your life if you was her? Keepin' up an old place like that's a lot of work, and Thelma's no spring chicken anymore."

"She's always done all right. Besides, unless Billy Ray's changed, he's likely to make more work for her instead of less."

"Yeah, but he's still a good-lookin' dog," Grant drawled. "And her feet'll stay warm on a cold winter night." This brought delighted chuckles from the group.

Chantalene's neck bristled. "Hey! Somebody want to take my money?"

One of the ditto brothers looked up from his cards. "Hi, Chantalene. Just help yourself. Register's open."

Amazing how much respectability she'd earned by working with Drew. Two years ago, these fellows would have kept a suspicious eye on her while she was in the store. Now they ignored her, like anybody else. It was disappointing.

She rang up her purchases on the ancient cash register and bagged the cans. From a nearby rack, Twinkies whispered her name, and she donated the last of her money.

The orange pop tasted sweet and cold and half of it was gone by the time she re-crossed the street to the post office. The old gossipers in the store might find it amusing, but Chantalene had felt uneasy about Thelma ever since, and a bit miffed because Thelma hadn't called. She decided to stop by and check on her.

Tiny brass bells tinkled above the wooden door as she shoved it open. A gust of wind fluttered the faces of the missing and wanted on a cluttered bulletin board beside the door. She glanced at the faces as she passed, a habit she'd picked up in sympathy for all those folks who wondered about missing loved ones. Not so long ago, she'd been one of them.

She moved past the bank of antique mailboxes and on to the window, expecting to see Thelma's smiling face. Instead, the pale visage of Annabelle Dickson peeked out at her, a monochrome in tan. Annabelle didn't wear make-up, and her cardboard-colored hair was always pulled back in a low pony tail. Even her eyes seemed faded, but straight white teeth brightened her smile.

"Hi, Chantalene. How'd you like that storm?"

"I liked it fine, but now it's too muddy to cut my asparagus."

"Save a few bags for me, will you?" Annabelle said in her cobwebby voice.

"Sure thing." Annabelle was one of her best customers. Mrs. Field Mouse had five healthy and well-mannered kids at home.

"Where's Thelma?" Chantalene asked.

"Off today. I'm the substitute, but nobody knows it because Thelma misses work so seldom."

"She's not sick, is she?"

A frown pinched Annabelle's forehead. "I don't think so." She looked ready to say something else, but just then they heard the back door of the post office open, admitting a gust of wind before it slammed shut. The suction rattled the wooden grate beside the window.

A male tenor voice called out. "I'm back from the route, Annabelle!"

Hank Littlejohn poked his head into the cubicle where Annabelle sat. "That old hermit out by the county line hasn't picked up his mail for three days. Wonder if he's dead in there." He glanced at the window. "Oh, hi, Chantalene."

Chantalene waved to Hank and caught a wink from Annabelle. The long-legged mailman looked like Ichabod Crane and was just as skittish. He'd made the same complaint before about one of their isolated mail patrons, but he refused to knock on his door, leaving Thelma to check on the old fellow. Chantalene had ridden along.

"I'd better get back to work," Chantalene said. "I'll bring the asparagus by as soon as I get it picked."

"Are you going to call Thelma?"

"Yeah. I think I will."

"I'm glad. She didn't sound like herself on the phone," Annabelle crooned. "Bye-bye." A librarian without her stacks.

Passing the bulletin board on her way out, Chantalene stopped cold. Pinned to the center was a face she recognized—the strange girl who kept appearing during her meditation sessions lately, and sometimes even in her dreams. The girl's aura was disturbing, as if something was drastically wrong. But Chantalene was sure she'd never seen the girl before.

She reached up and snapped the paper loose from its pin. The flyer was faded and curled at the edges. Beneath the photo ran the words, "Have you seen this girl?" Chantalene had undoubtedly seen the flyer before, but she hadn't connected the animated young woman in her visions with this grainy photo. Dark eyes engaged the camera knowingly, and the smile was one-sided. The photo looked like a blow-up from a high school yearbook. Most Likely to Seduce the Science Teacher.

It was the same face, all right. Those eyes must have tunneled into her subconscious memory and popped up like a prairie dog months later. Maybe years later. This flyer had obviously been there a very long time.

Huh. One mystery solved. Now if she could just find that darned missing hairbrush. On impulse, she folded the flyer into her pocket. Nobody would miss it, and maybe if she studied the photo later, she could figure why the girl's image got stuck in her brain.

Walking next door to the office, she tried to remember the last time Thelma had missed a day's work. Maybe never. She tossed her empty pop can in the trash—no recycling in Tetumka—and picked up the handset on the desk phone.

The message light was blinking so she punched that button first.

"*Hi, I'm home,*" Drew's baritone said. "*Call me.*" Then, singing, "*Maybe it's late, but just... call me.*"

Chantalene laughed, and the tiny office seemed suddenly lighter. When Drew was gone, she felt lost in her own home town. Worse, she couldn't seem to outgrow a fear that he simply wouldn't return. Like her mother, years ago, or the way Billy Ray had abandoned Thelma.

Knowing you're paranoid doesn't mean everybody's not out to get you.

Before calling him back, though, she dialed Thelma's number. Luckily Thelma answered instead of Billy Ray.

"Hi, stranger. Missed you at the P.O. Is everything all right?"

"*Oh, I'm fine!*" Thelma chirped. "*I just took a day off. As a matter of fact, I need to see you and Drew this afternoon—about my taxes.*"

"Your taxes?"

"*Yes, I have some—new information. See you later. Thanks for calling!*"

The buzz of the dial tone cut off Chantalene's response. She looked at the receiver. "What the hell....?"

They weren't doing Thelma's taxes. Thelma always did them herself.

Chantalene pushed the program button for Drew's number. "I just had the strangest conversation with Thelma," she told him.

"*Hi, I missed you, too,*" he said.

"Listen. She said she had some new information to give us about her taxes." He paused. "*That is odd.*"

"And she sounded weird. Too cheerful, as if she were covering up."

"*She probably was if Billy Ray was within earshot. Bet you a dollar she's decided not to file her petition in court.*"

Chantalene scowled. "I'd hate to see her back off. Showing up after twenty-eight years doesn't earn him any rights to her property."

"*That, partner, comes under the heading of nunaya.*"

Nun-a-ya business.

"Of *course* it's our business. You're her attorney, and I'm her honorary niece, sort of."

"*If she asks for legal advice, I'll give it to her. But I'm staying out of her love life, and so should you.*"

"Stop sounding so professional. I've seen you with your clothes off, remember that."

He laughed and his voice changed. "*Come over tonight. I'll cook for you.*"

"Umm. Wish I could. But I have a mid-term coming up in Early Brit Lit and about a hundred more pages of Middle English to wade through."

"*Yuk.*"

"Ye aulde yukke."

"*How's the data input going?*"

"It's boring as hell, but I've almost caught up with you."

"*Great. See you shortly.*"

He arrived an hour later carrying peanut butter sandwiches and two accordion folders which he laid on the desk beside the computer.

"What's this?" She opened one of the files and her eyes widened. "You took on more tax returns at this late date?"

"Just two."

"One of these is a corporation!"

"A very small company. Only five employees. If hail takes out my crop, I'll need all the customers I can get."

"Geez! You enjoy overworking, don't you? You get off on it."

"If you don't want to help, fine. I'll type them myself." He tugged on the back of the chair. "Get up."

"Forget it. Let go."

In the midst of their tug-of-war, the door opened and Thelma Patterson stepped inside. "Is this a bad time?" Clearly she didn't care. Her voice had a school-teacher edge.

Drew backed away from the chair. "Hi, Thelma. Come on in."

Chantalene's irritation passed straight to Thelma. "Why did you hang up on me earlier? And what's this about your taxes?"

"Sorry about that. He was right there. I couldn't talk." Thelma's face looked pinched behind her glasses.

"Don't tell me you've changed your mind about correcting your property deeds."

"No." She looked at Drew. "No, I want you to go ahead with that."

He motioned Thelma to the lone chair and assumed his favorite perch on the edge of the desk. "All right, Thelma. What's bothering you? I know good and well you filed your tax return a month ago."

Thelma's penciled eyebrows squeezed together, and her face flushed. She looked from Drew to Chantalene and back again, her mouth working with the effort to say what she'd come to say. "You're probably not going to believe me."

"Believe what?" Drew said.

Thelma's chin trembled, and Chantalene sat forward, alarmed. She'd never seen the intrepid Thelma so flustered. "Thelma? What is it? Is this about Billy Ray?"

Thelma's eyes settled on Chantalene as the most likely ally. She lifted her chin and her voice took on a tone of defiance.

"That man in my house is not my husband. He's an impostor!"

NINE

THELMA'S FACE TURNED re-entry red.

Chantalene's mouth fell open. Had she heard Thelma right?

"Thelma," Drew began gently, "everybody in town recognized Billy Ray." He was trying not to sound patronizing, a struggle he didn't entirely win.

Thelma set her jaw. "So what? I did, too, at first. Or thought I did. But I've been living with the man for three days now, and I'm telling you, he is *not* Billy Ray."

"People change," Drew said. "I imagine you aren't the same woman he remembers, either."

Thelma snorted. "I'd say not. He can't remember someone he's never met before."

Drew switched to his let's-look-at-this-logically voice. Usually this tone made Chantalene want to bite nails, but that was when he aimed it at her. Right now it seemed completely appropriate. "Is that it?" Drew asked. "He doesn't remember details you think he should? Things that were important to you?"

Thelma's face twisted. "Oh, he's got the details down. Too well. He knows more about my marriage than I remember." She started to say something else, but instead clamped her mouth tight.

Chantalene saw the distress in Thelma's eyes. Underneath the bravado, she was scared, and Thelma didn't scare easily. Chantalene imagined herself in Thelma's shoes. What if the man she'd taken into her house—maybe her *bed*—was a stranger?

Drew cleared his throat. "Then why do you think it isn't Billy Ray? Is it... something physical?"

Thelma's face blazed again and Chantalene sprang from the chair. "Drew, why don't you go get us some fresh coffee." She came around the desk and sank to her knees beside Thelma, handing her a tissue. The freckled hands were trembling.

Drew stayed on the edge of the desk, frowning. "You don't drink coffee." She gave him a withering look.

"Nevertheless...." He hopped off the desk. When the door closed behind him, Thelma slumped in the chair and blotted her nose with the tissue.

Chantalene nodded. "All right. But what is it that makes you certain, Thelma? What's different that the years wouldn't have changed?"

Thelma swallowed hard. "Mostly the little things. At first I thought I was imagining it, and I was too embarrassed to say anything to you. But then the other night when I was, um, really close to him... he doesn't smell the same."

Chantalene sat back on her heels. "I see," she said slowly. "Wow."

"I don't mean cologne or anything artificial," Thelma said quickly. "It's his own scent." Her eyes searched Chantalene's face for understanding.

"I can still remember the way my mother smelled," Chantalene said, "and my father. I'll never forget."

Thelma squeezed Chantalene's arm and nodded vigorously. For a moment she was too choked up to speak. "Thank you," she whispered.

Any doubts dissolved from Chantalene's mind. And she thought again of the cowboy's reference to prison time. Did Thelma know about that? Her skin crawled like a caterpillar farm.

Thelma twisted the tissue in her hands. "What's going on, Chantalene? Who is he?"

"We'll find out, I promise. But meanwhile, you should throw him out of your house—or move out yourself."

Thelma shook her head. "What excuse would I give? And what if he won't go? I don't think he's dangerous. He's been nothing but a gentleman so far, but if I cross him, that could change. And I will not move out of my own house and leave it with a stranger." Her voice was firm, but lower lip trembled and she bit down to stop it. "I can keep up the pretense for a few days."

Nothing Chantalene said would change her mind. Chantalene promised to act fast and Thelma agreed to call her every day.

"If he does anything that scares you," Chantalene warned, "I'm getting you out of there if I have to drag you."

"Believe me, you won't."

"IT'S LUDICROUS," DREW said, moving around Chantalene's kitchen that evening in a familiar way that gave her an odd sensation, like nesting. It felt homey, but alarming. After dinner, she would definitely shoo him away so she could study. Maybe.

Drew stirred the pasta loose from the bottom of the pot. "I tried to be patient with her, but the man looks like Billy Ray, he has ID, everything checks out. How else would he know things about their brief marriage, and about her farm? And about her dad, before he died?"

Chantalene dumped a heap of chopped vegetables into the wok. "I don't know. Maybe he's that brother who supposedly was killed in the car wreck. That could account for looking like Billy Ray. But a person's basic scent doesn't change, even with age. Maybe women are more attuned to smell than men. If I didn't see you for thirty years, I'd still remember your smell. Your *personal* scent."

He grinned and sniffed the back of her neck. "I like the way you smell, too."

"That tickles! You'll make me burn myself."

"I think you're over-rating olfactory memory," he said.

"No, I'm not. I read about it in one of my psych books." She shook her head. "I guess it's true about guys. They just don't get it." She added sauce to the vegetables and stirred lightly. "Take up the fettuccini, will you?"

"In my undervalued opinion," Drew said, pouring the contents of the steaming pot into a colander in the sink, "Thelma's having some natural panic about her impulsive decision to take the man back into her house. Like a bride who goes on a crying jag a week into the marriage."

"Bullshit."

"Of course she feels like he's a stranger," Drew went on. "He is. They've lived their lives apart. But for better or worse, he's still Billy Ray."

"Is not. Let's eat."

By mutual consent, they avoided the subject the rest of the evening. Chantalene was glad. His way she didn't have to tell Drew, at least tonight, that she'd promised not only to help Thelma find out the true identity of her would-be bedfellow, but also what had happened to the real Billy Ray.

Thelma was no flighty bride. She was a gutsy woman in a scary situation. If Drew didn't believe Thelma, neither would anyone else until they had some concrete proof. More than most people, Chantalene understood what it was like to know the truth and have no one believe you. She would not desert Thelma the way Tetumka citizens had once deserted her.

ON HER COMMUTE to class the next morning, Chantalene tried to review facts for her British Lit exam, but her mind kept returning to Thelma and her counterfeit husband. She figured they had two leads—the prison in California and the auto wreck in New Mexico. There was the sister in Tulsa, too, but she doubted the sister would tell her the truth even if Chantalene found her. She had the impression that Sunny had spent her life covering up for her brothers.

She would check out his prison story first. He had told Thelma that, under the influence of alcohol, he'd beaten a man in a bar fight, but that he'd paid his debt to society and not touched a drop of booze since. For Thelma's sake, Chantalene hoped that was true.

If her semester's credit weren't riding on this test, she would cut the class. At least she could make her long distance calls from campus, where Drew wouldn't overhear and tell her she was crazy. She checked the seat beside her to make sure she'd brought the file they'd compiled while searching for Billy Ray Patterson. She touched the manila folder, then grimaced. The file was there, all right, but she'd forgotten her lit book with her study notes in it. Great.

Oh well, if she didn't know the stuff by now, it was too late, anyway.

Dr. Davis's second-floor classroom smelled of chalk dust and jock sweat. The professor, a slight, effete man three times her age, clearly loved his job, especially on test days. His smile was evil as he passed down the aisle handing out essay questions.

"Choose two of the three questions and write your answers in essay format," he instructed.

Chantalene heard a few muffled groans and was careful to hide her pleasure. She'd never met a written exam she couldn't baffle. She scanned the questions.

Question 1. In the Beowulf epic, the hero Beowulf meets Grendel, the monster who is devastating the countryside, does battle and kills him, then immediately has to overcome Grendel's mother. After that he takes on a third enemy, a fiery dragon, and they fight until both are mortally wounded. Discuss the theme of the poem, including the values presented, and then evaluate whether this epic has any relevance to you as a student in the Twenty-first Century.

Ye gods. Dr. Davis wouldn't like her answer to that one. Quickly she outlined her answers to the two other questions, which weren't much better. Thank heaven he didn't expect them to write in Middle English.

An hour and a half later, she handed in her test booklet and gave Dr. Davis her best smile. "Could I please use the telephone in the English Department conference room? I have some business calls to make and need privacy. I promise to put any charges on my phone card." She produced the card as evidence.

"I'm sure you will." Dr. Davis patted her test paper. "I know how to find you."

The room was empty and she locked the door to avoid interruptions. She spread the Patterson file on the table along with an area code map from the phone book.

First, she dialed Tulsa information, but the operator found no listing for Sunny Ray Diehl, or anyone else with that last name.

No surprise there.

A clerk in the warden's office at San Juan prison confirmed that one Billy Ray Patterson had served three years there on a charge of manslaughter.

"Manslaughter could mean anything from reckless driving to a plea-bargained murder charge," she said. "What did he do?"

"The charge is a matter of public record," the man said, *"but we can't give out details except to a law enforcement agency. No matter how much I like your voice."*

Chantalene scowled. "Did I forget to say the attorney I work with is part of the Oklahoma State Bureau of Investigation?"

He laughed. *"Nice try."*

"Can we at least get a copy of his fingerprints?"

"Your local police can," he said.

Swell. Next she called the New Mexico State Police headquarters.

"This is the county sheriff's office in El Rio, Oklahoma," she said, crossing her fingers like a wayward child. "We're doing a background check on a Billy Ray Patterson, sometimes known as Donnie Patterson. Our information shows he spent some time in New Mexico," she paused, consulting her notes, "around 1972. Would you have information from that far back posted on computer?"

"Hold on, please," the woman's voice said. Chantalene heard the clicking of keys.

"We have no record on a Billy Ray Patterson, but under Donnie Ray Patterson we show a traffic fatality in 1972. Body burned beyond recognition but the officer who worked the scene found his wallet."

Bingo.

"Does it show who claimed his remains?" Chantalene asked.

"No, and it looks like the case file never was closed. Apparently, local police had some unanswered questions about the accident, but that kind of information isn't in the file."

"What about a name and number for someone who worked the case?"

Another pause. *"A detective Watson Wilson was the investigating officer for the Los Padres Police Department. I doubt if he's still around, but I can give you the department phone number."*

"Thanks. You've been a big help."

Chantalene scribbled the number and dialed.

In Los Padres, she got lucky.

TEN

DETECTIVE WATSON WILSON had risen through the ranks to become police chief of the small town in 1979, where he served until his retirement in 1998. He still lived in Los Padres, and his number was listed. He answered on the third ring.

This time Chantalene dropped the name of the Opalata county sheriff, for authenticity. If Sheriff Justin found out what she'd done, there would be hell to pay, but she had explained herself out of worse scrapes with him in their long and spotted history.

Watson Wilson's voice was gravelly and slow, like somebody's grandpa. He liked to talk and he had a clear recollection of the flaming wreck of Donnie Ray Patterson's pickup.

"Poor devil ran off the road and into a concrete bridge abutment right about daylight. Went to sleep at the wheel, most likely. Gas tank ruptured and blew. Happened just a mile or so out of town where our jurisdiction overlaps the highway, so the state police called me. Wreck was still smoking when I got there."

"Were you able to locate his family?"

"Nope. That one phone number—for the lady in Oklahoma—was the only lead we had. He had a Texas driver's license, I remember, with an outdated address. Couldn't locate anybody that knew him. County finally buried him as a transient, but I kept the file open hoping a missing-persons report would match up someday." Wilson wheezed, a sound meant for a sigh, Chantalene decided. "Somebody knew who he was, though. I don't think he was alone in that pickup."

"There was another body?"

"Nope. Motorist who reported the fire said he saw a fellow running along the highway, 'bout a mile before he came to the burning wreck. Said the fellow wasn't *trying to hitch, just hightailing like he was in a hurry to put some distance behind. Motorist didn't think anything of it until later."*

"Did the motorist give you a description of the man?"

"Now you're askin' my memory to be better'n it is. All that would be written down in the file, though."

So far everything matched the cowboy's story. Maybe he traded ID with his dead brother. But why?

"Would the police still have that wallet?"

"It's probably sealed up in the basement at the station. That's where we keep property from old cases we can't close."

She noticed that retired Chief Watson talked about his old job in the present tense. "Chief, if I came out there, could you help me get a look at that billfold?" She crossed her fingers again. "We just might be able to help you close that case."

His interest perked up. *"Somebody there knew the fellow?"*

"I'd hate to say anything yet. But we're making inquiries on behalf of the lady whose phone number was in that wallet."

Watson Wilson cleared his rocky throat. *"Sure, young lady. You come right ahead and I'll help you all I can."* He chuckled. *"Be the first interesting thing's happened since I retired."*

Chantalene hung up and dialed the Tetumka post office. "Thelma? Can you talk?"

"Nobody here but me. If someone comes in, I'll tell you."

Talking fast, Chantalene filled Thelma in on her conversation with Watson Wilson.

"Can you leave tomorrow?" Thelma said. *"I'll pay for your trip and your time. I'd go myself but I don't want to leave him alone in my house, especially since that oil company fellow might show up again."*

Chantalene bit her lip. Tax season. How could she abandon Drew before the deadline when she was supposed to be his partner? Especially when he'd think she was wasting her time, and Thelma's money? "Are you still doing okay at home?"

"So far. He's sleeping in the guest room, and he's very polite."

"I can go Saturday morning if you can hang on one more day," she said. "Before then, I need to know everything I can about the real Billy Ray. Do you have old pictures of him I could take? Photos of his family, samples of his handwriting, anything like that?"

"Nothing about his family, but I do have a scrapbook. You're welcome to anything we can find. My roommate," she said drily, "is helping Grant Selby work cattle today, so he's out of the house. If you can meet me at home this afternoon, I'll get Annabelle to cover for me here."

"I'll be there by two," Chantalene promised.

Several more hours lost from the office. Looks like an all-nighter with Gandalf. Just thinking about it made her neck ache.

CHANTALENE PULLED INTO Thelma's driveway at ten after two, finishing off the chocolate chip granola bar she'd bought from a vending machine at school. The black Cadillac crouched in front of the house, and Chantalene scowled.

The Suit was back. That oil company must think Thelma was sitting on a black gold mine. She'd have to wait him out and talk to Thelma alone. She parked beside the Caddy and walked around it toward the house. The sedan ticked like a lethargic bomb, expelling road heat.

Thelma's front door stood open behind the screen. Chantalene tapped on the door frame, then poked her head inside. "Thelma? It's me."

"Come on in!"

Chantalene opened the screen and stepped into the living room. Old farmhouses like this one didn't waste space on entryways.

"You'll have to excuse me now, Mister Hill," Thelma was saying. "My friend and I made plans."

"Of course." His voice took on a flirtatious tone. "I should have called before stopping by, but heck, I just enjoy visiting with you!"

Oh, brother.

Mr. Hill, today in a brown suit and turquoise-encrusted bolo tie, got up from the sofa and beamed her a smile that stretched upward to his crew cut. "Miss Morrell! Nice to see you again!"

She tried to decide if it was his phoniness or his bad taste that irritated her so much.

"You're good with names."

He winked. "No man forgets the name of a beautiful lady."

Chantalene gave him a phony smile. "I believe you have something stuck in your teeth." It was a metaphor, but it shut his mouth.

Thelma stepped between them and steered Mr. Hill toward the door. "I'll let you know as soon as I have things cleared up so I can sign your papers."

In the instant before he turned away from Chantalene, a look passed through Hill's eyes that startled her. *He's the kind of guy who would beat his wife.*

But the look had dissolved by the time Hill turned back to Thelma, all charm. "Our investors are getting restless, Missus Patterson. I'd sure hate to see you lose this opportunity."

By the front door, he stopped at the coat rack where a man's denim jacket hung alone on the hooks. He touched the coat and his eyebrows shot up like Roman candles. "Mister Patterson is back?"

"No." Thelma's tone was emphatic, and Chantalene knew she believed what she said. Hill looked unconvinced. Thelma held the front door open, lifting her chin. "The jacket belongs to a man friend, Mister Hill. I may be middle-aged, but I'm not dead."

Chantalene laughed aloud as Hill slid out the door and Thelma shut it firmly behind him.

"That fellow's beginning to get on my nerves," Thelma muttered, and motioned Chantalene toward the kitchen.

"With good reason. He's sure curious about your mister."

"That's what I mean. He's all flirty and polite, but when it comes to signing a lease, he acts as if my signature isn't good enough." She pointed to the kitchen table. "Sit. Have you had lunch?"

"Sort of. But I could use something cold to drink."

"I'll get it while you look through these." Thelma placed a scrapbook and a faded cigar box on the table. "Better hurry. I've no idea when he will get back."

Chantalene smiled at Thelma's refusal to call her housemate *Billy Ray*. She'd switched to a sort of capitalized He, un-deified by her tone of voice.

Thelma busied herself at the kitchen counter while Chantalene lifted the lid of the cigar box. Inside lay the letters Thelma's young husband had written before they married—the letters that made Thelma fall in love. Chantalene lifted one of the brittle envelopes but couldn't bring herself to open it. She set the box aside and opened the scrapbook.

On the first page, she found Thelma's marriage certificate, mounted with gold photo corners. Chantalene examined the surprisingly graceful signature of Billy Ray Patterson. She'd once read a book on handwriting analysis. From the large loops on his ascenders and descenders, the book's author would have concluded that Billy Ray had a generous nature.

She turned the page to a black and white snapshot of the newly married couple with a local magistrate, the Opalata County Courthouse rising above them in the background. Thelma looked young and slim, Billy Ray even younger, and blazingly handsome. The image definitely bore a resemblance to the mysterious wandering cowboy. Chantalene frowned. Could Thelma be wrong?

Thelma placed a glass of iced tea on a coaster, her eyes avoiding the snapshots. "I'll keep an eye out for him." She hurried toward the living room. Obviously she couldn't watch her past examined, even by a friend.

Feeling like a voyeur, Chantalene peeled back another page in the history of Thelma's one great romance.

Photo after photo of Billy Ray filled the album. Most seemed to be taken by Thelma. Billy waving from the tractor seat. A shirtless Billy Ray heaving bales of hay onto a flatbed truck. Thelma's adoration of him was obvious and unqualified. Had the affair been completely one-sided? A heartbreaking thought.

Occasionally, an anonymous shutterbug had captured the two together. One of those rare shots renewed Chantalene's faith. In the photo, Thelma posed playfully in a flowered dress and spring hat—her new Easter outfit, no doubt. She looked radiant, but it was the figure in the background that drew Chantalene's attention. His eyes fixed on Thelma, Billy Ray's smile bloomed with pride, his eyes shining. At that moment, love clearly etched the handsome face.

Chantalene loosened the photo from its corner holders and closed the scrapbook. Her throat felt tight as she sipped her tea. She took a deep breath before opening the box of letters.

Thelma had kept them in order by date. Chantalene unfolded the one on top, postmarked in June 19, 1969. Billy Ray's youthful handwriting inched across lined pages torn from a tablet. Chantalene read in silence, aware of Thelma's quiet movements in the front room—straightening the house, needlessly sweeping the mat by the front door.

The first letter was a travelogue of moving north with the harvest, impressions of a small town boy passing through country he'd never seen. Gradually, the missives grew more personal—journal entries of a lonesome young man who was sensitive to the natural world and articulate despite his faulty spelling and grammar.

> *This week I finally got to run the combine instead of just driving the truck. It takes some practice, but by the second day I had that big machine tamed like a bunny. I can turn it on a dime & pick up a little patch a wheat standin in a mud puddle without even gettin the tires muddy! Of course next thing I know I've ran the header to low and scooped up some dirt when the tires hit a bump. The boss hollered Hey Rookie! and that brot me down to earth real quick!*
>
> *But sometimes, sitting up so high above all that horsepower, I feel larger than life—like if I really tried, I could do anything. It's odd, though, cause the next minute I look up and I'm way out in some field that runs clear to the sky, and realize how small I am in this world. It's the closest I ever come to knowin what God is, I guess. And I gotta say, it's pretty lonesome.*

Chantalene bit her lip, goose bumps scattering down her arms. She knew just the feeling he meant.

The last letter read, *When I get back, I'm gonna take you to El Rio on a real date. We'll catch a movie and eat at that fancy place—Sandhill's, was it? You can ask a neighbor to stay with your dad one evening—I won't take no for an answer!*

Thelma hadn't believed he would really come, but it was easy to see why the letters charmed her. Chantalene fell in love with them a little bit, herself. Not only that, she kept remembering the stories the cowboy had told at dinner on his first night in town, and she had no trouble picturing him as the author of these letters.

Except for one thing. The newcomer's grammar was nearly flawless. Unless he conjugated verbs in prison or on the back of a horse, how would he have managed to polish his language skills so much?

If he wasn't Billy Ray, why was he pretending? Was it as simple as Thelma's money? And what had happened to the man who wrote the letters?

Closing the box, she kept one letter in which the handwriting and signature were clearest and carried it to the living room. Thelma stood by the window, looking out through a lace curtain. Chantalene doubted Thelma was really seeing the front yard or the road that led to her house.

"I'd like to take a photo with me, and make a copy of one of the letters for a sample of his handwriting."

"Certainly," Thelma said. "Anything you need." When she turned, Chantalene saw a telltale glisten at the corner of her eye. "I've put five hundred dollars cash in this envelope. Will that be enough for your plane ticket and expenses?"

"More than I need. I'm going to drive instead of fly."

Thelma frowned. "Are you sure? It's got to be six hundred miles!"

"I know. But I'd have to drive to Oklahoma City or Dallas and wait to catch a flight, then fly into an airport that's still a hundred miles from Los Padres, and rent a car. I think it'll be faster and cheaper to drive straight through."

Chantalene never knew quite how to react when people hugged her. Thelma smelled like flowers and felt like a warm pillow. She turned Chantalene loose and did her best to smile.

"I can't tell you how I appreciate this. I don't know what I'd do if nobody believed me. Speaking of that, have you told Drew that you're going yet?"

Chantalene chewed her lip. "No."

And she was planning to drive his car more than a thousand miles on a mission he'd consider a goose chase. Well, she had wanted some excitement. Be careful what you wish for, her mother used to say.

ELEVEN

IN BUSTLING DOWNTOWN Tetumka, Chantalene parked in front of the office—the only car on the street. Annabelle's dust-colored compact would be under the carport behind the post office, but Drew always parked his red truck in front and she'd expected it to be here now.

She fished for the key to the office door then realized it was open. Drew sat behind the desk looking like a wilted sunflower.

"Where's your truck?"

"Dead battery. I walked over to your place and rustled your horse."

Her eyebrows raised. "Whippoorwill let you ride him?"

"Behaved like an almost perfect gentleman. He's parked on the grass behind the building."

"That's amazing. Whip has never let anyone besides me ride him."

Drew shrugged. "Animals love me."

"Yes, we do." She set her notebooks on the bookcase, making sure the Patterson file was on the bottom of the stack. "That battery must have been defective. You ought to wring a new one out of that car dealership."

"I don't think so." Drew's expression turned sheepish. "Apparently I left the interior light on all night."

"Ah-ha. The absent-minded attorney."

"You should talk. The office door was unlocked when I got here."

She stopped in mid-motion. "Are you sure?"

"Yup. You must have forgotten to turn the latch when you left yesterday."

She glanced around the crowded office. "Is anything missing?"

"Nah. The computer's the only thing here worth taking."

"I'm sorry. I could have sworn I locked it."

"No big deal. That lock wouldn't keep out a thief, anyway. It just protects us from kids or the curious."

One of the things she loved about Drew was that he didn't get uptight about minor things. Usually. Of course, sometimes they didn't agree on what was minor. She debated whether the moment was right to tell him about her impending soiree to New Mexico.

Before she'd decided, he said, "I got one of those Oklahoma City accounts finished up this morning. All I have left to post is their state return."

"Wow. You must have stayed up half the night again. Want me to take over at the keyboard?"

"By all means." He leaned his head side to side and his neck crackled. "I'll go across the street and get us a soda. Orange for you?"

"Great," she said, still afloat in iced tea. "And a licorice stick, please."

When he came back, she would definitely tell him.

She sat behind the desk and tried to make sense of Anchor Brick Company's Schedule D. But when she glanced up at the steer's-head clock, a cold prickly scampered down her backbone. Something was wrong there. Something besides that ugly clock.

Sitting still, she concentrated on the warning. In a moment, she realized one of the filing cabinet drawers was standing open half an inch. This never happened in their office. Drew was a compulsive neatnik, and Chantalene hadn't taken anything from that drawer for a week. This wasn't earthquake country—so that left one explanation.

Somebody else had been in that drawer.

Who? And why?

Suddenly, she was dead certain she had locked the office door before leaving last night. She remembered doing it. Someone had picked the lock, not a difficult task, and looked through the files. For what?

She remembered to breathe again. Then another prickle. Did Drew really leave his interior light on in his precious truck? What if someone didn't find what they wanted in the office—the Patterson file?—and decided to look in his truck, under cover of darkness? If the culprit tried to shut the door quietly, the latch might not catch—and the interior light would stay on.

Ridiculous.

But possible.

She pictured herself telling this scenario to Drew, and heard his voice of logic. *Get a grip, girl. That's a lot of supposition.*

She was still debating this when Drew returned with two cans of soda, a licorice whip for her and a package of Ding Dongs for him. They might not have much else in common, but their love of junk food would hold them together. He pulled the spare chair up to the opposite side of the desk and cleared a space for his work by setting the "In" basket and phone/fax on the floor.

"Ten more days," he said, rolling his shoulders and stretching his back. "No matter how many hours we have to work between now and the fifteenth, it'll all be over by then."

Chantalene bit her lip. "I've got to take off this weekend. But I'll make up for it tomorrow and Monday."

His forehead crinkled. "*This* weekend? Seriously? It's the last one before the deadline."

"I know. I'm sorry."

"Sorry? That's it?" Then he hesitated. "Is something wrong?"

She took a deep breath. "I'm going to New Mexico for Thelma." She saw his face cloud and talked faster. "The cop who worked that auto wreck involving Donnie Ray Patterson still lives there, and I talked to him. They have the wallet that belonged to the dead man. And the cop says there may have been somebody with him who walked away."

"So what?"

"I don't know so what." She hated sounding defensive. "But Thelma asked me to check it out, and I promised to help. Drew, consider just for a minute that Thelma's right. If this fellow isn't really Billy Ray, who is he? Think how creepy it would be for her to have this stranger pretending to be her husband."

"It's a little hard to feel sorry for a woman who'd take a man home with her when the last she saw of him was his backside walking out the door thirty years ago. If she's changed her mind, why doesn't she throw him out?"

"What makes you think he'd go? His name's on her farm, and he has the whole town on his side, for some reason I can't fathom. Everybody seems to think he's just ducky. I can't understand why you believe them instead of her."

Drew huffed a tired breath and stretched his neck muscles. Chantalene heard his neck pop. "I can see how alarming it is to Thelma. But in a few days she'll change her mind again and realize this guy is her husband. She may not want to stay married, and that's her prerogative. But you saw them the other night. She certainly recognized him then."

Chantalene met his eyes. "Drew. If I didn't see you for fifty years, I could pick your tee shirt out of a line up if I was blindfolded. Just by remembering your smell."

He threw up his hands. "Oh, here we go again. Nobody knows what the nose knows!"

"Okay, don't believe me. Or Thelma, either. But you'd better believe *this*. When everybody in town thought my father was a criminal and I was a witch, Thelma treated me like a friend. I am going to help her, whether you agree with it or not. If you don't want me to drive your car, I'll borrow hers."

Drew's usually pleasant face turned darker than she'd ever seen it. "Why do I waste time trying to reason with you? You'll do what you want, anyway."

She kept quiet, except for the bass-drum hammering in her chest.

"Do at least one sane thing," he said finally. "Take Thelma with you. I can't go, because I've made promises to these clients." He swept a hand toward the tax forms scattered across the desk. "Two women on the road is at least a little safer than one alone."

"Thelma will not go off and leave him there in her house," she said quietly. "I'll be fine, really. I am not so sheltered and simple that I can't take care of myself." She paused. "But thanks for worrying."

He looked at her for a silent moment. Then he began to gather his work and stuff it into his valise.

"What are you doing?"

"I'm going home."

She waited two beats then said, "Take the car, so you don't lose your papers. I'll ride Whip home."

He left without another word.

She sat in the empty office, listening to the ticking clock, the silence loud in her ears. She took deep breaths that were scented by Drew's anger and her regret. It was another olfactory memory she'd never forget.

Had she just chosen her friendship with Thelma over her relationship with Drew?

Dread weighted her chest—or was it foreboding? Her eyes focused on the drawer of the filing cabinet, standing ajar.

TWELVE

ROSE-COLORED LIGHT streaked the eastern sky when Chantalene pulled onto the Indian Nation Turnpike, her headlights searching north. At this hour she had the highway almost to herself. A roadmap of the Southwest, folded open, was tucked above the visor, but she wouldn't need a map for hours. Farther north, the Turnpike connected with Interstate 40, which bisected Oklahoma east to west. Once she hit I-40 and headed west, she'd be on autopilot all the way to the Texas Panhandle.

The highway sang beneath the tires. She enjoyed driving, and she'd learned as a child to be comfortable with solitude. For security, Drew's cell phone sat beside her on the seat like a sleeping pet. *These are the good old days.*

Then she thought of last night, when Drew had given her the phone, and her moment of travel bliss evaporated. She had gone to his house to talk to him, hoping to make things right before she left for New Mexico. Instead they'd argued again. And somehow the argument shifted, as arguments do, to the big topics underlying the small ones. Usually the rational one, Drew had finally lost it.

"This crazy trip is just an excuse to put some trauma in your life," he'd accused. "You're *addicted* to it. You can't stand living like a normal person."

"Hey! I didn't go looking for this," she said, her voice rising. "Thelma asked for my help, and I'll be damned if I'm going to leave her hanging, like you and everybody else in town who choose to believe the woman can't recognize her own husband!"

His face went quiet. "You don't recognize yours."

He walked away from her then, and she felt a sinking inside.

They were back to the old theme.

He wanted a commitment, a settled life. Kids, eventually. The idea sounded good to her as a fantasy for the future. But not yet. In her heart lurked a terror that once she settled in Tetumka and had children, the boundaries of her life would be as fixed as the death date on a tombstone.

Alone in the car with the open highway ahead, she hunted for any truth in Drew's accusation. She wouldn't cop to needing trauma. Losing her parents and being a teenage runaway were enough of that for a lifetime. But she did want more than college classes and data processing. The truth was that she was on the road this morning not only for Thelma, but also for herself.

There was more to their argument, as well. She hated being dependent, and right now she was dependent on Drew's car and Drew's job. If it weren't for him, she'd might be serving fries through a window in El Rio for minimum wage. Drew was taking care of her as if they were married. He had accepted all the responsibility without getting what he wanted from the relationship, and that made her feel rotten.

Drew would never point this out, of course. Even in a fight he had rules he never broke. It was part of what she loved about him, but sometimes his ethics made her feel small. Maybe she'd won this particular battle, but he was the better man.

Chantalene took a deep breath and unclenched her grip on the steering wheel. The sky had lightened and she switched off the headlights, glancing at the car's digital clock. She pictured Drew just waking up, fuzzy-headed and warm from sleep, his eyebrows rumpled in all directions. She wondered if he felt as lousy about the argument as she did.

He'll come around when you prove Thelma right.

She thought about Thelma then, doing chores around her farm at this hour. Was the counterfeit husband afoot as well, or did he lie abed and let her feed the calves and chickens? She tried to imagine living with a man who pretended to be someone you used to love, when you knew he wasn't. Thelma had a lot of grit to hang in there while Chantalene went off in search of his identity.

In the early sunlight, redbud trees necklaced the creeks and watersheds with bright magenta, and sand plums bloomed white against a backdrop of new green. "Nature's first green is gold, her hardest hue to hold," she quoted. "Her early leaf's a flower, but only so an hour."

Robert Frost. But the poem ended sadly. "Then leaf subsides to leaf; so Eden sank to grief. So dawn goes down to day. Nothing gold can stay." She thought of Drew again.

At mid-morning she passed through Oklahoma City, grateful to miss rush hour traffic, and sailed west across increasingly flat land. She was making good time. Semi rigs whooshed past on both sides of the highway, rocking the Volvo with waves of diesel exhaust. In self-defense she nudged the cruise control up to seventy-five.

She crossed the Texas state line at noon and pulled into a truck-stop diner. Her joints crackled as she walked inside. The grilled cheese sandwich buttered her fingertips and the French fries were homemade—a fantastic mega-dose of cholesterol. In a frenzy of excess, she ordered a chocolate milkshake for the road.

A dark green pickup had parked too close to her car in the lot, and she could barely get her door open. "Inconsiderate jerk," she muttered, squeezing into her seat without caring if her car door added another ding to the pickup's dented side. Then she realized that inside the dark-tinted windows, someone was sitting behind the wheel.

With the sun glaring overhead, she couldn't see a face inside the truck, just a shadow of bulky shoulders. But she knew the driver could see her plainly, and Drew's warnings rose in her ears. She slammed her door quickly and locked it. Leaving the parking lot, she glanced in the rear-view mirror, but the pick-up hadn't moved.

The sun was high and hot when she left I-40 in eastern New Mexico, turning south on a two-lane highway that curved through semi-desert landscape spread with low mesquite and yucca spikes. For a hundred miles, she didn't pass one bona fide town. A phrase on her New Mexico map kept returning to her—*Jornada del Muerto*. Journey of the dead? She wished she knew Spanish. French, too, and maybe Italian. Next semester she'd definitely enroll in a foreign language class.

At mid-afternoon she stopped for gas and bottled water at a roadside store. The hand-lettered sign out front carried three lines.

Watermelon
Pool chemicals
Jesus Saves.

She turned west again on a narrow, empty road where a bullet-pocked sign pointed toward Los Padres. The Fathers? Or maybe in a broader sense, The Parents. The road began to climb, and the air that sliced through her windows felt dry and cool. She rounded a high curve around a rocky hill that in Oklahoma would constitute a mountain. There it was, a sudden oasis of stucco and greenery, accented with tile roofs and flowers. The road led directly to the main street and a grassy park that formed the village plaza. In the center of the park, surrounded by a low, spoke-like fountain, a sculpture of three stocky priests extended sandstone hands to all who approached.

The padres cast long shadows in the afternoon sunlight. Small shops, their doors open to the clear, dry air, bordered a one-way street around the plaza. Enchanted, she drove around the square twice, then turned off on a side street to find a travel-mart where she could get a cold drink and use the restroom. In the parking lot, she dug out the scrap of paper with retired Chief Watson Wilson's phone number. Drew's cell phone had free roaming service, so she dialed from there.

An hour later, she met Chief Watson Wilson in front of the police station. She identified him as soon as he stepped out of his ancient station wagon. He looked just like his voice.

His hair was silver, his face deeply tanned in spite of a wide-brimmed hat. Battered cowboy boots poked out beneath his loose-legged khaki pants, which Chantalene suspected were the bottom half of his old uniform. He wore a plaid sport shirt, open at the neck and tucked in over a slight paunch. And red suspenders.

"Glad you made it safe and sound," he said in the friendly, grumbly voice she recognized from their first conversation. "Hate to see a woman on the road alone."

Et tu, Watson?

"No problem," she said, and showed her teeth.

"You find the motel?"

"All checked in. Thanks." She'd also gassed up the car and eaten cheese crackers and fruit juice for supper. "Will we have trouble seeing the police records on a Saturday evening?"

Wilson adjusted the wire-rimmed glasses on his generous nose. "Actually it's a good time. The boys'll be busy finishing up the week's paperwork and won't pay much attention to what we're doing." He chuckled. "I still pretty much have the run of the place."

I'll bet you do. She liked Watson Wilson, and her conscience poked at her for the lie she'd told him over the phone about being with the El Rio sheriff's department.

He escorted her into a one-story adobe store front where a sign made from terra cotta tiles read Los Padres Police. Inside, two dark-haired cops glanced up from their desks. One held a phone to his ear while writing on some kind of form. The other was working on a very old computer.

"Buenos noches, el Capitan," they said almost in unison, and grinned. Watson Wilson returned their greeting and Chantalene saw their eyes switch from Wilson to her and back again. One of them rose to shake Wilson's hand.

"What can we do for you?" he said.

"This young lady came all the way from Oklahoma to check on a missing person that passed through here some years back," Wilson told him. "Thought I'd dig through the old files and see what I could find to help her out."

"Better you than me, eh?"

"Right. Wouldn't want to keep you from your paperwork."

The young cop laughed and retrieved a key from a desk drawer, tossing it to Wilson. *"Buena suerte."*

Chantalene followed him down a hallway and then a flight of cracked, concrete stairs that bent back on itself and ended at a metal door. Wilson unlocked it.

"Wait here until I get the light," he said.

In a moment she heard a snap and light flooded the basement room. She squinted. From a long cord in the center of the room, a bare bulb jittered shadows across the concrete floor. Fan blades began a slow swirl from another hanging fixture, and beneath the light sat a coffee-ringed card table. The place smelled like a cellar.

Chantalene paused in the doorway while a shiver ran across her back. She hated any enclosure without windows, especially basements and cellars. There was never enough air. Her chest tightened.

"Come on in," Chief Wilson said, "but watch out for spiders."

Perfect.

Wilson crossed to a bank of filing cabinets against one wall, checked the drawer labels, then opened one and fingered through files. In a moment he came out with a brown accordion folder tied with string and placed it on the card table. Chantalene checked the seat of the metal folding chair before sitting down opposite him.

The chief's thick fingers had trouble with the knot in the string—arthritis, no doubt—but finally he opened the fold-over flap and removed the contents of the file. A vision of the ragged, enigmatic cowboy who'd entered her office only last week rose in Chantalene's mind. Her heartbeat quickened. Was the secret to Billy Ray Patterson contained in this folder?

Wilson picked up a manila envelope and dumped something out. Before her on the table lay the billfold of a dead man—all that was left of one Donnie Ray Patterson.

If that's who he was.

Inside the wallet, behind a plastic window, a faded Texas driver's license bore the name, but no photo. The wallet contained no other cards, no pictures. A ten dollar bill and three ones still resided in the money compartment. "Honest cops you have around here."

"Everything here is just like we found it," Wilson said, and he didn't smile.

From a second envelope, he removed a creased slip of paper about two inches square, holding it carefully by one edge. He laid it before her. Seeing Thelma Patterson's first name and phone number written there, the same number she had now, gave Chantalene an unexpected ripple of shock. The numbers and letters, written in pencil in a dark, firm hand, were well-formed.

She swallowed. "I recognize this writing."

"Izzat right?" His tone was noncommittal.

From the file folder in her bag, Chantalene produced the letter from Thelma's scrapbook and laid the envelope next to the scrap of paper. It didn't take a handwriting expert to see the resemblance. A unique stroke forming the *T* on Thelma matched exactly.

"I'll be durned," Wilson said. "Who wrote that letter?"

"A man named Billy Ray Patterson, who was married to Thelma nearly thirty years ago. Donnie Ray may have been his alias. Or his brother."

The chief nodded, his brow creased. "Either that, or the dead fellow really was Donnie Ray, and Billy Ray was his alias."

Chantalene met his eyes and blinked, thinking that over. "Or the billfold belonged to the guy running from the scene."

"Yup." Wilson nodded, chuckling. "Ain't detective work fun?"

"I don't suppose we could lift fingerprints from the wallet after all this time," she said.

"Time wouldn't matter so much as the fact that every cop in the department, including me, handled the thing. Besides, we don't have fingerprints from the burned guy to match up with."

"No, but we have a live one back in Oklahoma, claiming to be Billy Ray Patterson. We have reason to believe he isn't who he says."

"Have fingerprints from him?"

Chantalene hesitated. "No. But I ... we could get them."

She had a bizarre vision of sneaking into the cowboy's bedroom at night, rolling his limp fingers on an ink pad. Too many detective novels.

But Thelma could save something in the house that he'd touched—a glass, the raised toilet seat. Then she remembered the prison. His prints would be on file in California. *If* he was the same Patterson that served time there.

But Wilson was shaking his head. "Not a gnat's chance in a swarm of blackbirds you could get a useable print off the outside of that billfold. And if you did, it'll likely be one of ours."

"Could we give it a shot? I don't have much else to go on."

"We could try that little plastic window inside it." Wilson shrugged. "I've got nothing better to do today. There's a kit upstairs, and I used to be a pretty good hand with it."

She caught a quick spark in his eyes. Some people just weren't cut out for retirement.

While he went upstairs for the kit, Chantalene read the police reports on the accident and fire that ended the life of the supposed Donnie Ray Patterson. There wasn't much in it. From the torso up, the body was burned beyond recognition. He'd been wearing cowboy boots and jeans. The report identified the boots as Justins.

If there was enough left of them to identify the brand, where were they?

She asked Watson Wilson that question when he lumbered back down the stairs.

"Should be over there in property storage." He nodded toward one end of the room where tall, unpainted plywood shelves stood in rows like library racks. "I'll take a look after we do this."

He spread a clean newspaper on the table. From a beat-up plastic tackle box, he set out a baby-food jar of white powder, a tiny, soft brush that looked like a feather duster for Barbie, and a long-handled magnifying glass.

Her eyebrows pinched together. Was this how they did it in Dallas or L.A.? He saw her eyeing the magnifying glass. "That'll help us see if we've got anything. If we do, we'll take it upstairs and have Carlos photograph it to send off for ID. We don't have all that fancy computer stuff here."

She nodded, and felt her pulse rise to her neck as he opened the wallet on the table, dipped the brush in the powder and delicately sifted it across the plastic window that covered Donnie Ray Patterson's driver's license. "I've always wanted to know how to do this."

Wilson glanced up at her and smiled. For a moment their eyes met like two kids in complicity over a homemade science project.

"This is magnetic powder," he said. "It sticks to the oils and perspiration left behind from the top ridges of skin in a fingerprint."

"Would the oils still be there after all these years?"

"If we're damned lucky." Wilson picked up the magnifier and began a centimeter by centimeter inspection of the whitened rectangle.

"Nothing," he said at last. "Want to take a look?"

She took the glass and leaned over the billfold. The power and clarity of the instrument impressed her; smudges and streaks outlined by white powder leaped into huge detail. But nothing resembled even half of a fingerprint. She sighed and put down the magnifier.

Wilson turned the wallet over and dusted the outside, repeated his examination and handed her the glass. *Nada.* He re-sacked the wallet and replaced it in the file. Then he took out the crinkled note.

"You can get prints from paper?"

"They got one of Hitler's from a book he'd handled years before," he said. "For paper, it's a different process, though." He produced an aerosol can from the tackle box. The label said *6% Ninhydrin Solution.* "Move back. These fumes can be toxic."

Holding the paper by one corner with a pair of tweezers, he shook the can twice and sprayed both sides. "This stuff reacts with the amino acids left by skin contact. It'll turn a fingerprint dark purple," he said, holding the paper suspended to let the solution dry. "Trouble is, it usually takes 24 to 48 hours for it to work."

"*Two days?*"

"You don't want to hang around Los Padres a couple days and check out the night life?" Wilson smiled. "Guess we'd better speed things up, then. Hand me one of those baggies out of the box, will you?"

He slipped the dry paper into a plastic bag she held open for him. Then he put everything, including the plastic bag, back in the tackle box and said, "What time is it?"

She glanced at her watch. "Six thirty. But that's Oklahoma time. Five-thirty here."

"Maybe we can still catch Sammy Sung at his dry cleaning shop. I'll give him a call upstairs."

"What?"

"Come on. Hurry."

Upstairs, Wilson thumbed quickly through the thin yellow pages of a phone book and repeated the number to himself as he dialed. Chantalene had no idea what was going on, but in the belief that Wilson's odd behavior had something to do with the slip of paper in the baggie, she kept quiet.

"Sammy?" Wilson boomed after a few moments. "Glad I caught you. Watson Wilson. Need a little favor, and I'm at the station now. If I hightail it down there, can you wait for me? Yeah. Great. Appreciate it."

He hung up. "Let's go. It's only two blocks. We'll walk."

Chantalene took two quick steps for each one of Wilson's long strides as they hustled over Los Padres' uneven sidewalks. "Heat can speed up the chemical reaction of the ninhydrin," he told her. "We're going to use Sammy's pressing machine."

Sammy Sung, a slight man with a wrinkled brown face, smiled and nodded them toward the back room of Sung's Cleaners & Laundry. He'd been pressing somebody's suit pants, so the big, alligator-shaped machine was already hot.

"Switch off the steam, please, sir," Wilson said. From the tackle box, he produced a sheet of folded white butcher paper, which he laid flat on the ironing table, shiny side up. He took the treated note from its bag, laid it on one end of the butcher paper and folded the other end on top of the note. When it lay smoothed and ready, he instructed Mr. Sung to lower the presser head and hold it down.

Heat emanated from the machine and Chantalene smelled hot paper. It felt like a full minute before Wilson motioned Mr. Sung to raise the presser.

Wilson carefully peeled back the top fold of butcher paper. All three of them leaned forward to see. Before Chantalene could examine the slight darkenings that appeared on the creases of the note, Wilson folded the paper back over it and said, "Hit it again, Sammy."

Sammy did.

This time when Wilson unfolded the butcher paper, definite purplish-black markings appeared on the note.

"Ahhhh," Sammy Sung pronounced.

"Hmmm," Wilson said.

Chantalene smiled. Without waiting for permission, she scooped the magnifier from Wilson's kit and leaned over the ironing table. Heat floated up to her face.

Purple etched the crossed fold lines of the paper like thin veins. She examined each flat quadrant for any swirls that might delineate a thumb or finger, then raised her head, disappointed. "I just can't tell."

Wilson took the glass. "This could be a partial in the top left corner."

Sammy Sung and Chantalene leaned forward in unison while Wilson held the magnifier over the spot. The drycleaner's dark eyes squinted into slits, his oily head nearly touching hers. The odor of garlic cut her inspection short.

"Is it enough to identify?"

Wilson shook his head. "I doubt it. There's no center ridges."

The three of them stood silent for a moment, appraising the stained note.

"You bring that letter along?" Wilson asked.

"Yes. Right here." She patted her file folder. "Why?"

He looked at her. "You're sure this lady's husband wrote the letter, right?"

"Yes."

"If we could get a latent off it, and you could get a print from the fella back in Oklahoma, at least you could tell if it's the same guy or not. Wouldn't solve our mystery here, but it might solve yours."

Chantalene hesitated a moment, thinking of Thelma's precious letter stained with purple. What would Thelma say?

"Good idea." She handed the envelope to Chief Wilson. Fifteen minutes later, they left Sung's Cleaners with a clear, purple thumb print etched on Thelma's letter.

But how the heck would she get that cowboy to hold still while she inked his fingers? Or if Thelma could manage to save a useable print on his iced-tea glass, what could Chantalene tell Sheriff Justin—who considered her a menace anyway—that would convince him to dust and identify a latent fingerprint?

And speaking of Justins, what about those boots?

THIRTEEN

MISSION BELLS CHIMED a peaceful Sunday morning in Los Padres as Chantalene drove out of town with a dead man's boots on the back seat of her car. She'd just finished breakfast with Watson Wilson and turned onto the main road out of town when she noticed a dark green pickup at the stoplight on a cross street.

Surely it couldn't be the same vehicle she'd seen at the Amarillo truck stop. There must be thousands of green Ford pickups in Texas and New Mexico, even with dark-tinted windows. The light changed and she moved on, but for the next mile she kept glancing in the rearview mirror.

Earlier, over huevos rancheros that Watson Wilson paid for, she had convinced him to let her carry the boots back to Oklahoma on the chance Thelma might recognize them. They'd switched to first names by then, and she'd also cleared her conscience, admitting that she didn't work with the Opalata County sheriff's office, wasn't even a private investigator in any official sense.

Watson didn't even glance up from his eggs. "I knew that."

"You've known all along?"

He slurped his hot coffee in a quiet, friendly way. "Since yesterday. You don't act much like a cop."

"Oh." She didn't know whether to be insulted or say thanks. "Then why did you help me?"

Watson never hurried his answers. She was learning the rhythm of conversation with the retired chief. It was like a badminton game. No matter how hard you struck the birdie, the thing floated in its own timeless arc before being swatted back. In the interim, daily business at the small café hummed around them. Quick commands in Spanish drifted out from the kitchen, along with the scent of last night's chili relleno special.

"This lady, Thelma. She's a friend of yours. Right?"

"Yes. A very close friend."

Watson chewed. "She's in a tight spot and she can't get anybody official to help her?"

"Yes. In fact, I'm the only one who believes her."

He nodded. "Right. That's why I helped you."

Chantalene let her fork rest idly a few moments while she thought about that. Watson added green chili salsa to his eggs and kept on shoveling.

"So you helped me," she said slowly, "because somebody you don't know is in trouble."

"That's about it."

She watched him and waited.

He lowered his voice so it didn't carry beyond their table. "When I was a rookie on the force, I saw a lot of folks who needed help. Mexican families, especially, who came to the police about a missing husband, or a son or daughter. And the guy who was chief back then just blew them off. Took the name and description but did nothing. Or a guy with one arrest on his record, maybe some crazy kid stunt, and later on when he needed help from the law, he couldn't get it." Leathery wrinkles bunched at the corners of Watson's pale eyes. "I swore if I was ever in a position to do things different, I damn sure would. And I did."

Chantalene looked at him a moment before she spoke. "I wish I'd known you years ago." *You'd have helped a twelve-year-old orphan whose father was hanged and whose mother disappeared without a trace.*

Her tone brought a frown to Watson's face, but he didn't ask. She looked away quickly and drank her tea.

Watson cleared his throat. "Anyway, can't much harm come from poking around in a twenty-year-old case. Always bothered me that we couldn't find that fella Patterson's family and notify 'em. Figured someday somebody would come looking for him, and you're it."

"Yes. I am."

So she told him the story from the beginning, even the part about the 28-year-old farmer's daughter who was wooed by an itinerant harvest hand nine years her younger, and how he won her heart with his letters. Especially that part, because Watson Wilson had a warm gold aura that made her believe he was a romantic at heart.

She told him about Billy Ray Patterson's desertion, about Thelma being so flustered by the phone call from New Mexico a few years later that she couldn't even ask questions. About their recent search for the missing husband and his popping up like a fishing cork when he thought he might inherit.

And lastly, about Thelma's certainty that the man her neighbors accepted as her missing husband, the man living under her roof and sharing her meals, was an impostor.

Watson listened closely. Chantalene could see his eyes soften. When she thought he was ready, she said, "So I want to take the boots back with me. If they were her husband's, she'll know it. And we'll know that he died in that car accident."

"They're evidence," Watson said. "We were never positive that wreck was an accident. The boys can't release evidence to you just because you have a pretty face."

"But they would release the boots to you."

He shook his head. "I don't have any official status, either."

Ha. Those cops idolize you. She spread jalapeño jelly on her last bite of toast. "How long do you think it's been since anybody looked at those boots in that basement?"

Without even looking up, she felt his eyes narrow.

"Twenty years," he said, guardedly.

"So if they were gone for a few weeks, who would know?"

"I would."

Chantalene wiped her hands and rummaged through the folder beside her on the seat of the booth. On a clean spot beside Watson's plate, she carefully laid the photo of Thelma Patterson, newly married and wearing her Easter dress, and her handsome young husband whose eyes focused only on her.

Just as she'd hoped, Thelma's smooth face, so obviously in love, drew Watson's attention. He picked up the photo and held it at a proper distance for his bifocals. Held it for a long time.

"That's him in the background?"

"Yes."

"And the guy who showed up still looks like this?"

"Enough," she said.

Watson's eyes went back to Thelma. "She has a nice face. Reminds me a little of my wife when we were young."

"I didn't know there was a Missus Wilson."

Watson nodded his graying head. "She's been gone a long time."

Chantalene waited.

"Maybe it's really him," Watson said. "What if all her neighbors are right?"

"And what if they're not? How does the fellow know so much about their past? And what does he want? He spent some time in prison, remember."

Watson finished his third cup of coffee and picked up the check. "Come on then. We'll make one last visit to the property room before you leave town. I'll get a copy of that fingerprint, too, and see what I can run down."

She carried the boots out of the police station in a brown grocery bag. Returning the property room key to its desk drawer, Watson waved to the cop on duty, who was on the phone. The cop returned the retired chief's salute and gave Chantalene a smile.

On the street, Watson opened her car door and waited until she was inside and had rolled down the window. He shut the door firmly and pushed down the lock. "You drive careful, you hear? I'm glad to see you got one of those portable phones in the car."

Chantalene smiled up at him. Why did she enjoy it when the grandfatherly chief fussed over her, but when Drew did, it ticked her off? Someday she'd have to figure that out. "If you're ever passing through southeastern Oklahoma, stop and say hello," she said.

"Will do. And do me favor. Check in with the local law when you get back. If that fellow's got a prison record, he might be a harder character than he looks."

"Darn! I meant to ask you to check on that. Would you be able to find out why he was in prison?"

"Sure. I'll ask the boys to run his name. Did you say California?"

"Yes. San Juan Prison. And something else, for what it's worth. He told Drew that he and a couple buddies stole a pile of money from a crooked Indian bingo hall in Oklahoma thirty years ago. Seems the family that ran it was connected with the mob, and they sent some thugs after Billy and his pals. It's kind of far-fetched, but he says that's why he left Thelma—he didn't want the bad guys to connect her to him. Of course, if he's not Billy Ray, he might have made all that up."

Wilson sucked his teeth. "This gets worse and worse. Give me the number on your little phone there and I'll call you when I see what I can find out."

Watson Wilson withdrew a tiny notebook and stubby pencil from a hip pocket and wrote it down. Chantalene smiled again. She'd seen Sheriff Justin do that same thing. She bet every old-time lawman carried a notebook and pencil until the day his case closed forever.

THERE IT WAS again. In the rear view mirror, Chantalene watched the green pickup on the road behind her while a spidery feeling crept up her neck.

At the first gas station, she pulled off the road and watched the truck cruise past. It had oversized tires, not whitewalls, and though it wasn't going fast, she couldn't see if there was a dent on the door. The dark windows hid whoever was inside. She used the ladies' room, bought a Coke and a licorice stick. In the car, she plugged Drew's cell phone into the cigarette lighter so the batteries wouldn't run down.

The miles rolled by and she stayed alert, her eyes scanning each vehicle that came up behind her. She saw groups of tiny pronghorn antelope on the dry plains, but she didn't see the pickup again all across the Texas Panhandle or western Oklahoma.

An hour past sundown and ninety miles east of Oklahoma City, she exited I-40 onto the Indian Nation Turnpike. Traffic thinned dramatically as she cruised southward, lost in speculation about the twin mysteries of Donnie Ray and Billy Ray Patterson. When the cell phone warbled, she jumped like a pronghorn, goosing the accelerator.

She fumbled with the buttons. "Hello?"

"*Chantalene?*"

"Hi, Chief Wilson. What's up?"

"*Got that make on your Billy Ray Patterson fellow.*"

"What'd you find out?"

"*The good news is he's stayed clear of the law since he got out of San Juan. The bad news is he served three years for manslaughter after a bar fight down in Salinas. Seems he beat a guy to death with a pool cue.*"

"Damn. I was afraid of something like that."

Watson grunted his agreement. "*No luck on the bingo hall heist. I've requested fingerprints from the prison so we can see if they match the one on your letter. Course we still won't know if it's same guy who claims to be the long lost husband. Either way, you better keep a close eye on your lady friend.*"

"Will do." Chantalene signed off and gripped the wheel. A bar fight wasn't like cold-blooded murder, and the cowboy had told them he quit drinking because it always got him in trouble. Still, the man was obviously capable of violence. With a pool cue for a weapon, you probably didn't kill somebody with only one blow.

If the fingerprint on Thelma's letter matched the cowboy's, Thelma had herself a serious situation. And if it didn't, she might have a worse one. Who the hell was he?

Headlights flashed in the side mirror, approaching fast, blinding her for an instant. She held up a hand to avert the glare, but it didn't help.

A loud, dark vehicle roared up beside her in the left lane.

"*Shit.*" Her foot hit the brake but it was too late.

Sparks flared in the corner of her vision and the Volvo rocked as metal screeched against metal. Her hands locked on the wheel but when the vehicle struck again, she couldn't hold it on the road.

The Volvo leaped the edge of the shoulder and careened down the steep slope beside the highway.

The wheels jolted through thick grass, too fast, out of control. She braced her arms, her breath frozen, the headlights lurching pell-mell toward a line of trees a hundred feet from the road.

In the few seconds before the airbag deployed and knocked her senseless, her last conscious image was a flash of dark metallic green.

FOURTEEN

DREW STOOD UP from the desk and stretched his arms behind him until his back popped. His neck muscles burned. He'd been at the desk until midnight last night and was back in the chair at seven this morning. Now it was dark outside. When he closed his eyes, he still saw numbers crawling across Gandalf's blue screen.

For the third time in half an hour, he glanced at his watch. Chantalene should have been home by now. Why hadn't she called? Probably she was being stubborn, after their argument. He was stubborn, too, but he still wanted to know she was back safely. He picked up the phone and dialed the number to his cell phone.

No answer. Maybe she hadn't even turned it on.

He walked to the window and peered into the quiet night. The post office and market were closed on Sunday and the street had been empty all day. His red pickup sat alone in a puddle of shadow beneath the single street light. On Tetumka's crumbling main street, nothing moved except the wind.

He paced the tiny office, rolling his stiff shoulders. Stupid of him to argue with Chantalene. Hadn't he learned anything from his failed marriage back in New York? Life was too short to battle over the small stuff.

Still, it didn't feel like small stuff when he thought of her taking off to New Mexico. The trip made no damned sense. Thelma was a friend of his, too, but she'd backed herself into a corner with this cocky cowboy and now she was having second thoughts. He felt certain that, unconsciously or not, she'd come up with this mistaken identity thing to get herself out of a bad situation.

Besides, Chantalene was supposed to be his partner in their tax business, and these were the busiest weeks of the year.

Okay, that last part was self-pity. But dammit, his shoulders were pinched up like a calving heifer and his carpal tunnels bawled for mercy. He didn't need the extra worry of her on the road alone. She took too many chances, thought she could handle anything by herself. Sure, that's part of what attracted him, but it also attracted trouble. He should have chucked these tax returns and gone with her. But he'd given his word to his clients, and that meant something to him. Where the hell *was* she?

The phone warbled and he leaped to snatch the receiver. "Chantalene?"

He felt a pause on the other end of the line. *"No, Drew. It's Emily."*

"Emily?"

The voice turned dry. *"Yes. Remember me? My name's on your divorce papers."*

"Of course I know who you are, dammit. I just didn't expect you to call."

"Obviously. You were expecting Chanticleer."

"Chantalene. So, did you call me up late at night just to be shitty?"

Another pause. *"No. I'm sorry. I guess old habits die hard."*

Emily huffed a sigh and Drew winced. This was not a woman who sighed unless she wanted something.

"I called because I need to ask a favor."

"Really." *Here it comes.*

"It's kind of complicated to explain. I need to see you in person."

Right. So she could use her considerable physical charms to get what she wanted. "Forgive me, but I doubt that. Just tell me what it is, Emily."

"My father died last week."

Drew's next flippant remark dissolved in his mouth. Emily's father, a robust man in his early sixties who had once been Drew's boss, had seemed indestructible.

"Oh. I'm sorry to hear that." And he was. Sam Savolini had begun a small import/export company that had expanded into more than a dozen high-end construction products. He ran his financial empire with a ruthless decisiveness that pushed legal limits, but he'd always been fair with Drew and he'd doted on his only daughter. Emily's mother had died in an accident when she was small. Drew had ethical objections to the way Sam ran his business, but as a father-in-law, Sam was likable and loyal. "Had he been ill?"

"On the contrary. He had a coronary on the jogging trail at the country club."

The tremble in Emily's voice shook him. In their five years together, he'd never seen her cry. Not even about the divorce.

"My god. That's awful."

She sniffed and her voice went back to normal, cool as diamonds. *"In more ways than you could guess. I'm now the majority owner of Savolini, Inc., and all its subsidiaries. I'll have to learn the goddamned business, I guess, after resisting it my whole life."*

"You poor thing. All that money." Surely she didn't want him to sign back on with the company he'd quit to avoid falsifying tax returns. "So what's the favor you need from me?"

"Daddy hadn't revised his will in two years. It says I inherit everything, but it names you, as his son-in-law, executor of his estate. Along with William."

"Me? Why in the world would he do that?"

She snorted. *"You know he thought your socks didn't stink. He depended on you to keep me financially responsible."* She paused, her voice softening again. *"He kept hoping we'd change our minds and get back together."*

"For a tycoon, he could be awfully naive."

"Sometimes. But you're still executor and have to sign off on everything we do to settle the estate."

"I'll sign. Just have William handle it."

"There are... some difficulties, a lot of details." She hesitated again. *"Drew, could you please come to New York for a few days? I really need your advice on some of this stuff."*

Not frigging likely.

"I'm trying to start my own business here, doing taxes, and I'm way behind. It's that time of year, you know."

"Do I know. The company accountants want me to sign the tax reports, and I have the feeling even they don't think they're accurate. That department just went to hell after you left."

"Don't whine, Em. It's unbecoming."

"You're a real shit, you know it? I've just lost my damned father!"

Drew clenched and unclenched his jaw, fighting for an even tone. Exactly when in their flammable history had it become impossible to conduct a civil conversation? He couldn't recall, but it hadn't always been that way.

"I can tell you're grief-stricken," he said, "but you have Uncle William at your disposal, and he's more than competent." William Bratten, Esq. was her uncle only in the sense that he'd taken care of Sam Savolini's business, part of which included Sam's mercurial daughter, since long before Drew knew them. Good old William had even handled her end of the divorce. Despite all that, Drew liked William, too.

Emily's voice turned hard. In his mind's eye, he could see her light eyes narrow and the slim Barbie face solidify like china. *"Fine. I should have known not to depend on you for help. Five years together obviously doesn't count for anything."*

He opened his mouth to respond but heard an emphatic *click* and then the dial tone.

As usual, Emily had finished early.

He dropped the receiver into the cradle. "Bat shit," he said, with feeling.

And the feeling was mixed. She had a lot of nerve asking him to fly to New York and straighten out her daddy's crooked affairs. On the other hand, William probably didn't know anything about the tax department, and he'd have his hands full with all the details of the impending probate of a huge estate. Drew could see the potential for Savolini, Inc. getting in perilous trouble with the IRS. Once those snappers targeted a company for audit, they didn't let go until it thundered.

Though Emily would never say it, daddy's little girl must feel like a highwire walker with the safety net jerked from beneath her.

Beneath his hand, the telephone rang again. Ye gods. Was there some name she'd forgotten to call him?

"Yes?" he said irritably.

"Drew Sander?"

It was man's voice, and that irritated him further. "Yes. Who's this?"

"Sir, I'm Officer Bob White of the Oklahoma Highway Patrol." Bob White like the quail? Was this a crank call? *"I'm out here on the turnpike with Chantalene Morrell...."*

"Oh, no." Drew's body stiffened. "Is she all right?"

"She's okay. Just a little shaken up. She ran off the highway and met head-on with a blackjack tree. Her car won't run... actually, it's your *car*, she says."

"Did she go to sleep?" But that wasn't logical, the woman hardly ever slept, let alone in the car.

"I'll let her tell you about it. But right now she needs a ride home."

"Sure. Can I talk to her?"

"The EMTs are still finishing with her, but they tell me she's fine. And she insists on it."

Drew could picture that.

"I'll drive her down the turnpike to Exit 63 if you can meet us there," the officer said. "There's a Love's station on the west side, south of the Highway 69 junction a few miles. You know where it is?"

"Yes."

"Your car's close to mile marker 79, north of McAlester. I tagged it, but the longer it sits here, the better chance it'll get stripped."

"Okay. Will it pull, do you think?"

"Hard to tell, in the dark. The front bumper's mashed in pretty good."

"I'll come take a look in the morning."

"Okay. Meet you in thirty minutes."

"No problem. Thanks, Officer."

Drew hung up with his ears ringing. *No problem, my ass.* Chantalene could have been killed. This was just the sort of thing he'd been afraid of. Well, no, his fears had been worse. At least she wasn't hurt. But his car was wrecked, his ex-wife was calling him on the phone, and how would he finish these tax returns?

He shut down Gandalf, turned off the lights and locked the door behind him.

Half an hour later, Drew pulled into the Love's travel stop at Exit 63 on the Indian Nation Turnpike. Three semi rigs sat at the diesel pumps, rumbling like giant metal grasshoppers. He circled them and spotted a black-and-white parked beside the brick building. On the drive, he'd rehearsed a dozen ways to say I told you so, then promised himself not to say them.

When he pulled up, Chantalene got out of the patrol car with a Styrofoam cup in her hand and a dazed look on her face. In the glare of the halogen lights he detected a reddish bruise on her forehead and a scrape on the end of her nose. A lump settled in his gut. He wanted to wrap her in a hug, and then strangle her. He did neither.

"You okay?"

She nodded. "I'm sorry about the car." Her voice sounded hoarse. "You can take the deductible out of my wages."

"I'll just take it out of your hide." He'd meant it as a joke but it didn't quite work and he sounded pissed, instead.

A fit of coughing seized her. "Air bag dust," she wheezed, and took a drink from the cup. When he slipped an arm around her shoulders, she flinched. "Looks like I'm going to be sore tomorrow."

Patrolman Bob White came around the car and introduced himself. He was several inches taller than Drew, six-three at least, an impressive figure in his two-tone uniform.

"Thanks for your help," Drew said.

"Just glad nobody was hurt." Patrolman White handed the Volvo keys to Drew and a printed card to Chantalene. "I'll be in touch if we learn anything."

"Thanks," she said. The officer touched the brim of his Smokey Bear hat and climbed into his car.

Drew opened the right-side door for Chantalene and gave her a hand climbing up onto the pickup seat. When they were out of the parking lot and on the road to Tetumka, he'd waited as long as he could. "Tell me what happened."

She took a deep breath and kept her eyes on the two-lane road that stretched ahead into the night. "A dark green pickup ran me off the road."

He glanced sideways at her and frowned. "Was he drunk?"

"I doubt it. He did it on purpose."

Again he looked over at her, but she kept her eyes straight ahead, her chin set in a defiant line he recognized only too well. He kept his tone neutral. "What makes you think that?"

"I first saw the pickup on the way out, at a truck stop in Amarillo, then again in Los Padres. I thought it had to be a coincidence—not the same truck—until it followed me part way out of New Mexico. Then I didn't see it for a long time and thought I'd been imagining things." She glanced at him. "But I definitely saw it run me off that embankment."

"Nobody else saw it?"

She shook her head. "Not that I know of."

Drew's jaw muscle tightened. "It's a miracle you aren't hurt."

"No kidding. I'm now a Volvo fan."

"Sounds like you have a stalker."

She turned toward him on the seat. "I had some evidence in the car that would have told us whether the guy in Thelma's house is the same one she married. The collision stunned me, and when I came to, the stuff was gone."

Her face was white and urgent in the glow of the dashboard lights. The bruise on her forehead was getting darker. This was no time to remind her she shouldn't have made that trip. "What kind of evidence?"

"A pair of boots that belonged to the fellow who was killed out there in that wreck. And a fingerprint on one of Thelma's love letters."

"And you think whoever was driving the green pickup took the stuff?"

"What else could have happened? Officer White searched the car. The boots and letter were gone, but not my purse or your phone." Reminded of that, she pulled his cell phone from her bag and set it in the drink holder of the console. "Whoever it was knew what he wanted."

"Did you see the driver?"

"No. The pickup had those really dark windows. Didn't they make those illegal? They ought to. It was a Ford, fairly old, with big tires. But not a dualie."

"Maybe the boots and letter were knocked out of the car when you hit."

"Yeah, right."

She laid her head back on the seat and fell quiet. It wasn't like her to be too tired to argue. She must be in shock.

Drew's hands wrung the wheel and he wished it were the neck of that crazy driver. What if the green truck really was tied to Thelma's cowboy somehow? Had the guy sent someone to follow Chantalene and prevent her from finding out about his history?

It was just too far-fetched. If Chantalene was wary of a green pickup, she might have imagined it in the darkness when some sleepy driver swerved out of his lane. Tomorrow when he went to get the car, surely he'd find the boots and papers scattered along the highway.

He turned off the paved road onto the red shale that led toward Chantalene's house. She was quiet, her eyes closed, but she wasn't asleep. He wished she'd stay at his place tonight, but it was useless to bring it up. She guarded her independence like a farmyard dog, and besides, the argument they'd had before she left hung unresolved between them.

The pickup lurched over the rutted, quarter-mile driveway toward the house where she lived alone with her animals and the ghosts of two peculiar parents. The house glowed white in the headlights, bright with new paint he'd helped her apply. On the front porch, Chantalene's black-and-white mongrel stood up and barked, doing her watchdog thing. When Bones recognized his truck, she settled into tail-wagging. Across the yard, Whippoorwill stood sleeping against the corral fence.

Drew left the motor idling as Chantalene opened the pickup door.

"You going home?" she asked.

"Actually I was going back to the office, unless you need me to stay."

"No. I'm okay." Her tone was weary. "What time is it, anyway?"

"Ten-thirty."

"I'll be there early in the morning and type taxes while you go after the car."

"See how you feel tomorrow. You may need to stay in bed."

"Yeah, right."

She slammed the door, a sure sign she was getting back to normal. That made him feel better.

AT SEVEN O'CLOCK Monday morning Drew phoned Monkey Jenks, knowing the old farmer would have been up since dawn. "Monkey, it's Drew. You happen to own a tow bar?"

"Yup," Monkey drawled. *"Think I've got one out in the barn."* When it came to hardware, Monkey owned just about one of everything.

Drew told him about Chantalene's accident and why he needed the tow bar. Monkey volunteered to ride along and help with the car. "I'd appreciate that," Drew said. "Pick you up in fifteen minutes."

Montgomery Jenks's farm was only three miles from Drew's, his closest neighbor except for Chantalene. He raised wheat and cattle on 480 acres that had been in his family since homesteading days. Monkey was a true steward of the land, but since his wife Martha was gone, the old farmhouse didn't receive the same attention it had once enjoyed. When Drew drove in, he noticed fewer chickens milling around the barnyard, replaced by several stray cats.

Monkey was waiting beside the huge red barn, wearing his usual faded jeans and a cowboy hat with a sweat-stained band. He laid the tow bar in the bed of Drew's pickup and climbed into the cab.

"Morning," Drew said.

"Mornin'," Monkey drawled. "Chantalene okay?"

"She's bruised up, but luckily that's all. I went by early this morning to check on her—too early, actually. Woke her up. I told her to go back to bed and stay home today, but she said she'd go to the office. You know Chantalene."

Monkey bobbed his head. "Yup."

Indeed, Monkey knew her as well as anyone. He'd served as Chantalene's foster dad during some stormy teen-aged years. Drew hoped that at some point in the future Chantalene would re-establish a relationship with Monkey. He had to be lonely in that big old house.

They rode over the red shale roads in silence, windows rolled up far enough to keep out the dust until they hit the paved road that led to the turnpike. The morning was cool but warming quickly in the April sunshine. A humid wind stirred the rye grass along the roadsides.

"You know of a good body shop in El Rio?"

Monkey thought for a moment. "Bubba's, prob'ly the best."

That was pretty much a full conversation for Monkey these days. Not that he'd ever been loquacious. Monkey was the age of Drew's father, and in fact had been Matt Sander's closest friend. If it turned out they could tow the car to El Rio, the only town of any size within thirty miles of Tetumka, Monkey would point out the body shop and Drew would know he could trust its owner.

They sailed along the highway with the wind ripping through open windows. It was good to get away from that desk for a few hours. He'd never set out to become a number jockey, but farmers had to supplement their income these days. At this point the tax business was a necessity. He'd stayed up until one a.m. to get all the returns calculated, and if Chantalene made it to the office, she'd likely have most of them posted by the time he got back. She was faster on the keyboard than he was. Maybe they could make their deadline after all.

On the turnpike, Drew watched the mile markers. When they passed number 77, he slowed the truck. A minute later, Monkey pointed across the road.

"There it is."

Drew took the next exit and headed back on the southbound side. The Volvo sat at the bottom of a broad slope, nosed into the trees as if it were parked there for a picnic. From the back, it didn't even look damaged. Drew eased the pickup onto the shoulder and down the incline.

Brake marks sliced the grass going down the hill. Chantalene hadn't frozen up at the wheel like some people would. In fact, she was a darned good driver. He pictured her in the Volvo, fighting for control as the car careened down the embankment at three times his current speed. The image made his stomach lurch. She must have been terrified. What if the car had rolled?

When he got to El Rio, he would enlist Sheriff Justin's help in locating the son of a bitch who had crowded her off the road. Most likely a drunk driver, though there would be no way to prove that by now. With no witnesses and no license plate to go on, the odds of finding the culprit weren't good. But if they did, Drew could at least file charges for reckless driving.

He parked close to the Volvo and both men crawled out to inspect the damage. The front bumper and grill were mashed in, but he had no sentimental attachment to the Volvo—a car was just metal and paint. He'd driven this one back to Oklahoma from New York a year and a half ago, and in a way it was his last tie to a former life. Except for an occasional phone call, of course. But he put that out of his mind.

Standing in front of the damaged car in the wind-whipped grass, he decided to get the Volvo repaired and sell it. Maybe buy a convertible—Chantalene would love driving that. It would have to be red and black, of course.

Drew hadn't known Chantalene's mother, but he knew that Chantalene wore only red and black in honor of her mother's memory.

Monkey tested the crumpled bumper with one foot. It didn't fall off, so he lay on his back in the grass and peered underneath the car. "I think we can hook it up."

The Volvo was still in gear, the inflated airbags sagging like after-party balloons. Drew cramped the wheel and together he and Monkey pushed the car far enough away from the trees to back the pickup in front of it.

While Monkey set to work hooking up the tow bar, Drew searched inside the car, then walked the roadside from the point where Chantalene left the highway to the spot where the car came to rest. He kicked through the calf-high grass for a hundred feet on both sides of her path but found no sign of the boots or Thelma's letter.

He scanned the roadside in both directions. The letter might have blown away. And anybody who traveled the highway since last night might have spotted the boots in the grass and picked them up.

His Okie-to-the-bone grandmother would have said that explanation had more mights than a chicken's butt.

He was beginning to get a bad feeling about this.

FIFTEEN

A FULL MOON hung round and butter-colored against the blue-black sky when the old man took up his post in the windbreak, fifty yards from the small frame house. A southwest wind tossed the limbs above his head, and a whippoorwill cooed in the distance. He sat cross-legged, his back against a bois d'arc tree, and waited. Soon he saw her shadow against the blinds as she moved from room to room.

The shapeshifter was a night owl. But because she didn't sleep long hours, she slept deeply. He envied that. Liddy always had been a deep sleeper.

He liked watching her. It gave him power. Sometimes he lost track of time, but it didn't matter. Time was out of sequence now, anyway, a blend of memories and visions.

When he looked up again, the moon had melted into a small ivory coin among the stars. Finally, in the darkest hours, the last light blinked off inside the house.

As long as a light was on, the dog had stayed awake, restless, listening to the night sounds. Now it settled on the front porch, just inside the line of shadow where the moonlight didn't reach.

The old man's knees crackled like dry wood when he rose. He moved down the tree line parallel with the house, crouching beneath the low-hanging branches until he was past her bedroom window. Then he left the trees and circled behind the house, approaching the porch from the north side, downwind. He crouched beside the house and peered around the corner.

The dog's head was down, facing away from him, into the wind. The animal was long-haired with a slim muzzle, part shepherd like the ones used to work sheep, but larger. He stood slowly and removed the small chunk of beef from his pocket. Taking careful aim, he lobbed the meat over the dog's body so that it landed with a soft *thunk* on the south end of the porch.

Immediately the dog's head came up, looking toward the sound. It woofed softly. When it scented the fatty meat, it rose and padded over to sniff the lump, cautiously. But if it smelled the pinch of sleeping weed inside, the strong smell of the raw beef outweighed the danger. The dog gobbled it down.

The old man smiled. While the shepherd sniffed and licked the porch where the meat had lain, he circled soundlessly back to the windbreak and waited. He waited until he was sure the dog was asleep, and then he waited some more. Patience was a virtue, one of few he still possessed. The wind ebbed and the night sounds swelled—crickets in the brush, the mournful call of an owl, the faint, distant yap of a pair of coyotes. He smelled the earth cooling.

It was time. He slipped off his shoes and left them in the windbreak with his battered canteen.

The ground felt cool beneath his leathery soles, damp from recent rain. This time he walked directly to the front porch, like an invited guest. His feet were silent on the wooden steps. He knew where to place them so the warped boards didn't squeak. He drew a folding knife from his pants pocket and opened the long blade.

The dog lay on its side snoring softly, limp as an airless balloon. He stepped over its body once, twice, holding the knife ready. But the weed had taken effect. The dog snored on.

This was good. He didn't like the dishonor of killing an animal he didn't hunt. Tomorrow the dog would have no ill effects except an excessive thirst.

The hinges of the screened door scraped lightly when he opened it just far enough to test the knob of the front door. It was locked. He thought it would be, but he never overlooked the obvious. He stepped off the porch and walked around the house to the back. When he'd gone inside before, she wasn't home. He had climbed through the window in her bedroom in daylight, and memorized the layout of the house. The rooms smelled like licorice and cloves.

Now he pictured her bedroom, the white bedspread, everything else red and black like the clothes she wore. This seemed peculiar to him. Liddy used to like autumn colors. He had gone into every room, touching her things to leave his mark on them, to let her feel his presence and know what she was dealing with.

But she was still here. Neither warnings nor exorcisms had driven her away.

Her bedroom window stood open to the spring wind. He stopped beside the screen and listened. When his ears adjusted, he could hear her breath, soft and regular behind the whisper of the shifting curtains.

He moved along the wall of the house to the next window and used the tip of his knife to pop off the screen. This window was in the second bedroom, used mostly for storage, where she kept the blinds down and the door closed. He had unlocked this window on his last visit, believing she was unlikely to notice. He was right. When he pushed up on the wooden sash, the window stuck at first but then slid open. He reached inside and found the cord to the blinds, pulled it slowly so the slats rose without noise. Then he hoisted himself over the window sill and crawled inside.

After the moonlight outdoors, the darkness inside was total. He squatted on the floor, listening, inhaling the scent of the house while his eyes adjusted. When he could make out the shape of the painted door, he turned the knob with exquisite care. He stepped into the hallway and moved silently down the darkened corridor to her bedroom.

She lay on her stomach, the sheet pulled up to her waist, the bare skin of her back luminous in the dark. He stood over the bed, listening to her breathe.

Now, Liddy. My turn to appear to you in your sleep.

A blade of moonlight fell across her face and the scent of lilacs sifted through the bedroom window. He saw her eyelids twitch and knew she was dreaming.

Let her dream. At least for a while.

He turned away and moved back down the hall, through the small living area and into the kitchen.

She spent most of her time in this room. The wooden table lay strewn with papers and heavy textbooks. The window over the sink was open, the curtain puffing out then sucking against the screen.

He touched each book and notebook on the table, moving their positions slightly. Among the books he found a small sheet of paper edged with flowers—a letter written in her slanted, feminine hand. He squinted at the words in the moonlight from the kitchen window.

Nothing was more personal than someone's words. The rafters of the house creaked in a sudden gust of wind and his heart beat like a loose shutter. Carefully he folded the letter into its envelope and stuck it in his pocket, feeling the heat of the words against his skin.

He turned then, and that's when he saw her, watching him from the wall.

Liddy's face, pale in the darkness, stared out at him from a paper tacked to a message board by the phone. The paper fluttered lightly, and his heart stopped. When he could breathe again, he licked his lips and pulled the picture from the wall.

It was one of the flyers Naomi had sent out years ago, when guilt caught up with her about her missing daughter. Just like the one on his bureau at home. The shapeshifter had put it here for him to find, taunting him.

His breath came in short, painful bursts. He could smell her scent. Liddy was filling him up, and her power was strong.

The paper crinkled in his fingers. He folded it carefully and slipped it into his back pocket. His feet pulled him back through the living room, down the hall, the braided rug in her bedroom like knots beneath his soles.

He leaned over the bed, breathing her in. Reliving the shock and shame of the first time Liddy seduced him, the thrill of her teenaged flesh against his skin. He thought of the summer nights in his tiny cabin, the hot sheets beneath them and the owl's warning on the wind.

Why keep playing the game? He could end it now.

He could have her again and forever.

The curtains huffed and sucked against the screen. Her hair splayed out on the pillow, the nape of her neck white and fragile. A gust of dizziness left him sweating.

He wouldn't need his knife. He could feel the snap of her neck in his hands, the way he'd learned in the jungle years ago. The way he'd done Naomi's white bird. And Liddy, too, once before.

He reached out his hand.

And heard the sound of a vehicle outside the house. A car door slammed.

The old man dropped flat on the floor, his heart battering his chest. The girl stirred in the bed, turned over, made a low noise in her throat.

He heard footsteps on the porch, the screak of the screen door opening. His head pounded. He crouched and scuttled down the hall to the room where he'd come in.

Knuckles pounded the front door and a man's voice called out. "Chantalene?" The old man closed the door to the spare bedroom and released the knob by millimeters, feeling each click like the tumblers on a safe. He heard the girl's groan and then her footsteps on the hollow floor. With his back pressed against the door, his temples throbbing, he heard her steps moving down the hall, crossing the living room to unlock the front door. Her voice sounded muffled and groggy at first, then she laughed.

His chest constricted. Disgust welled up and burned in his belly, blotting out the pure vision of her moments before.

She had won. She'd seduced him again and left him wanting. His hands shook and the metallic scent of his own sweat burned his nose.

Cool earth met his feet when he dropped out the window, the night air welcome as water against his face. His breath came in sharp jerks as he padded toward the shelter of the trees. The moon had disappeared and the pale glow that fanned out above the eastern horizon surprised him. Once again he'd lost track of the hours.

Next time he wouldn't be so careless. He'd get her on his own territory, where he had the power. And next time he wouldn't hesitate.

We'll meet again, Liddy. You won the skirmish, but not the war.

SIXTEEN

DREW AND MONKEY rolled into El Rio at mid-day, trailing the mashed-in Volvo. Monkey pointed directions to Bubba's Body Shop, and Drew left the car on a lot among the other metal mishaps. Bubba was out to lunch, but an employee with appropriately grease-lined fingernails promised the boss would be back by one o'clock. If Drew would come back then, Bubba would give him an estimate.

They had time for lunch and a visit to Sheriff Justin's office.

Drew parked his pickup near the town square, whose centerpiece was the Opalata County Courthouse, a three-story limestone structure that housed the county records, county sheriff's office and the jail, in addition to courtrooms. While Drew went inside to see if Sheriff Justin was in, Monkey moseyed down to the Feed & Seed store to look over the crated baby chickens.

The sheriff was in his office on the first floor, catching up on paperwork. Drew tapped his knuckles on the doorjamb and the sheriff looked up from his desk.

"Mister Sander," he said with mock formality. "What brings you to town this morning?" His gray eyes assessed Drew with the sort of grudging respect attorneys were used to getting from lawmen.

"A car wreck."

The sheriff put down his pen and gestured toward a chair. Drew sat. "Just left my Volvo over at Bubba's with the front end cratered."

The sheriff's spring-loaded desk chair squawked when he shifted his weight. "Nobody hurt, I hope."

"No, but there could have been. Some jerk ran my car off the Indian Nation Turnpike last night and didn't hang around to say he was sorry. I was hoping you had enough stroke with the Highway Patrol to make sure they won't just blow it off. I want that driver found."

"Don't suppose you got a tag number."

"Afraid not."

"Description?"

"Dark metallic green pickup, an older model, with big tires."

The sheriff grunted. "That's a big help. See the driver?"

Drew hesitated. "Actually, I wasn't in the car when it happened. Chantalene was driving."

The sheriff grunted louder and leaned back in his chair, running a hand over his thinning hair. "Now why doesn't that surprise me?"

"Don't jump to conclusions. She was just driving home, that's all. She'd seen this green truck a couple of times, then got a glimpse of it in the dark as it crowded her off an embankment."

The sheriff frowned. "You mean intentionally?"

"Apparently so."

"Why?"

"Good question."

The sheriff heaved a sigh, shaking his head. Drew knew what he was thinking. The sheriff and Chantalene had been at odds for years after her father was killed, Justin having failed to investigate the death as a homicide. It was uncomfortable history for the sheriff. Nobody likes to be reminded of his mistakes.

"It could be a stalker," Drew said, "or it could be random maliciousness. But if there's a green metallic pickup within six counties that has scratches of silver Volvo paint on the right side, I'd like to talk to the son of a bitch that owns it."

"So would I." Justin searched the cluttered desktop for a notepad. "Let me write down the details."

Drew repeated everything he knew about the incident except why Chantalene had been on the road in the first place. "The guy may have stopped, because a couple of things were missing from the car, and I didn't find them anywhere near the accident scene," he added. "Chantalene was knocked out for a few minutes and didn't see anybody."

"What was missing?"

"A pair of cowboy boots. And a letter. Not valuable to anybody but Chantalene, really." *And Thelma Patterson.*

"A letter? Why would anybody steal a letter?"

Drew shrugged. "Or maybe it just blew away."

Sheriff Justin's chair squeaked as he leaned forward and crossed his arms on the desk, regarding Drew closely. "Chantalene's never worn a pair of cowboy boots in her life," he said, and waited.

"Right. That brings me to the other favor I wanted to ask."

"Here it comes."

"Can you trace down the prison record of somebody who served time in California?"

"Are these two things connected?"

"I sure hope not."

BY THE TIME he picked up Monkey on the cracked sidewalk in front of the Feed & Seed, it was past noon and Drew's trained nose detected the scent of barbecue in the air. They drove to the edge of town where the Hickory Pit café offered an all-you-can-eat lunch buffet. The parking lot was crowded, which Drew considered a good sign.

Drew piled up his plate, despite a guilty vision of Chantalene back at the office, bruised and tired, clacking out tax data on the computer and probably skipping lunch. Well, shoot. Even if she were here, she wouldn't eat barbecue. How anybody could exist without meat was beyond his comprehension. He balanced a long sausage on top of a mound of pork ribs and made a mental note to take Chantalene a piece of the café's homemade cherry pie. He'd never seen her turn down dessert.

Drew and Monkey carried their plates to a red vinyl booth by the front window. It was definitely a three-napkin meal. When Drew's main course had shrunk to a pile of bones, Monkey shoved the plastic basket holding the rest of his French fries across the table. Drew dumped them on his plate.

Monkey's tone held respect. "I never seen a slim fellow could eat like you."

"Bachelor cooking is no fun."

"Tell me about it."

Monkey's wife Martha had been the best cook in the county. Her absence was something neither of them wanted to think about.

"Guess you knew Thelma Patterson's long lost husband showed up last week," Drew said.

"Yup. Ran across him at the co-op the other day."

Drew looked up from his food. "Did you recognize him?"

"Well, sure. He ain't changed all that much, 'cept for some gray in his hair. Course I'd already heard he was back in town."

Drew attacked the fries and mopped up barbecue sauce with his Texas toast. "What do you remember about Billy Ray, from before?"

Monkey gave him a puzzled look, then he frowned as if trying to remember. "Nice enough kid, none too serious. Everybody reckoned he married Thelma for her farm. But he seemed to treat her good and God knows she needed a man around there to help out with the work. And she was happy as a settin' hen with a new hatch."

"Any idea why he left?"

Monkey's broad shoulders shrugged. "Nunna my business." He paused. "Course Martha had her theory."

Drew dunked the last French fry in catsup. "Which was?"

"That Billy Ray had another lady friend somewhere else. Said a guy that good lookin' wasn't likely to limit hisself to a plain gal like Thelma."

"What did you think?"

Monkey thumbed the rim of his coffee cup. "I thought that opinion was a mite unkind to both of 'em." He frowned. "You worried about Thelma?"

Drew tossed his wadded napkin on the table and signaled for the waitress. She filled their coffee cups and Drew ordered a piece of homemade cherry pie to go. "No, make that two pieces, please." It wouldn't be polite to make Chantalene eat dessert by herself.

Monkey declined dessert but added two packets of cream and three sugars to his coffee mug.

"It just surprised me when Thelma took him back so fast," Drew said. "After so many years, she can't really know this guy."

Monkey nodded. "Thelma always was impulsive in some ways. But I hope it works out for her. No fun to grow old alone."

"Umm." The voice of experience.

When the waitress returned with the pie carton, Drew grabbed the check before Monkey could get it. "This is my treat, no arguments. I appreciate your help with the car."

They climbed back into Drew's pickup bearing the universal sign of a barbecue dinner—toothpicks clamped between their teeth. It was after one o'clock. Bubba should be back by now.

Before Drew backed out of the parking space, Sheriff Justin pulled in next to them and rolled down the right side window of the cruiser. He leaned across the seat. "I found that Patterson fellow's record on the computer database."

"And?" Drew said, the truck engine idling.

"He pleaded guilty to assault and battery and manslaughter after he killed a guy in a bar fight."

The barbecue in Drew's stomach turned heavy as stone. Damn. "Thanks for the information."

Drew swore and gunned the engine, pulling out of the parking lot into the path of an oncoming car. His tires squealed as he waved his apology.

Monkey glanced over at him, probably understanding more than Drew would have wanted.

"Sorry," Drew said.

He'd bet money Chantalene found out about Patterson's conviction while she was in New Mexico. If so, she knew the guy was capable of violence and purposely didn't tell him about it last night.

What else was she not telling him?

He bit his toothpick in half and blew the splintered ends out the window.

SEVENTEEN

SUNLIGHT ANGLED THROUGH the open window of Chantalene's bedroom and woke her from a troubled sleep. All night she had careened down a highway embankment again and again, trees looming ahead in the jerking headlights. Normally an early riser, this morning she felt drugged. After Drew had stopped by in the early dark to check on her, she'd fallen back into bed and slept, but the chain of nightmares returned.

Outside her window, morning sounds chirped and rustled. She shoved herself upright on the edge of the bed and rubbed her face. Seatbelt bruises striped her hips and her muscles felt like tenderized meat.

Suddenly her head buzzed like an electric shock. She straightened, instantly alert.

Something was wrong.

She held her breath, listening. No unusual sounds, nothing out of place in the room. Just an awful, prickling sensation that she wasn't alone. Only when she inhaled again did she pinpoint the source of her alarm—a faint, peculiar smell. Not Bones's wet doggie smell. This one was foreign.

"Bones?" Her voice came out a spindly croak. She tried again, louder. "Bones!" If somebody were here, Bones would know it and warn her.

From the front porch came a reassuring woof. Her knee joints ached as she made her way to the living room and opened the front door. The yard sat empty and quiet, Whippoorwill asleep in his corral.

What was she expecting? A green pickup parked out front?

Bones looked up at her through the screen and made a small, forlorn sound. Her water dish was empty.

"Morning, girl. Good grief—when did you turn into such a heavy drinker?" Chantalene ran water in a pitcher and refilled the dish. Bones lapped it up, wagging. A fresh breeze wafted up Chantalene's nightshirt and shivered her skin. She thought of falling back into her warm, soft bed again and sinking into oblivion. But Thelma would be fidgeting behind the post office window already, anxious for her to appear and report in.

She couldn't leave Drew hanging with all those tax forms due, either. He'd taken the first step toward patching up their argument when he stopped by this morning. She barely remembered his visit, just the reassuring warmth of his presence, which had relieved her of some particularly scary nightmare. To return the favor, she would report to the office this morning and data-process like crazy.

Too sore to sit for meditation, she splashed cold water on her face, tied up her hair, and pulled on holey jeans and a red tee shirt for doing chores. But in the hallway she caught that foreign scent again. A feeling like spider legs skittered down her back. The house felt drafty, too, and she thought unexpectedly of the girl on the post office flyer. A shard of remembered nightmare flared in her mind—the girl was in it again. Why?

Maybe the girl's spirit was haunting her house.

Yeah, right. And maybe it had borrowed her hairbrush. Don't let that jerk in the green truck spook you like this. Get over it.

She put out dog food for Bones and oats for Whippoorwill, then attacked the asparagus bed, which was now wild with spiky shoots, some of them knee-high. Only the tips of those would be edible. She moved down the rows cutting crisp stalks and stuffing them into plastic sacks. Bending over the plants was agony for her sore joints, but the sun on her back and smell of chlorophyll soothed her nerves and revived her will. Sometimes avoidance behavior was a good thing.

She stuffed three giant sacks of asparagus into the fridge and headed for the shower. That's when she remembered she had no car. She would have to jolt to the office on horseback. Damn.

While she saddled Whip, she rehearsed telling Thelma that she'd failed to bring home the proof they needed, and in fact had no clue what to do next about the puzzle of Billy Ray Patterson. The only thing she had for sure was an opinion. If the guy in Thelma's house wasn't Billy Ray, he must be Donnie Ray—only brothers could look that much alike. Was he so desperate to keep his identity secret that he'd followed her to New Mexico, run her car off the road and taken the boots and letter? She was anxious to know if Thelma's house mate had been at home all weekend. If he had, then who was driving that green pickup?

She guided Whippoorwill out of the corral and commanded Bones to stay. The shepherd retreated to the front porch with a truly hangdog face.

Along the roadside, fields of ankle-high spring wheat rippled brilliant green in the sunshine, and early wildflowers bloomed in hilly pastures. The air felt soft and warm. Chantalene stopped fighting the bumps and relaxed into the horse's rhythm, resolving to spend more time outdoors. In the spring morning, the charming but phony cowboy seemed benign, the green truck episode less menacing. Thelma's predicament would probably resolve itself without dire consequences.

On the pocked main street of Tetumka, she hitched Whip to the flagpole in front of the P.O. and pushed open the door, chattering the windchimes and fluttering the faces of the missing and wanted.

"Who's there?" a sharp voice demanded. Hank Littlejohn stuck his bony head through the customer window. "Oh. It's you."

Ichabod Crane was cranky today. "Morning, Hank. Where's Thelma?"

Hank's eyes darkened, his neck extending farther through the window. "That's a darned good question! Ever since that shiftless husband of hers showed up, she's about as dependable as March weather. And we have you and your lawyer friend to thank for that, don't we!"

Taken aback, Chantalene didn't try to dispute the point. "Have you tried to call her?"

"Of course I did! Then I called Annabelle to come help put up the mail. Meanwhile, this window is closed." He slammed the wooden gate over the window and disappeared into the inner sanctum.

Chantalene stood still only a moment while a dark premonition washed away her spring-induced optimism. Thelma was never late. Never. And if she wasn't answering her phone, something was wrong.

She ran back to her startled horse and mounted up like a rodeo cowgirl. "Whip! Let's go!"

Whip sprang into a gallop. She leaned over to his neck and clamped her legs to his sides, urging him on.

THELMA'S RED CAR wasn't in front of the house and the door to the detached garage was closed. The barn door was closed, too, so she couldn't see if the white pickup Thelma let Patterson drive was there. Chantalene slid off Whip's back before he'd completely stopped and flipped his reins around the gatepost. Her fist rattled the screen door.

"Thelma? Billy Ray? It's Chantalene!"

No response. She stood on tiptoes to peer through the high window in the white door behind the screen. The house looked dark inside. When she opened the screen and pounded on the door, it swung open.

"Thelma?" She stepped into the potpourri-scented living room and called again before walking farther.

No one in the kitchen. The table was cleared and the dishes done, Thelma's yellow kitchen gloves hanging across the faucet spout. Everything looked as if Thelma had gone to work—except that the coffee maker was hot and half full, its yellow light still glowing. She walked through the living room and paused at the hallway.

"Billy Ray?"

The bathroom door stood open with no one inside. Thelma's bedroom was empty, the bed made. If the cowboy was gone, too, why was the coffee pot still on? Her shoulders stiffened.

Down the dim hallway, the door to Thelma's sewing room, on the left, was closed. But the door to the spare bedroom at the end of the hall stood open. Chantalene moved quietly down the hall.

Her eye went first to dark smears on the light-colored rug in the open doorway. The big galoot had tracked mud... but no. This was too red even for Oklahoma mud.

This was blood.

Her breath froze. She stepped inside the bedroom.

Oh, man.

Beside the bed, a china lamp lay smashed on the floor, its cord still attached to the wall, shade wildly askew. Beside it a lace doily and a small, hardbound copy of the Bible lay where they'd fallen from the night stand. Thelma's antique rocking chair lay on its side, one runner pointing toward the long-legged body that lay spread-eagled on the quilt-covered bed.

Billy Ray Patterson—or whoever he really was—wore only his Wranglers and socks, as if he'd been surprised in the act of dressing. The handsome face was barely recognizable with its lower lip split and bleeding, the left eye swollen like a flesh egg. His dark-haired chest, arms and hands were smeared with blood.

He hadn't gone down without a fight.

Still holding her breath, Chantalene squinted hard at his chest. Please, please, breathe!

Nothing. She leaned over him and tried twice before she could speak.

"Billy Ray?" His eyes didn't open.

She raised her voice. "Donnie Ray?" *Rumpelstiltskin?*

Beneath his head a red sunburst bloomed on the pillowcase, and above his ear in the dark hair, she saw a neat, round hole. Jesus. He'd been shot! Her stomach lurched.

She turned and ran to the kitchen. On the wall beside Thelma's phone hung a framed needlepoint bearing local emergency numbers in blue and red stitching. But all the numbers were for El Rio—half an hour away. Tetumka's promised 911 service had yet to materialize, and Drew had gone to retrieve his wrecked car.

She punched in Monkey Jenks' number. No answer. *Shit.*

Quickly, she dialed the red-stitched numbers for "ambulance." The dispatcher for Emergency Transport Service calmly took her name and directions, promising to send a "unit" as fast as possible and to notify the county sheriff.

Chantalene hung up, her hand shaking. Nothing to do but wait, the very thing she did least well.

She counted breaths and tried to calm her pounding heartbeat. Who could have done this to him, and why? And where was Thelma?

Oh, my god....

She ran back to the closed sewing room, the only room in the house she hadn't searched. Her throat tight, she turned the doorknob and pushed, switching on the light.

Everything was in order. She breathed again, then spotted the closet. She forced herself to open the closet door.

No Thelma. Thank god.

Quickly, she checked the closets in Thelma's bedroom and in the hall, then returned to Patterson's battered form on the bed. His swollen eye was turning purple. Would it do that if he were dead? She had no idea. One arm hung off the edge of the bed, the knuckles split and oozing blood. You oughta see the other guy....

She grasped the dangling wrist between her thumb and fingers and felt for a pulse. She thought of the evening they'd had dinner together at Drew's house, how polite and genuine he'd seemed, his stories full of magic. Imposter or not, she liked him. A lot. And as for his prison time, a bar fight wasn't the same as calculated murder. She knew from cold experience how the right circumstances—or the wrong ones—could push a person over the edge.

She found no pulse.

Who was this fellow, really? She looked again at the swollen face, and then the bloody fingers, hanging limp.

Her eyes widened. Silence ticked in the room.

The EMTs couldn't get here for at least ten more minutes. Probably.

She ran to the kitchen, grabbed the notepad by Thelma's phone and snatched the rubber gloves from the faucet. Back in the bedroom, she put on the gloves, picked up the fallen Bible, and knelt beside the cowboy's outstretched hand.

His fingers were still limber. Supporting her work on the flat surface of the book, she carefully rolled his bloody thumb print onto the paper.

The Moving Finger writes, and having writ, moves on. Was that from the Bible? Nah. Omar Khayyam.

She held the paper up to the light. Not bad. Watson Wilson would be proud of her. Or not.

Alert for the sound of a vehicle outside, she printed the index finger next. The house was eerily quiet except for her own noisy breathing. Outside the bedroom window, wind swished the shrubbery and a mockingbird sang from the trees. Her scalp crawled. She inked the other fingertips, using blood from his knuckles. In a few minutes, five oval fingerprints stained the notepaper. One was smeared but the others looked readable. She laid the paper on the night stand to dry and replaced the Bible on the floor exactly as she'd found it, careful to avoid getting blood on its cover.

An image of Sheriff Justin arose in her head and accused her of tampering with a crime scene. She told him to buzz off.

When the fingerprints looked dry, she placed another piece of paper from Thelma's notepad on top and folded the papers in half so they fit into the hip pocket of her jeans. In the kitchen, she replaced the notepad, washed the rubber gloves with dish soap, and returned them to their place on the faucet.

Then she stood at the open front door and watched down the long lonesome road.

She wished Drew were here.

Wished to hell the ambulance or the law or somebody would get here. Her eyes fell on the closed door of Thelma's detached garage. In three leaps she was out the front door and off the porch, scattering chickens. Whippoorwill whinnied.

She ran to the side door of the garage and peered in the window. Thelma's car was gone.

EIGHTEEN

SHERIFF JUSTIN ARRIVED at Thelma's house even before the ambulance. He carried a toothpick clamped between his teeth and the smell of barbecue on his uniform shirt. Obviously, the call had interrupted his Sunday lunch. Chantalene led him to the back bedroom and stood against the wall while he analyzed the crime scene with narrow gray eyes.

Sheriff Justin had served Opalata County for nearly forty years, counting his time as deputy. He knew everybody in the county by first name and treated them all the same—gruff and point-blank. Today he wasted no time in pissing Chantalene off.

He removed the toothpick and stored it in his shirt pocket, then shook his head. "Beware a woman scorned."

"That's ludicrous," she snapped.

"Let's see—he deserted Thelma, but shows up again when he thinks he might inherit. If she can't get his name off her property, he'll own half of everything. Now he's dead and she's conveniently missing."

"Look at the guy's face, for crying out loud! Do you think Thelma beat him up like that?"

"Revenge is full of adrenaline."

"Don't be asinine. Thelma's obviously in danger. What if the killer took her with him?"

The sheriff sucked his teeth. "Now that'd be the ransom of Red Chief, wouldn't it?"

"Of all the snotty, unprofessional—"

"Most people don't get kidnaped in their own cars," he cut in. "Now move out of here before I have you arrested as an accomplice." He turned toward the corpse, dismissing her. "But don't go anywhere because I'll want to ask you some questions." When she hesitated, he pointed to the door. "Out."

She retreated to the front porch, fuming.

The EMTs came shortly after that, a young man and a woman driver in her forties. It was too late for their services, but at least they could help remove the body. Opalata's onion-headed medical examiner arrived next in his private conveyance, a 1970s-era hearse painted Mary-Kay pink. Doc Baker, along with his wife, owned a funeral parlor in El Rio, which seemed to Chantalene like a conflict of interest. But not in Opalata County. She directed Doc Backer inside and sat on the porch swing to await her interrogation.

A white car bearing the gold sheriff's department seal rolled in and parked beside the ambulance. Chantalene recognized Deputy Bobby Ethridge, whose older brother was a former school buddy of Drew's. Bobby was a decent guy, for a lawman.

"Anybody hear from Thelma yet?" he asked, coming up the porch steps.

"No. And your boss seems to think she beat Patterson up and shot him."

The deputy frowned but didn't comment on the sheriff's bedside manner. "We'll get out an APB."

Bobby went inside and in a few minutes the sheriff came out.

She did her best to cooperate. Sheriff Justin perched on the porch railing and took notes while she told him everything she knew about Billy Ray and Donnie Ray Patterson, and about the green pickup that had run her off the road. In return, the sheriff managed to sound concerned instead of oafish when he warned her not to go searching for Thelma alone. And she managed to keep her temper in check and not refer to his pompous ass. Finally he closed his notebook and went back inside.

Chantalene retreated to the shade of a mulberry tree next to Thelma's garage. Beside the henhouse, she found a bucket and ran water for Whip, who was tethered to the mulberry tree, switching his tail nervously. Together they watched the EMTs descend the porch steps with a shrouded stretcher.

The last roundup for one mysterious cowboy.

Who wanted him dead? And why beat him first? She could think of only two reasons—punishment, or information. Either the attacker intended to inflict pain out of rage or retaliation, or he'd believed the cowboy knew something he wasn't telling.

Where did that leave Thelma?

Thunderheads towered in the mid-afternoon sky as the EMTs secured Cowboy Patterson's body in the back of Doc Baker's hearse, slammed the doors and retreated to their boxy truck. Chantalene stood sweating in the muggy heat. A whirlwind spun through the yard, raising dust and scattering chickens. In its wake came an eerie silence. The mulberry leaves above Chantalene's head went limp. Even the chickens froze in their tracks.

Chantalene had the distinct feeling that she wasn't the only one watching this scene. A shiver ran over her skin, the same sensation she'd felt in her house that morning. Squinting, she scanned the surrounding fields and the long country road in both directions. No movement, not even a likely place to hide. But she was dead sure that somebody was out there.

Sheriff Justin lumbered down the porch steps and stood beside his car talking on the radio. When he'd signed off, he called to her. "You need a ride?"

She shook her head and pointed to the horse. The sheriff folded himself into the car, rocking the shocks, and pulled out of the driveway followed by Doc Baker's weird hearse. The diesel-engined ambulance rumbled to life and lumbered after them, bringing up the rear of the sad little caravan. Only Deputy Bobby Ethridge was left to guard the scene until the OSBI arrived.

The dust that powdered Chantalene's lips tasted bitter. Whoever the mysterious cowboy was, he was gone now. What if something awful happened to Thelma, as well?

Too many secrets, too much death in this damned town.

She swore aloud and kicked the gravel. The toe of her sneaker caught something square and shiny in the dust and sent it flying. A matchbook?

She picked it up. The booklet was covered in gold foil and looked as if it had been run over. She wiped the dust on her jeans and examined the bold print on its cover: Ballenger Energy Corp. Dallas and Oklahoma City. Wasn't that the company who wanted to lease Thelma's land? She pictured the guy in the brown suit who had smelled like cigarette smoke and insisted on getting Thelma's mister to sign the papers. Hill, wasn't it?

The matchbook was empty and showed no address and no phone. She could picture Hill using the last match and tossing his trash out the car window. Had the oilman been here this morning? She remembered that flash of evil in his eyes when she'd irritated him, the impression of a definite mean streak. What if the oil company was bogus, and Hill was really looking for Patterson? What motive could Hill have to kill him? Did it have something to do with Billy Ray's real identity?

She rubbed a thumb over the gold foil. Anybody could get these things printed, just like business cards. Come to think of it, she'd seen Hill hand Thelma a business card and ask her to call him. Thelma had tossed the card into a basket beside the kitchen phone.

Chantalene scanned the horizon where the shale road disappeared toward the distant purplish haze of the Kiamichi Mountains. In the old westerns Drew liked to watch on TV, she could have leaped onto Whippoorwill and galloped off to find Thelma. But this was no oater. Without a car or any clue where to start, she had to trust that job to Sheriff Justin, at least for now. She could check out Ballenger Energy, though, and try to learn something about the man named Hill.

A shadow passed over the yard and she looked up at thickening clouds. She and Whip had better get back to town before the storm hit. A rider on horseback was a target for lightning. But there was one thing to do first.

Chantalene untied Whip and led him to the gate. The deputy sat in a white Adirondack chair on Thelma's front porch, behind a strip of yellow crime scene tape anchored to the porch posts.

"Looks like you're going to get wet," he said. "You should have let the sheriff give you a ride."

She gave him an innocent smile. "I guess so. I'll get going, but do you think I could go in and use Thelma's bathroom first? Not many restrooms between here and Tetumka."

Bobby laughed. "Okay. Just don't go into the bedroom, and don't touch anything else."

"Thanks." That was just too easy. She mounted the steps, ducked under the tape, and let the screen door slam behind her.

Inside, she went straight to the scrapbook in Thelma's bookcase, extracted one of her young harvest hand's letters, and shoved it into her pocket. Moving quickly, she searched the basket by the kitchen phone for Hill's business card. Nothing but grocery lists, freebie ballpoint pens, and a packet of wildflower seeds. Where would Thelma have put it? If she searched any longer the deputy would get suspicious. She slipped into the bathroom and shut the door.

When she came out, she thanked Bobby again, mounted Whippoorwill and goosed him with her heels. Whip hit the road at a lope, happy to get away from all those flighty chickens.

Lightning zig-zagged among the clouds and random, quarter-sized drops of rain splattered her shirt. Home was closer than the office. She turned right at the next mile line and gave Whippoorwill his head.

By the time they trotted up her long driveway, both of them were damp and winded. She rode Whip beneath the lean-to in the corral and left him saddled. When the rainstorm passed, she'd have to ride him back to town. How many El Rio mechanics does it take to repair a Volvo? Three—one to spit, and one to whittle while the other guy does the work.

Bones pranced on the dry strip of front porch next to the house, begging to get in as thunder rumbled. Chantalene went straight to the phone and dialed Drew's number at home, then tried the office. Where the hell was he? Shooting the breeze with Monkey Jenks?

"Call me at home," she said to the machine. "It's urgent."

A gust swept through the house, rattling the spare bedroom door and filling her with an acute sense of loneliness. Her knees melted. She sank into a chair at the table and laid her head on her folded arms like a lost child.

The world had gone crazy. Patterson murdered. Thelma vanished. A phantom in a green truck that nearly killed her.

And where was Thelma now? Was it really possible she'd shot Patterson? What if he threatened her or tried to force himself on her? Maybe she was defending herself—

But that didn't explain Patterson's bloody face. Thelma couldn't do that, and Chantalene was pretty sure the only gun Thelma owned was a shotgun.

Thelma must have fled in her own car. Was Patterson's killer after her? Had he found her already?

She emptied her pockets onto the kitchen table and named her loot—the matchbook, Thelma's letter, the folded papers with Patterson's fingerprints printed in blood. Luckily they'd stayed dry in her jeans pocket. If she sent the bloody prints to Chief Watson Wilson, she might at least find out if his prints matched the ones on Thelma's letters. But how would that help Thelma now?

The cowboy's identity, Thelma's disappearance, and the guy in the brown suit had to be connected somehow. She stared at the items on the table and asked herself what Watson Wilson would see here that she was missing. His grandfatherly voice rose in her ears. *Take this stuff to the sheriff. Trust the law to sort it out.*

Even the bloody fingerprints? *How can I explain those?*

Watson had no answer for that.

Rain peppered the roof and dimmed the room, but the lightning had moved on. She went to the living room and booted up the computer.

Her PC was old and the modem moved at Tetumka speed. She ran a search for Ballenger Energy Corporation, tapping her fingers while the machine ticked and whirred. The search came up empty—plenty of Ballengers, but nothing connected with oil. She tried Ballenger+petroleum—no matches. She switched search engines but got the same results.

On Google and Dogpile, at least, Ballenger Energy didn't exist.

She signed off and tried calling the office again. No answer. What if Drew had disappeared, too? Her stomach rolled.

She stood for a moment peering out the front screen, watching the rain slacken. *Thelma, Drew, send me a message. Where are you?*

As if in response, the door to the spare bedroom rattled again.

Why did it keep doing that?

Her body moved like time lapse photography. Her breath stopped and she saw herself as if from the outside, walking to the pantry with exaggerated slowness. Her hands found the old shotgun behind the door. She chambered two shells as quietly as she could.

She paused beside the kitchen table. Her throat was too dry to swallow, her voice quiet as dust. "Bones, come with me." Bones left her hiding place beneath the table, a ruff of fur standing up on her neck. She stood by Chantalene's leg without a sound.

Together they crossed the living room, slowly, walked into the hallway and stopped at the spare bedroom door. Leaning her head close, she heard—or imagined—something moving on the other side. She braced the butt of the shotgun under her right arm, finger on the trigger, and placed her left hand on the knob. She counted to three.

Bones barked when she threw the door open.

Nothing moved.

She reached inside and switched on the light. No one there. The room was just as she'd left it.

Except for the raised mini-blinds—and the wind puffing wet curtains at the open window.

NINETEEN

WHEN THE PHONE rang, she screamed.

Then thought, *it must be Drew. Thank God.*

She slammed and locked the window, the wood floor wet beneath her bare feet. Still carrying the shotgun, she ran to the kitchen and snatched the receiver. Bones hustled back under the table.

"Hello!"

A pause. *"Miss Chantalene? Is something wrong?"*

The voice was unmistakable. "Chief Wilson! I was thinking about you just a minute ago."

He sounded wary. *"Oh really? Why is that?"*

"Thelma's missing. And the imposter husband is dead. And somebody's been in my house."

"Good Lord, girl. What's going on out there?"

"I wish I knew." She spilled out the main details of Patterson's death, her fear for Thelma, and the discovery of the matchbook, thankful for Watson Wilson's rational voice, though it was two states away. She even told him about getting the dead cowboy's fingerprints.

That impressed him.

"You've got guts, girl, I'll say that."

"You wouldn't if you saw the way my knees are knocking. I don't know what to do next."

"What's this about somebody being in your house?"

She told him about the open window. "And this isn't the first time, I'm certain. I don't see how it could be connected to Thelma, though. It may be a stalker. But last night on the way home, somebody ran my car off the highway and stole the boots and the letter with the fingerprints." She told him about the green pickup.

"Holy jalapeños. This gets worse and worse. Did you tell the sheriff about that?"

"Yes, he knows." She paused. "I'm sorry about losing the boots. Maybe if I can find Hill, I can get them back."

"That's the least of our worries. Let's concentrate on finding Thelma."

She liked the way he said our worries.

Watson cleared his throat, but the rocky quality didn't change. "Do you trust Sheriff Justin?"

Good question. "We don't get along, but he's honest, I think. And he's good at his job—with one notable exception. But that was a long time ago."

"Give him the matchbook and tell him about your Mister Hill, every detail you can. He has resources available to him that you don't. He can cast a net for the guy, and at the same time have people checking Hill's background."

She rubbed the knot between her eyebrows. "Okay. You're right. I'm just afraid he won't do enough."

"I didn't say you and I would quit looking. But take advantage of the law. Call the sheriff just as soon as we hang up."

"Okay. I will."

"Give me Sheriff Justin's number," Wilson said. "I'll see if I can have a talk with him myself, one lawman to another."

She read him the number from memory. "What about these fingerprints? Justin will kill me if I give him those. Or have me arrested, anyway."

"Umm. Then let's keep quiet about that for now. Why don't you overnight the dead fellow's fingerprints to me. I got the prints for Billy Ray Patterson from San Juan, and they don't match the one from your letter. We'll see if your set does."

She jotted down his mailing address and stuck the paper in her pocket. "I really appreciate this."

"Actually, I had a couple of other reasons for calling. Somebody came nosing around the station the morning you left, wanting to know what you'd found out about Billy Ray Patterson."

"Who was it?"

"I didn't see him, and he gave the boys some phony name. They said he was late thirties, probably, medium build but wiry and tough looking, crew cut."

"Oh brother."

"Hill?"

"It sure sounds like him. Did they see what he was driving?"

"I'll ask, but I doubt it. The other thing is I found an old lawman friend from Oklahoma who has a history as long as mine. He knew the name of the man that ran that Indian bingo joint that got burglarized back in the 70s. It was a Texan named Kingman."

"Okay, thanks." Chantalene scratched the name on a pad, though it probably didn't matter now that all the thieves were dead. "One more thing. Patterson's supposed to have a sister in Tulsa. Her name is Sunny Ray Diehl. I tried Tulsa information but there was no listing. Any idea how to track her down?"

"Sunny Ray, Donnie Ray and Billy Ray? Good grief. What were those parents thinking?" He had her spell Sunny's last name. "San Juan might have an address on next of kin. It'd be old, but it's a start. I'll see what I can find. Now hang up this phone and call Sheriff Justin, you hear? Don't be stupid about this."

"Okay, I promise."

True to her word, Chantalene dialed the sheriff's office as soon as Watson signed off. Surprisingly, the sheriff was in, and even more surprisingly, he took her call immediately. She told him about the matchbook and Ballenger Energy, and that Hill might have been nosing around in New Mexico after she'd gone.

"I'll have Deputy Ethridge come by. Give him the matchbook and the best description you can of this Hill fellow. We'll put out an APB on him and run a background check on Ballenger Oil." He stopped to say something to someone in his office. "I gotta go. You at home?"

She thought again of the open window. She wanted out of her violated house. "Have Bobby meet me at Drew's office in Tetumka. I'm headed there now." Surely Drew would be back by then.

She threw a towel on the wet floor in the spare bedroom, her spine crawling. An irrational image of the missing girl on the P.O. poster popped up, but somehow she was certain the scent she'd detected this morning was masculine. Try explaining that one to Drew.

If it was Hill, why would the creep invade her house? What did he hope to find?

Before shutting down the computer, she called up Google and typed in "Kingman." The search netted several thousand hits, including Kingman, Arizona, and Kingman, Kansas. That gave her an idea and she tried Kingman+Texas. Three of those results were sites that purported to trace ties to organized crime. *Hmm.*

The first site looked as if it has been posted by a twelve-year-old. But the second was supposedly run by an ex-cop who'd made it his life's hobby to catalog the names of everyone who'd ever had dealings, or been rumored to have dealings, with known mob figures. Frank Sinatra was there. So was the Pope. *Paranoia alert.* Nevertheless, she scrolled through pages of names, looking for Kingman.

There. Joseph Kingman of Dallas. Born 1914 in Lewisville, died 1988 on the Kingman Ranch sixty miles southwest of Dallas. Wife, Ophelia, and two daughters, Juliette and Cassandra. *Hmm. A Shakespeare fixation.* The family owned homes in a wealthy suburb of Dallas, in Boca Raton, Florida, and a lodge in northern Montana. Holdings included ownership or controlling interest in Kingman Cattle Company, Kingman Shipping, Exeter Petroleum, Roster Publishing Company and the Arctic Blue hockey team, with minor holdings in a dozen more companies. Known associations with the Beretta family of Chicago and with Mavis Davis, hostess to senators, royalty, and presidents in Washington D.C.

So the patriarch was dead. Who ran the family enterprises now? The entry didn't say, and it was dated a year ago. She selected the text and hit print, scrolling down to read the entry for Pope John while she waited. "Granted an audience to Vincent Vansetti, reputed Italian crime don." Okay, so the Pope wanted to save his soul. Or get a loan for art restoration at the Vatican.

She closed the site and clicked the third and final link.

This one didn't identify its webmaster, but the listings were detailed and well-written and got her attention immediately. There was so much information, searching it would take hours. She printed the address and bookmarked the site.

What if the Kingman's were still after the Patterson boys? Could Hill be one of their henchmen? If he'd traced Patterson to Tetumka, that could explain why he'd been bugging Thelma about her missing husband. And it might explain Patterson's battered face, maybe even the shooting. On impulse, she went back to the second site and scrolled down searching for anybody named Hill. No luck. But if he was hired muscle, his name might not show up.

She logged off, her mind zinging like a ping-pong ball. The rain had let up and she needed Drew's calm, analytical influence. She left the spare bedroom door open and all the lights blazing when she rode away.

A damp wind swept the clouds eastward and the air temperature had dropped by at least twenty degrees. She wished for a jacket but didn't go back. The muddy driveway sucked around Whip's hooves as he moved. He tossed his head and snorted.

"Stop fussing. It'll come off when we hit the shale."

But Whip kept complaining and shying sideways until she finally had to dismount. She found a stout stick along the roadside and knelt beside him, scraping the mud loose from each of his shoes. Damp hair fell across her face and she shoved it away, leaving a muddy streak on her nose. She swiped at it with her sleeve. *Get a car.*

Mounted up again, she poked Whip in the ribs. "Okay, you big baby. Now vamoose!"

They trotted into town twenty minutes later, her hair standing out like a black tumbleweed. Everything on her was sore, including her attitude.

Drew's pickup was nowhere to be seen. Instead, a white limousine stretched like a cat along the muddy curb, its windows dark. At first she thought it was another hearse and nearly swallowed her heart, but the rear end wasn't configured for transporting corpses. Beyond the limo's immaculate profile, the old creamery building with its cracked paint and rotting window frames appeared slightly off plumb. A light shone through the café curtains in the front window of the office. Why the hell would Drew rent a limo?

She looped Whip's reins around the flagpole, stalked to the office door and yanked it open.

In the desk chair sat a striking young woman with short, spun-gold hair, her slim legs propped up on the cooler that served as the office refrigerator. She had small features, classically beautiful, and the most calculating eyes Chantalene had ever seen.

"How did you get in here?" Chantalene demanded.

A smirk appeared on the flawless face. "That lock wouldn't keep out a five-year-old," the woman said. She shrugged narrow shoulders encased in a creamy turtleneck that Chantalene thought must be cashmere. She wasn't sure because she'd never seen real cashmere before.

The blonde ran an appraising look over Chantalene's rain-induced Afro and mud-streaked jeans. Her smirk deepened. "You must be Chanticleer."

"*Chantalene.* Who the hell are you?"

"I'm Emily." She flipped her manicured nails. "You know. Drew's wife."

TWENTY

WHEN DREW WALKED into his office carrying a to-go carton of cherry pie, Chantalene and his ex-wife stood faced off like gamecocks, a nightmare come true. He'd seen the limo out front, the uniformed driver coming out of the market across the street with a can of soda. The limo was a rental from the airport in Oklahoma City—it carried the security sticker. He should have guessed who brought it here.

But he hadn't guessed, and the sight of his ex-wife in his Spartan country office struck him dumb. He stood in the open door, arrested by the contrast of the two women—Emily's cool sophistication and flawless style—Chantalene's untucked red shirt and mud-streaked jeans. Chantalene's eyes had that wild look he'd come to know so well, and her hair was a licorice explosion.

The glare Chantalene turned on him would have melted granite. Emily's would have frozen the sea.

"Emily," he said, his vocal chords tight. "What are you doing here?"

Even when Emily smiled, there was no warmth in it. "I came to see you, of course."

Drew closed the door behind him. The clock ticked. "I'm not getting involved in your father's estate, Em."

"Of course," she said sweetly. "But we need to talk. Privately."

Emily swung her legs off the cooler and stood up. She was cigarette-slim, her caramel-colored stretch pants outlining long legs punctuated by matching ankle boots. Her sleeveless sweater showed arms that were firm and tanned. If anything, she looked better than when he'd last seen her, more than a year ago.

He had waited too long to respond. Chantalene's jaw clenched.

"Don't mind me," she said. "I was just leaving."

Mud streaked her cheek like war paint. What the hell had she been doing?

She turned abruptly, her sneakers leaving a track on the Berber, and jerked open a file cabinet drawer. She snatched an Express Mail envelope before heading for the door where Drew still stood.

"You don't have to leave," he said.

"Sure I do." She pushed past him. "And by the way," she paused only an instant in her exit. "Patterson has been murdered and Thelma's missing. But you two have a nice chat."

The door slammed.

"Murdered?"

"She's probably just being dramatic," Emily said. "But at least she left us alone."

Drew tossed the carton on the desk, sprinted out the door and caught Chantalene a few paces down the sidewalk. "What's going on?"

Her face hard, she looked at his hand on her arm. He removed it.

"Funny, I was wondering the same thing," she said.

"I had no idea Emily was going to show up here. She called last night and told me that her father died suddenly. She wants me to help straighten out the estate. I told her no. But I guess I'm the closest thing she has left to a family member, and I imagine she's feeling pretty lost. Though she'd never admit it."

Chantalene met his eyes, assessing. "Okay." She pushed a strand of hair out of her face. "I'm sorry about her father."

He waved it off. "I'll talk to her and send her back to New York. What's happened to Thelma and Billy Ray?"

"Thelma didn't show up for work so I rode out there and found Patterson beaten like a rag rug. He's dead. Thelma's gone. The sheriff is looking for her."

"Jesus. First somebody runs you off the road, and now this...."

"Yeah. Must be a connection, huh?"

"Any idea why Thelma took off?"

"To escape the same fate as Patterson, no doubt. *If* she left on her own."

Emily stepped out of the office onto the sidewalk. She stood with her legs apart, gold bracelets circling the fist that she propped on her hip. "Drew! I went to a lot of trouble to get here. Must I pay you by the hour now, to get some of your time?"

Drew's clenched his jaw. "In a *minute*, Emily."

She tossed her head and went back inside.

"You never told me she was gorgeous," Chantalene said.

"That's not what I remember about her," he said.

They glanced up as an Opalata County Sheriff's Department car rolled down the pot-holed street and parked across from them. "That'll be Bobby Ethridge," Chantalene said. "He's come to get some information from me." She started across the street toward the cruiser. "You better go talk to your ex."

Drew frowned. "It won't take long. Bring Bobby down to the office."

"Forget it. You're on your own."

"Thanks a lot."

Drew watched her crawl into the car with Deputy Ethridge. He wanted to hear that conversation. But he had another problem.

Reluctantly, he retreated to his office, where Emily was pacing the floor, smoking. "This is a non-smoking office."

She just looked at him, blowing smoke toward the ceiling. "Since when don't you smoke?"

"Since eighteen months ago." *But man, the idea sounded great right now.*

Emily strode to the restroom beside the back door, which she had propped open, he noticed. She earned one point for that consideration. He heard the cigarette drop into the commode and the water flush. She came out and sat on the edge of the desk, crossing her legs. If he sat in the chair, he'd have to look up at her. With Emily, everything was deliberate. He chose to stand.

"You look good," she said, the cool eyes assessing his body. "I'm glad to see you aren't wearing overalls."

Drew crossed his arms and waited.

"Okay, then. No small talk. I need you to help me sort out the mess Dad left me in."

"No, you don't. You have Uncle William. We've been over this already."

"For the past month, William has been undergoing chemotherapy for prostate cancer."

That stopped him. "I'm sorry to hear that."

"He's still working, but he isn't up to his usual level and may never be again. In fact, he's planning to retire soon and strongly recommended that I make you an offer."

"An offer of what?"

"Vice-president in charge of the financial department. You'd oversee the company investments, as well as the accounting departments of all divisions."

"Forget it."

"Let me finish. You can hire whatever staff you need—attorneys, accountants, whatever. William trusts you to do this." She paused. "And so do I. We both know something's wrong in that area of the company, and we need someone from the outside to fix it. You're outside, but you're also familiar with the company structure. Everybody knew Daddy was grooming you for bigger things. Apparently you told William about some of the problems you saw back then, and he thinks you were right."

He'd forgotten how fast New Yorkers talked. "I'm flattered by his confidence," he said. "But I don't have any credentials as a manager."

"Screw credentials. We need somebody who's honest and smart, and not part of the good-old-boy fraternity that's been there for too many years. You do get a newspaper out here, don't you? The SEC is out for blood." Emily leaned forward, bracing her arms on the desk edge. "We're offering you an annual of two hundred thousand to start, plus profit sharing, stock and bennies."

"Two hundred thousand? Suddenly I'm worth three times what I was making when I quit?"

"And you don't even have to re-marry me." She fidgeted, glancing at her handbag slumped on the floor. "Are you sure I can't smoke?"

He scowled.

"Okay, okay, never mind. I told William it would take a very attractive package to lure you back from Dogpatch, and this is what he put together. The board of directors is behind it because we have them by the balls. They're scared to death, partly of the feds and partly because Daddy left the company to me. William convinced them you can avert the disaster. As a VP, you'd have a seat on the board, of course." A tiny smirk pulled at her mouth. "They'll try to convert you to the good-old-boy club."

Drew sat in the chair. "This is crazy. They don't even know me."

"No," she said drily, "but they know me. Or they think they do. And that's what scares them."

Emily slid off the desk as smoothly as a house cat and paced the small space in front of Drew's spread knees. "Maybe we weren't good as a married couple, but if there's anything I learned about you in five years, it's that you're honest to a fault. That's what we need right now. The IRS has been making threatening noises, and an officer in the import division suspects something fishy going on over there, too. William and I have common goals here. He's a major stockholder, of course, so if the company fails, he loses a lot of his retirement. He has a wife and kids, and grandkids ready for college. If the cancer gets him, he wants to leave them well off."

"I can understand his motives. I just don't know yours."

She took a deep breath. "I've learned a lot about the company in the last few weeks, enough to know I hate it. I'm an interior designer, not a corporate desk jockey. If we can iron out the internal problems and get somebody trustworthy to run the company, then I can do whatever the hell I want. And have plenty of money to do it with."

Now that was a motive that had the ring of truth. He shook his head and started to speak, but she stopped him.

"Don't shoot down the idea until you think it over. Please." She picked up her leather bag, the exact color as her outfit, plopped it on top of the tax returns Chantalene had been posting, and dug out an envelope which she laid on the corner of the desk. "This is an airline ticket in your name. I'm asking you, as a personal favor, to come to New York and talk to William. He'd have come here himself but he's not up to traveling. You may not trust me, but I know you trust William. Just talk to him."

"Emily, I know you can't understand this, but I'm happy here."

In the few moments their eyes connected, he saw that she believed him, and that she truly didn't understand. And he saw something else, something he'd never seen in all their history together. Emily was scared.

She swallowed and looked away. "I don't think William's going to make it, Drew. And if he dies, I'm up shit creek. Unless you help me."

The steer's head clock ticked in the silence. Emily glanced at it. "How do you stand that thing? I've got to have a smoke." She grabbed her purse and swept out the door in a gust of expensive perfume.

Drew slumped in the chair, legs spread before him, arms inert in his lap. What the hell.

He thought of William Stratten, possibly dying of cancer. He thought about Manhattan, their apartment with the view of the river, the little bar on Fifty-ninth Street where he used to go to drown his frustrations. It wasn't all good. But it wasn't all bad, either.

He found Emily on the broken sidewalk, pacing and puffing. The deputy's car was gone from across the street, and so was Chantalene.

The limo driver approached Emily. "Miss Savolini? If you're going to make your return flight, we'd better go."

So she'd gone back to using her maiden name. It was no surprise, really. In some circles, the Savolini name carried a lot of power.

"All right," Emily said to the driver, dismissing him. He climbed into the car and started the engine.

Emily dropped her cigarette on the sidewalk and ground it out with her boot. She stepped close to Drew, facing him. "See you in New York." He could have sworn her eyes were wet.

She placed her palms against his chest, raised up on her toes and kissed him lightly, then laid her forehead against his shoulder.

He held her for a moment. But only a moment. Emily turned way and slid into the back seat of the limo, disappearing behind the darkened windows. He watched the limo drive away, tasting cigarette smoke on his lips.

When he turned back to the office, Chantalene was standing in the open doorway.

TWENTY-ONE

WHEN DREW HAD first met Chantalene, her eyes carried a haunted look, a blend of pain and fear. It had taken a year for that look to melt away, as her life settled into some kind of normalcy and he won her trust. Now, in the moment she stood in the office doorway before turning away, he saw that look in her eyes again.

Damn. Why was everything falling apart?

He followed her inside and closed the door. She was heading out the back way.

"Chantalene?"

"I need to get home and feed the animals."

"I'll drive you."

"No. I don't want to leave Whip here overnight." There was no heat in her voice, just a heavy fatigue.

"You mean you don't want to talk to me."

She stopped and turned toward him. The doubt on her face cut him. "It's been a hellish day. I don't want to argue, or say something I'll regret." She walked out the back door where her horse waited beneath the carport.

Drew followed and watched her mount up. "Please call and let me know when you're home safely." By the time she got home, maybe she'd be ready to talk. Without looking at him, she turned Whip's head toward the alley and they rode away.

Watching her go, he felt like shit. He tried to work up some righteous indignation—nothing was going on between him and Emily, after all. What Chantalene had seen was a sympathy hug for someone with whom he had a lot of history. She ought to understand that. Usually she was extremely perceptive to what other people were going through. If she didn't understand, he decided, it was because she chose not to.

She was pulling away from him. It went deeper than their difference of opinion about Thelma. He had scared her with the idea of marriage and kids. Ironic. Wasn't marriage and kids what most women wanted?

Of course, Chantalene wasn't most women. Not even close.

Neither was Emily, for that matter. Freud would have had something to say about his managing to connect with two women in a row who didn't want children. But Freud would be wrong. Drew really did want kids, always had. Even back in college, when he was too young to be ready, he'd always pictured his future as somebody's daddy. And for the past year, he couldn't picture anyone but Chantalene as their mom.

Now the mother of his future children was riding off into the sunset. And he knew going after her would be a mistake.

He turned back inside but left the door open to the rain-cleansed air. The desk chair squeaked as he dropped heavily into the seat and glanced at his watch, timing Chantalene's ride home. She ought to be there in half an hour or so. But would she call?

Meanwhile, he dialed Sheriff Justin's office in El Rio.

It was well after five, and the sheriff answered the phone himself. His voice sounded tired and impatient, more bark than greeting.

"Sheriff, it's Drew Sander. I know you're busy, but can I find out what's happening with Thelma Patterson's disappearance? I'm her attorney."

Drew could picture the Sheriff pushing back in his chair, running a hand over his thinning hair, and wishing he hadn't picked up the phone. But since he had, he answered Drew's question.

"*We have an APB out on Thelma, and also for one Henry Carl Hill, the fellow Chantalene told us about who's supposedly with Ballenger Energy Corporation. Turns out he's a son-in-law to the Kingman family of Dallas that the Patterson brothers ripped off twenty-some years ago. Old money, political connections. A tough bunch to mess with.*"

"Hill's a suspect in Patterson's death?"

"*Right now he's wanted for questioning. But so is Thelma.*"

"So Hill's out to get the Kingmans' money back."

"Probably, and also to prove something to his in-laws. No rap sheet on him, but the Dallas County office had a pretty thorough background. Late thirties, grew up in a blue-collar family that had too many children, served four years in the Army after high school. Had a rough go in the service, bullied by some toughs, and when he got out he adopted their tactics. He's been in some fights, but only one of them resulted in charges."

"How did a guy like that marry into a family with money and clout?"

"Not with the family blessing, that's for sure. There were three girls in the family, no Kingman sons. He married the youngest daughter, a country club airhead. The family gave him a job with one of their companies in order to keep their thumb on him. It's a crumbling dynasty now, run by the aging mother and eldest daughter and her husband. Henry Carl gets no respect."

"That's pretty good research on such short notice."

"It helps to have a friend on the force in Dallas," the sheriff said.

"So maybe Hill's trying to prove himself by recovering long lost money?"

"Who knows. Apparently he's not the sharpest knife in the drawer, but sometimes it's the dull ones that cut you."

"Is there anything I can do to help?"

"Yeah, now that you mention it. I know Chantalene's sort of adopted Thelma, or vice versa, and this hits her hard. Don't let her do something crazy."

"What do you mean?"

"You know damned well what I mean. We don't need Chantalene putting herself in danger with some cockamamie idea she can rescue Thelma." He paused. "I don't want her finding Thelma before we do."

Drew's mouth went dry. "You think Thelma's dead."

"I didn't say that. I'm hoping she'll show up and give us some information. But one man's already dead, and if Thelma didn't kill him, she may be the only one that knows who did."

Drew pressed his thumb on the bridge of his nose. "Okay. Thanks for the information."

When he hung up, he saw the envelope Emily had left and picked it up. Inside was a flight itinerary in his name, for a first class ticket on Delta

Airlines. The flight left from Oklahoma City the next day at eleven. To catch it, he'd have to leave before sunrise, or else drive to the City tonight and stay over. The return date on the ticket was open.

There was also a note from William Bratten, Esq. on his cream-colored, embossed stationery. William's once-beautiful handwriting looked shaky and old.

Dear Drew,

I know you can't be thrilled to hear from me, but I'm counting on the mutual respect we had when we worked together. Sam's death has come as a shock. There's nothing like the death of a close friend to remind you of your own impermanence.

It's imperative, for personal reasons and for Emily's sake, to get Sam's estate settled quickly and the company on sound footing. You understand, perhaps better than most of the company executives, some of the problems we'll encounter. You have some friends on the board, men who have been with the company for years but came to their board seats recently—Bob Shanks, Leonard Leoni. And you have my trust.

I realize you owe nothing to us or to the company, which is another reason you're the right man for the job. I'm asking you, as a personal favor, to meet with me and hear our proposal. After that, if your answer is no, you won't hear from me again.

With all best wishes,
William

Not one mention of his illness, but Drew read it clearly between the lines. William did not expect to beat the cancer.

From the beginning, there had been a professional respect between Drew and William that went beyond the fellowship of attorneys. William was a rare breed, a shrewd corporate lawyer but tempered by compassion. He was also a family man, a collector of fine art, and possibly the brightest intellect Drew had ever known. When Drew had pointed out the problems in the accounting wing of the company, William listened. He kept his opinions to himself, but Drew knew that he'd taken those concerns to Sam. It was Sam's decision to ignore them in favor of the bottom line. William had thirty years with the corporation. He'd helped shepherd the expanding companies from infancy to Fortune 500. Savolini, Inc. was a work of art to him, and he wanted it restored to fiscal beauty before he died.

How could Drew refuse to see him one last time?

He tossed the envelope on the desk next to the computer and saw a colored paper he didn't recognize beneath the keyboard. He pulled it out. It was a flyer from a museum somewhere out west, with a note to Chantalene scrawled on the top. Drew's eyes scanned the page. The flyer outlined details of a one-year internship offered by the museum. Attached to the flyer was an application, filled out in Chantalene's neat printing.

So that was it. She'd found her escape. Maybe that's why she'd been keeping her distance. He laid the paper carefully on the desktop and smoothed out the wrinkles made by his fist. He had no right to prevent her from going. And also no chance if that's what she wanted.

His stomach felt like lava. He picked up the plane ticket and put it in his shirt pocket. Perhaps he should keep his options open.

TWENTY-TWO

AWAKE FROM A feverish dream, the old man lay sweating, his heart stopping for long seconds between bursts that shook his chest. His bed was full of terrors old and new, so he rose and prowled the dark, like last night, and the one before.

But he needed rest. By afternoon, fatigue pulled on him, weighted his eyes. In the long afternoons, dangerous things happened. His mind spiraled away, out of control.

He settled into his chair by the window and pulled the cord to raise the blind. One corner accordioned up. The string that threaded the slats on the right side had broken years ago. Through the exposed triangle of dirty windowpane he could see across the weedy yard to the orchard. Maybe the fox would come back. He needed something like that, something natural and real to anchor his mind.

The old padded chair had memorized the shape of his body, and that was a comfort to him. He laid his head back and gazed out the window. In moments he drifted to half-consciousness and instead of foxes in the orchard, he saw a kaleidoscope of faces reflected in the glass. And all of them were Liddy.

He closed his eyes, giving in. Nothing he could do now to stop it. The kaleidoscope shifted and turned, and at its center were the golden eyes, full of surprise and betrayal the only time he'd ever struck her.

BENEATH A PEAR tree thick with white blossoms, the two of them bent over a hole in the earth, digging. His new pickup truck was parked nearby at the abandoned house next to the orchard. He had a shovel, Liddy a length of board. She was digging for treasure, her eyes alive.

"Are you sure it's here? Is this the right tree?"

He didn't answer. Grass overgrew the spot where he and the kid had buried the bag nearly a year before, and they'd buried it deep. But he knew this place.

By the time his shovel struck something solid in the hole, he already regretted telling Liddy about the money. He'd told her to keep her with him, but he saw that was a mistake.

Liddy heard the *whump* of his shovel and sucked in her breath. She jumped down into the hole and finished uncovering the canvas bag with her hands. He helped her lift it onto the grass. From the look in her eyes he knew he'd have to hide the money again. If he didn't, she'd take it and leave him, just as her mother had done.

But for now, she was jubilant. Liddy plunged her hands into the bag and ran them through the bundles. She laughed and danced beneath the trees, white blossoms raining down on her hair. He saw her in a golden haze, everything else fading into shadow.

He decided they should stay at the abandoned house until the hired thugs stopped looking for the money. For Liddy it was a great adventure. They were hiding out, like Bonnie and Clyde. She tied up her hair and threw herself into cleaning while he repaired the plumbing and the roof. Remarkably, the electricity hadn't been turned off. He bought a used refrigerator and stove at a flea market and disabled the electric meter so that whoever owned the property wouldn't notice an increase in usage.

They found discarded furniture along roadsides where it waited for trash haulers. Liddy hung curtains at the three small windows and did her best to scrub the rust stain out of the sink, a reddish splatter the shape of a scalp. She said it gave her the heebie-jeebies, but no amount of scrubbing or bleach would remove it. It was still there, like the mark of Cain.

Those first months in the little house were the happiest of his life. She helped him catch fish and snare rabbits. For her it was all a game, but he knew Liddy had a short attention span. One night when he was sure she was asleep, he hid the money in the cistern.

She began to complain about living in the sticks, with nowhere to shop and nothing to do. They had all that money. Why couldn't they spend it? He had to keep reminding her of the dangers, why they must stay hidden. He planted a garden. All he wanted was to live simply and have Liddy to himself. The longer they stayed, the more he reverted to the old ways his grandmother had taught him, and the more she hated it.

When they needed supplies, they didn't go into the closest town. They drove to different ones, at least fifty miles away. Before those outings, she washed her hair and put on lipstick, and he worried that she'd slip away. In town he kept her constantly in sight.

He couldn't use the money without Liddy finding it, so he kept his eyes open for easy marks where he could sneak in at night. Liddy begged to go along, and she proved to be an efficient thief. The danger was addictive. She wanted to go every night, but he was careful. They did break-ins far from home and far apart. He didn't like stealing. But Liddy did, and that's exactly what she was doing one autumn afternoon when he came up from the pond early and caught her carrying her raggedy suitcase to the truck.

She looked up and saw him, the stringer of perch hanging limp from his hand. The smell of fish still reminded him of betrayal.

The lid was off the cistern box, the rope he'd used to suspend the money bag dangling over the outside, its knot empty. Caught mid-way between the truck and the cistern, she watched him take it in with a glance. Her face was blank, like a fox frozen for an instant on the road, deciding which way to jump.

But for Liddy there was nowhere to jump.

She didn't move when he went to her slowly, with more sorrow than anger. He took the suitcase from her hand and felt the weight of the money inside it. She stood straight, her chin level, eyes unafraid.

He struck her once, without warning, and heard the fine cheekbone crack beneath his fist. Blood erupted from her nose, and her eyes went wide as a child's, accusing him. *What have you done?*

She never made a sound. She staggered backwards, her feet tangling, and fell full length against the concrete platform of the cistern. He heard the sickening thunk of her skull as it struck the corner.

There was too much blood. He knelt beside her limp body and slipped his forearms on either side of her head, the long hair cascading over his skin like honeyed water. Her neck made a sound like popcorn when it snapped.

THE OLD MAN jerked awake in his chair, mouth-breathing, his skin slick with sweat. He rose heavily and steadied himself while the room flowed like a river around him. When the motion stopped, he went to the kitchen sink and drank a full glass of water. The rust stain stared up at him from the sink bottom.

Everything was wrong. His days were jumbled and his appetite gone. He couldn't remember what he'd done yesterday, whether he'd eaten. He heard warnings in his head. Now one of the Patterson boys had come back, nosing around, asking questions.

It had to stop.

Killing the shapeshifter wouldn't be enough. She would only take some other form. Liddy's anger must be purged, the evil purified, and for that he must bring the shapeshifter here. This required penance, like the death of the baby fox.

TWENTY-THREE

WHIPPOORWILL'S HOOVES THUMPED like a slow heartbeat on the damp shale road, the horse's reins hanging slack in Chantalene's hands. She turned at the first mile line and took the long way home. A neon sun teetered on the horizon, casting long shadows that changed the familiar road into an alien landscape. Wind stirred the roadside grass and the eerie moment passed, but her sense of otherness, of not belonging here, remained.

For a second time in her life, she stood to lose the two people she loved.

Recently she had begun to believe that Drew wouldn't disappear as her parents had, that he would be part of her life permanently. Now her doubts rushed back. She pictured Emily Savolini Sander, so svelte and stylish and easy to hate, with Drew's arms around her as they said good-bye. Watching them together, she'd felt like a clumsy, countrified clod.

In truth, she didn't believe Drew would go back to his ex-wife. Emily couldn't give him what he needed—and neither could she. If Drew left, it would be the result of her own failing. The magnitude of the impending loss softened her bones.

Then she thought of Thelma, out there somewhere, and Patterson's killer on the loose. Deputy Ethridge had radioed the information about Hill and Ballenger Energy and the Kingmans of Dallas to Sheriff Justin, and the manhunt was launched. But the worry on the deputy's face confirmed her fear that she might never see Thelma again.

It was nearly dusk when Whip finally turned the last corner and clopped west toward home. No comfort in that thought. She spent a moment hating the bastard who had violated her house and made her dread going back there alone.

Whippoorwill snuffled and tossed his head, and Chantalene reached down absently to pat his neck. Not until he shied sideways in the road did she notice the car squatted on the wrong side of the road beside a clump of trees. Its left-side tires sat off the roadway on the grassy shoulder.

Even in the failing light, she knew that car.

She urged Whip forward. The car's lights weren't on, and she couldn't see if anyone was inside. She halted the horse a few yards behind Thelma Patterson's red compact and slid down, dropping Whip's reins to the ground. The horse stood.

"Thelma?" Her voice was loud in the stillness. Whippoorwill snuffled.

She approached the car cautiously. No sound, no movement. She cupped her hands against the glass of the passenger-side window and peered inside. It was Thelma's car all right, with the keys dangling from the ignition. On the damp roadway, Chantalene saw heavy tread marks—like a pickup—that angled into the grass and across the path of Thelma's car. She had been heading to Chantalene's house when she was run off the road.

The metal hood above the engine felt cool as the evening. The car had been here a while. Nevertheless, her eyes searched the fields next to the road and squinted into the darkness under the clump of trees.

"*Thelma?*" She heard nothing but her own fast breathing. She thought of Billy Ray sprawled on the bed, his face a mass of contusions and blood blooming on the pillow beneath his head.

Her hand didn't want to open the car door. Didn't want to pull the keys from the ignition and fumble at the trunk lock until one key fit inside.

The key turned and the latch popped.

"*Ourfatherwhichartinheaven, hallowedbethyname....*" She looked out across the pasture, heard the distant call of an owl as the trunk lid rose beneath her hand with a nauseating squeak. She forced herself to look inside.

The trunk was absolutely empty. She let out her breath.

Not only was it empty, the carpet was spotless. Compared to the trunk of Drew's Volvo—littered with her college papers, both their old sneakers, the water-smoothed walking sticks they kept for impromptu hikes in the Jack Fork Mountains—the cleanliness of the yawning space felt ominous.

But this was Thelma's car, her prized baby. It was absolutely typical that Thelma would *vacuum* the trunk of her car.

She slammed the lid and pocketed the keys, wishing she still had Drew's cell phone so she could call the sheriff. She slid inside the car without touching anything else and examined the front and back seats, the floorboards and dash, in the weak interior lights. No purse, no personal belongings, no clue to Thelma's whereabouts.

Chantalene locked the doors, ran back to Whip and mounted. *"Adelante!"*

She didn't have to tell him twice. They galloped home and slid to a halt at her porch, sending Bones in to a paroxysm of barking. She took the porch steps in one leap while digging the house keys from her pocket—and stopped cold at her front door.

Her breath came shallow in her mouth. The house was dark.

And she knew damned well she'd left on all the lights.

The doorjamb was splintered. *Jesus! He's been here again.*

Bones whined, and she looked down. The dog was favoring one leg, and a dark patch of blood matted one ear. She knelt and carefully smoothed her hand over Bones' back. Bones seemed okay except for the damaged ear.

Anger flashed through her like a fireball. *The son of a bitch.* She leaned back and kicked the door open, screaming. The door slammed against the wall and rebounded, the doorstop twanging in the echo.

Shadows shrouded the living room furniture. Her eyes adjusted to the gloom and she smelled a faint, foreign odor—but not the same as before. This was aftershave.

The aftershave worn by Hill.

"Show yourself, you slimeball!"

No movement, no sound. Then she saw an unfamiliar shadow lumped on the center of her braided rug. She slapped the wall switch and light flooded the room.

A single cowboy boot sat in the middle of the living room floor. One of the Justin boots she'd brought from New Mexico.

So it *was* Hill who had run her off the road.

Cautiously, still listening for sounds in the house, she approached the boot and picked it up. A folded paper the size of a business card stuck out from the loop of the right pull-strap. She slid it out and read the five words printed in heavy black ink and double underlined. *"NO COPS OR SHE DIES."*

Something rattled in the bottom of the boot. Chantalene tipped it over and caught a small, heavy object in her palm. A clip-on earring, encrusted with tiny beads.

Thelma Patterson was perhaps the last woman in the world who wore clip-on earrings. Chantalene had seen her wear this one.

She looked at the card again, turning it over. It was printed with the logo for Ballenger Energy Corporation. The only other printing was the name Henry Carl Hill and a phone number.

His calling card. Was the man an idiot?

Either that or egotistically insane. She thought again of the cowboy's battered face.

The number was undoubtedly a cell phone. She flipped on the kitchen light and dialed the number, her heartbeat pounding in her throat. Her knuckles turned white on the receiver before the phone on the other end began to ring. Five times, six.

"Chantalene! I need help—"

"Thelma? Are you all right?"

But the next voice was masculine, arrogant and cold. *"Just to prove Thelma's with me. That's the last time you'll ever talk to her unless I get the money."*

"*What* money?"

"Don't play dumb! Thelma has convinced me—with some discomfort—that she doesn't know where it is. If Patterson didn't have it, the other guy does. You've got till noon tomorrow."

"What other guy?"

"Don't mess with me, sweetheart. You're such a smart ass, I'm sure you know everything."

"Patterson's brother died twenty years ago—"

"Noon tomorrow. If you call the police—if you tell anybody—your friend dies. Two hundred fifty grand of Kingman money, and I want it back. If you want to see the old gal alive, be at home when I call."

"What *other* guy?"

But the connection was dead.

She gripped the receiver and closed her eyes. This couldn't be happening. How in hell could she find out what happened to the long-lost Kingman money? Let alone between now and noon tomorrow.

Her mouth felt like sandpaper. Did Thelma's face look the way Patterson's had? She felt like throwing up but her stomach was too empty.

She couldn't borrow, beg or steal that kind of money between now and noon tomorrow. Hell, she couldn't even rob a bank without a car.

There was no way to meet his deadline. And she had no doubt he'd kill Thelma if she didn't. Thelma had to be rescued *tonight*.

What would Watson Wilson do?

She replayed Hill's phone call in her mind, memorizing. The connection definitely sounded like a cell phone, but she'd heard something in the background, like a television. The evening news? So he wasn't in his car.

No cops.

Screw you, Hill. She dialed Sheriff Justin's number. The law Chantalene had never trusted was Thelma's only hope.

TWENTY-FOUR

SHERIFF JUSTIN WAS not one of those lawmen who resents getting assistance from another agency. By ten p.m. the Oklahoma State Bureau of Investigation had identified a fingerprint taken from Henry Carl Hill's business card, printed copies of his Army picture, and installed a tracking device on Chantalene's phone. Chantalene sat at her kitchen table with Sheriff Justin while the phone technician, a man of about forty whom the sheriff introduced as Devereau, finished stringing wires and hooking cables to his laptop computer.

The two of them had arrived after dark driving Drew's crinkled Volvo, which Justin had appropriated from Bubba's car lot before repairs were finished. "We don't want police cars in the driveway in case he checks the house," the sheriff said. They had even left Thelma's car alongside the road as if its whereabouts had gone unreported.

In appreciation for his caution, she didn't remind the sheriff that she was right about Thelma's being kidnapped. She did tell him that someone had broken into her house, possibly several times.

"Probably Hill. He's been a busy man," the sheriff said.

She thought of the two distinct odors she'd discerned but decided not to mention it. Like Drew, she was sure the sheriff would give no credence to olfactory evidence.

With a ten-o'clock shadow, Sheriff Justin's face looked even sterner than usual. "You did the right thing to call us instead of trying to deal with this guy yourself. We've done some background checks, and this is the kind of weirdo who tortured animals when he was a kid. As the only male left in the family, he's on a mission to become the new kingpin of the Kingmans. And he has no conscience about how he achieves that status."

Chantalene had a bad moment picturing what a man like that might have put Thelma through. She closed her eyes till it passed.

The sheriff gave her a minute, then softened his tone. "At least we know Thelma's still alive. Are you sure you don't know anything about what happened to the stolen money?"

She shook her head. "Patterson told Drew his partner probably spent it years ago, and he thought the guy was dead."

The sheriff frowned. "Maybe he was wrong. Or lying. Maybe that's the 'other guy' Hill was talking about. Do you know his name?"

She shook her head. "Patterson called him Songdog. That's all I know."

Devereau finished his work and sat down at the table. Both men had headsets that would let them hear any conversation on her phone. Devereau's was linked to his laptop, where the screen now showed an image that resembled an Etch-a-Sketch map of Opalata County.

"Are you OSBI?" Chantalene asked him.

"No," Devereau said. "I work for the wireless company that owns towers all over this part of the state." He pointed to yellow dots on the screen. "In McAlester, there's a central switch that feeds several municipalities in the southeastern counties. At that site, they can pinpoint the originating tower for any cell phone call within this area. We have a lot of towers out here because of the hills and tree cover, so if we pick up the signal, we'll know the call was made within a fifteen mile radius of the originating tower."

"We have two deputies and four OSBI agents ready to canvass the targeted area," Sheriff Justin said. He narrowed his grey eyes at her, all business. "Are you ready?"

Her stomach lurched, but she nodded.

"Okay." The sheriff's voice was calm and deliberate. He shoved a notepad in front of her where he'd written Hill's phone number from the card. "If he answers, tell him you're doing your best to comply but can't find the money. Ask him who this other guy is, and where you can find him. Ask for more time—ask anything you can think of to keep him talking." He paused. "Do you want to rehearse it?"

She shook her head. "What if he's turned his phone off?"

The muscle in the sheriff's jaw tightened again. "Then we're screwed. But people who live with cell phones tend to leave them turned on. We'll hope he's one of those."

"Okay." Chantalene picked up the notepad and moved to the red phone on her kitchen wall. The sheriff put on his headset and nodded.

She dialed.

After five rings, the phone cycled to voicemail and Justin motioned for her to disconnect. Her heart sank.

"What now?"

"Wait a few minutes and try again."

They waited in silence.

Again, the ring signal trilled in her ear. Three times, four. She squeezed the receiver tightly and closed her eyes. *Answer the damned phone, Hill.*

The buzzing stopped. The line clicked.

"What are you doing still at home, Miss Morrell? Shouldn't you be getting something for me?"

A chill ran over her. His cell phone had caller ID.

"Look, I'll do it. I'm trying. But I have no idea where to start." It was no stretch at all to put panic into her voice. "Who is this other guy? Where do I find him?"

"The third man. Finding him is your problem." His tone had finality in it and she raced on before he could hang up.

"Patterson said he was dead and the money spent!"

"Patterson lied."

Was that true? At the table, Devereau leaned forward attentively. She saw the map on the computer screen jump to a smaller radius. "Look, I'll get it, I swear. Just tell me his name—give me *something* to go on!"

"If I knew all that, I wouldn't need you, would I? You work for a lawyer. Use your resources."

The sheriff motioned, *keep it going.*

"Yes, I do... I'll get Drew to help. I can trust him."

"Well I can't. He was useful in helping me find Patterson, but that part's over. Call the lawyer and Thelma's dead."

Shit. She tried a different tone. "I demand to talk to Thelma. If I don't know she's okay, I'm going straight to the police."

"Whining has cost you two hours. You've got until 10 a.m."

The line went dead.

Chantalene pounded the receiver on her fist. The sheriff took off his headset, watching Devereau fiddle with his dials.

"We got it," the tech said.

"Which tower?"

"The one just this side of El Rio."

"That's no help," Chantalene shrieked. "The whole town of El Rio's within the fifteen-mile radius!"

Sheriff Justin ignored her, thinking aloud. "The countryside's no problem. We can canvas the farmhouses pretty quickly. I heard the TV in the background, so he's not outdoors somewhere." He glanced at his watch. "But we can't do a door-to-door in all of El Rio before ten a.m."

Chantalene looked at him. "He has to be staying somewhere and I doubt he has any friends. A motel?"

"That's what I'm thinking. We'll start there." He picked up his radio and pressed a button. "Number one calling home base. You there, Bobby?"

A spurt of static answered. "Have Tim and Oscar start a house-to-house in the rural areas within a fifteen-mile radius of that cell phone tower northeast of town. Give them a photo of our suspect and a description of Thelma Patterson. We're looking for someplace where there's a TV, so skip the barns and outbuildings unless there's an electric line."

The deputy's voice crackled. *"Roger. Want me to go with them?"*

"Negative. I want you to mark all the motels in El Rio on a map and have the OSBI fellows canvass those. When I get there, you and I will start on the east side and take every house in town that has a light on. We've got until 10 a.m. And tell the boys to consider this guy armed and dangerous."

The sheriff signed off and stood.

"I'm going with you," Chantalene said.

"Absolutely not. Stay by the phone in case he calls again. Devereau will stay with you. We'll check in as soon as we find anything."

"I can't just sit here—"

"You *have* to. We don't have time to worry about a civilian." He hefted his considerable torso and reattached the radio to his belt. "I know you're worried, but you can do Thelma the most good by staying out of the way. You hear me?"

"Loud and clear."

Bones heard him, too, and set to growling from the front porch. Bones never had liked Sheriff Justin. Maybe he was a cat person.

At the door the sheriff turned. "Get Drew over here to wait with you. But first corral this mutt of yours until I get to the car."

Chantalene held Bones' collar while the sheriff stepped off the porch and folded himself into the Volvo. When he started it up, something under the hood rattled like rocks in a blender.

"The fan blade's hitting the radiator," she mumbled. Thank God, the noise stopped as the car lurched down the driveway. She turned Bones loose and the shepherd launched mournful howls into the night. Chantalene stared after the tail lights.

Waiting. Her least favorite thing to do.

Inside, Devereau stared at his computer screen as if some answer might magically appear. She put a mug of water in the microwave and took down the jar of tea bags. "Want some coffee?" She saw him eyeing the jar. "Or tea?"

Devereau had pale blue eyes and thin, colorless hair that didn't quite cover a pink scalp. "Do you have Earl Grey?"

"Yeah, I think so."

She rooted through the jar and held up a tea bag. Dimples creased his cheeks when he smiled.

"I thought all lawmen drank coffee," she said.

"They probably do. I'm a communications engineer."

"Of course. I forgot. I apologize for the insult. What do you take in your tea?"

"Honey, if you have it. And a drop of milk. Thanks." He went back to monitoring his equipment.

She set a second mug of water in the microwave, choosing one with no cracks in honor of Devereau's refined taste. When the timer beeped, she dropped in the tea bags and set his beside him, along with a saucer and spoon and the honey bear.

"Okay if I use the phone to call my friend?"

"Use my cell, and we'll keep your line free." He laid a tiny, expensive-looking phone on the table and then gave his attention to brewing his tea. She took the phone into the living room.

The buttons were so small it was hard to dial. She tried Drew's home number and got no answer. At eleven p.m.? She pushed the disconnect and dialed the office.

Drew answered on the second ring. *"Why didn't you call me?"*

"Sorry. I've been a little busy here—"

"Never mind. I found your application for the internship at that museum."

She frowned. "I wasn't hiding it."

"No. You left it where I could find it instead of talking to me about it."

"Excuse me. I was busy finding a dead body, and worrying about Thelma, and then your ex showed up—"

"You filled this out before Emily came," he said.

The last thing she wanted was to argue about petty stuff, with Thelma's life hanging like a fly in a web. Before she could explain what was happening, Drew surprised her again.

"I'm driving to Oklahoma City tonight. I'll deliver these tax returns and then catch a flight to New York."

Chantalene was dumbstruck. "You're going back to Emily?"

"No. I'm going to visit an old friend, a man I respect who's dying of cancer. He's asked me a favor, and I can't turn him down."

"I see." But what she saw was something else—Emily Savolini snaking her arms around Drew's neck. Everything she wanted to tell him log-jammed in her throat.

"I hate to leave before we know about Thelma, but there's nothing I could do, anyway. I'm sure she'll turn up."

"Right." She couldn't believe he was going—especially now.

"I'm not sure how long I'll be gone," he was saying. *"But a few days away might be a good thing. Give us both a little perspective."*

Horseshit. "Hey. Do what you gotta do." *Run away like a yellow dog.*

She jabbed the off button and clenched the tiny phone in her fist. Something huge and dark rose up and curled over her like a monster from a nightmare.

Bad things come in threes, her mother used to say. The cowboy was dead. Drew was leaving her. Now Thelma would die.

TWENTY-FIVE

CHANTALENE JERKED AWAKE on the sofa, enveloped in the thick darkness of pre-dawn. She lay still, panting, her face damp with sweat. She had dreamed of the girl on the post office flyer again. But this time she was the girl, and she was trapped in an earthen dungeon, trying to claw her way out with her fingernails.

From the kitchen came the sounds of Devereau microwaving another cup of tea, and reality rushed back to her. It wasn't much better than the dream.

"What time is it?" she called.

"Five a.m."

"No word?"

"Nothing."

She sat up slowly and massaged the cramp in her neck and a spot below her right eyebrow where a headache spiked red flashes to her brain. Two hours' sleep was worse than none. She felt like crap with a wagon track through it.

The dream wasn't hard to explain. Her subconscious had done a bang-up job of symbolizing real life by tossing her in a dark, claustrophobic place—her worst fear. But why the P.O. poster girl? What did she have to do with anything?

The house felt stuffy and she got up and opened the front door. Cool air sifted through the screen and she breathed deeply. Ironically enough, it was going to be a beautiful spring day.

On the porch, Bones lifted a sleepy head and looked at her. *What are you doing up?* Better question, *What was she doing here?* Thelma was out there in the dark somewhere, in mortal danger and undoubtedly terrified. And Drew was traveling back to his old life, after she'd given him up without a struggle. What a spineless worm she was. A mollusk. A legless lizard.

She slumped down the hallway to the bathroom, splashed water on her face and brushed her scummy teeth. Her face in the mirror looked haggard. Maybe she shouldn't have called the sheriff. What if Hill found out and took it out on Thelma?

No. No second guessing. A dozen men were scouring the countryside for Thelma, and those odds were a hell of a lot better than if she hadn't called the law.

The mirror shimmered eerily before her eyes. She laid her fingers on the cool glass to regain her bearings, and made a wish for yesterday to disappear. In that moment she understood Drew's longing for a normal, quiet life. A house with a two-car garage and a swing set in the yard. Was it too late?

She combed her hair back from her face and fastened it with a banana clip. But when she glanced in the mirror again, the girl from her dream looked back at her.

All the breath went out of her. Until now, she hadn't seen the resemblance. For a nerve-jangling moment, she was inside the skin of the girl on the poster, just like in her dream. A metallic taste like dirt stained her tongue.

She dropped the comb in the sink and ran to the kitchen, past Devereau at the table reading yesterday's newspaper, to the cork bulletin board beside the phone.

It wasn't there.

"I had a flyer stuck on this board. With a girl's picture on it. Have you seen it?"

Devereau looked up, his face blank.

"It was a missing-persons flyer," she said.

"I don't think it was by the phone yesterday, or I'd have noticed it when we were wiring things up," he said.

She looked on the floor, dug through the stack of books on the back of the kitchen table. Last week, the hairbrush. Then the letter she'd been writing to Gamma Rose. Now the poster was gone. Again, she tasted dirt in her teeth.

It didn't make sense. What would Hill want with that stuff? Of course, if he was a psycho, nothing would make sense—including logical efforts to find him. And Thelma's chance of surviving was thinner than blue milk.

She squeezed her eyes shut and sent Thelma a message. *Hang in there, girl. Stay alive, no matter what. We're trying to find you.* She glanced at Devereau, placidly looking over yesterday's news, and wanted to scream at him. *Someone's been stealing random items from my house! How can you sit there drinking tea?*

Okay, stop freaking. He's not a crime stopper. He's just a communications engineer.

Waiting was making her nuts. She had to *do* something. *As God is my witness, I'll never be carless again.*

"Could I please borrow your phone again?"

"Sure." Devereau gestured to the miniature phone on the table.

She dialed Drew's cell number and carried the phone into the dark living room. No answer. He was on his way and taking no calls. And it was too early to call Watson Wilson in New Mexico. He couldn't have received the Express Mail package yet.

Calm down. Nothing's changed since last night. You're still stuck waiting for Hill's next call, or the sheriff's, whichever comes first. She took a deep breath and slipped the phone into her shirt pocket. She would try Watson later.

Oblivious to her panic attack, Devereau glanced up at her and smiled. He'd been sitting in that wooden chair all night. His butt must be made of leather.

"Want some breakfast?" she said.

"Toast would be nice."

Tea and toast. It figured.

She put two slices of wheat bread in the toaster and broke eggs into a bowl with shaky hands. Maybe Devereau could live on toast but she needed protein. Bones heard dishes clatter and woofed from the front porch. "Keep your fur on. I know who gets the scraps." The eggs sizzled into the skillet.

The phone shrilled.

The toast popped up.

She dropped the spatula, splattering egg goo on the stove top. Devereau snatched his headphones and she grabbed the receiver.

"Hello?"

Sheriff Justin's voice was rough and tired. "*We found Hill, but Thelma's gone. A car's on its way to pick you and Devereau up.*"

"What—?" The sheriff had hung up.

She looked at Devereau, who shook his head. "Your eggs are burning."

WHILE BONES WOLFED down the scorched eggs and Devereau packed his equipment, Chantalene paced the front porch watching for dust on the lightening horizon. It didn't take long. The squad car must have been halfway there before Justin phoned.

Deputy Ethridge sat behind the wheel, his face somber. She met him at the window before the car came to a full stop.

"Tell me the truth, Bobby. Where's Thelma?"

"We don't know. We found Hill dead in a motel room, but no Thelma. We don't even know for sure that she was there. The sheriff wants you to look at the room, see if you recognize anything."

Devereau came out of the house with a load of equipment. Bobby popped the trunk and helped him. "Thelma's ex was killed by a bullet to the brain. We found a thirty-eight caliber on Hill's body that could be the murder weapon. But Hill wasn't shot. His neck was broken."

"The third man," she said.

"Who?"

"I have no idea."

Devereau put the rest of his equipment in the trunk and crawled in back, leaving Chantalene to ride shotgun. The deputy drove fast. In minutes they were off the shale roads and onto the two-lane highway, spearing toward El Rio.

The third man. Nobody knew who he was or what he looked like. If he had Thelma, what chance did they have to find her?

They dropped off Devereau and his equipment at the sheriff's office in the Opalata County Courthouse and drove to the edge of town, where a splattering of no-frills motels dotted the state highway that entered El Rio from the north. The deputy turned into the parking area at the White Buffalo Inn.

The motel's stucco facade reflected orange light from the sunrise. A mural of a white buffalo, its pink eyes more fierce than welcoming, was painted in the gable above the office.

Bobby drove down the row of one-story units to number thirteen, the last room at the end, where Sheriff Justin's county car hunched beside a black-and-white El Rio Police unit. Across the parking lot, she saw two other vehicles she recognized.

She pointed. "That's the truck that ran me off the highway."

Bobby nodded. "That's Hill's. The black Caddy's a rental."

Doc Baker's homegrown hearse and a coupe marked OSBI were the only other cars in the lot. If the Inn had any other guests last night, they'd already fled. Bobby killed the engine and they got out. Now that she was here, Chantalene dreaded going inside.

Deputy Ethridge opened the door to number 13 and let her go first. The cubicle looked like a fraternity game in progress—how many cops can squeeze into a cheap motel room. She and Bobby stood in a narrow space between the double bed and the front window.

The bed was made but rumpled, the faux Indian-blanket bedspread askew as if someone had been lying on top. A guy with a camera squatted on the other side, photographing the body of Henry Carl Hill that was sprawled on the floor. Chantalene glanced at the body in spite of herself. Hill might have been sleeping, except for the waxy texture to his skin. He lay on his side, his knees slightly bent and his arms relaxed in front of him. He wore jeans and a burnt orange tee shirt with a Longhorns emblem on the back. There was no blood. The only thing that looked unnatural was the slightly odd position of his head in relation to his shoulders. She looked away, tried not to inhale the sour stench of death that pervaded the room.

Doc Baker was packing up his kit. Everybody else stood around watching. From the bathroom doorway, Sheriff Justin motioned to Deputy Ethridge. "You two wait outside a minute while we remove the body." Not even a *please*.

Chantalene and Bobby slipped back outdoors and stood on the sidewalk that ran in front of the numbered doors. The sun sat roundly atop the horizon now, its brilliance piercing. The morning was chilly and Chantalene hugged her arms, wishing she'd brought a jacket. "Too bad we don't smoke."

Bobby smiled. "I used to."

"Still miss it?"

"Only at times like this."

"Never could afford it. But when I turn 80, I'm gonna start. A pack a day."

"You don't want to live forever?"

"I'm not that brave."

Two men entered number 13 with a stretcher, and a few minutes later Henry Carl Hill went out, zipped up in a bag. Doc Baker and the photographer followed, then the local cops. Finally Sheriff Justin stuck his head out and motioned to Bobby.

The only one still inside besides the sheriff was the OSBI investigator, poking around the room with his plastic gloves and a flashlight.

"Don't touch anything," Justin warned her. "Charlie's chemical evidence will give us clues, but that takes a while. You know Thelma better than anybody. I want to see if you notice anything that indicates she was here."

"What if she wasn't?"

"Then it's going to be a whole lot harder to find her, now that Hill's dead."

Harder to find her body, his tone said.

Chantalene stood still and tried to read the room. The tan carpet looked worn but newly cleaned—a K-Mart lamp and end table beside the bed held a phone and courtesy notepad. The only other furniture was a tiny round table and two chairs, a black windbreaker thrown over one of them. In the open alcove that served as a closet, two white shirts hung next to Hill's brown suit. Below sat his brown shoes and a pair of dingy sneakers.

Apparently, he'd stayed here several days. She could see his shaving kit beside the sink. She walked around the bed, looking on the floor, in the corners. Thelma hadn't exactly had time to pack, so there wasn't much she could have left in the room. Was the indention on the pillow made by her head? Was she bound and gagged?

The reality that Thelma might be dead hit her hard. Until now she hadn't really believed it. Chantalene's eyes filled and she kept her head down.

She cleared her throat. "I guess you've looked in all the drawers."

The sheriff grunted.

She looked inside the lavatory for a curly, gray-brown hair, but found only a rust stain. She stepped into the white-tiled bathroom. The shower was dry, the towels undisturbed. The commode stood open with the seat and lid tipped up against the tank.

Thelma would hate that. She liked to quote Phyllis Diller. Even cats cover it up. The thought made Chantalene smile, and her nose burned again. Forgetting Justin's command not to touch anything, she closed the lid.

A folded paper, tucked between the upright lid and the commode tank, fell on the floor. She picked it up. It was a page from the motel notepad, with a number scrawled in the center: *1-73*.

"Sheriff Justin!"

Sheriff Justin appeared in the door. "Where did you find that?"

"Where a man would never look." She handed him the paper.

"Does 1-73 mean anything to you?"

"Not that I can think of. January 1973, maybe?"

"Is this Thelma's handwriting?"

Chantalene examined the numbers again. "I think so. Thelma makes her threes like that."

The sheriff nodded. "I'll need to keep that with the other evidence."

The OSBI investigator appeared beside them. "Look what I found under the bed."

In his gloved palm, he held up a beaded clip-on earring.

"It's Thelma's," Chantalene said, her hope rising. "The other one was left in my house with the note. Thelma must have still been alive in this room."

"Looks like your friend is helping us out. Smart lady."

Smart and brave. Somehow Thelma had managed to write those numbers and hide them behind the toilet lid.

But what did they mean?

TWENTY-SIX

THE WOMAN WOULDN'T stop talking.

The old man was used to silence. He couldn't think straight with her constant noise. Even after he tied her arms behind the kitchen chair and each ankle to a chair leg, still she talked. He searched for something to tie around her mouth.

"They're looking for me right now. I left a clue and Chantalene will know what it means. She'll bring the sheriff."

He heard her words but not their meanings. He opened a drawer in the bureau, Liddy's drawer, and found a scarf patterned with autumn leaves. He ran the soft length of it through his hands. He had left her things just as they were all these years, but after today he would leave this place, anyway. He twisted the scarf into a long strand and turned back to the Talking Woman. She was a necessary nuisance, the bait that would bring the shapeshifter to him.

"You'd better escape before they get here. I'll tell the sheriff you killed Hill in self-defense—or to protect me. He'll believe that, and you'll be off the hook."

When he came toward the woman with the scarf in his hands, he saw her eyes widen, her breath catch. Still, she didn't beg or tremble. Her flowered dress had lost a button in front and there was a reddish bruise around one eye. Perhaps the man with no color had lost patience with her chatter and struck her. Couldn't blame him, though he felt no sympathy for the bristle-haired thug named Hill that he'd dispatched in the motel room. The old man had watched him for days and knew his motives.

But the buzz-head's greed had worked to his advantage. Hill had made it easy to appropriate the Talking Woman.

He moved to place the scarf around her mouth.

"What do you want from me?" the woman demanded. "Hill wanted the money he said Billy Ray stole, but I don't know anything about that. You don't seem like a man who wants money. What do you want?"

He tightened the scarf. Her brown eyes fixed him with a look of reproach.

No, he didn't want money. He had the money, and all it ever brought him was sorrow and trouble. He should have given it to Liddy years ago. She'd have gone away and left him in peace. As it was, he'd lost her anyway, and set himself up for her revenge. Too late to fix things with money.

The woman tried to talk around the scarf, coughing and gagging. At last she fell silent, but her frown followed his every move. The brown eyes reminded him of his grandmother. Apokni had disciplined him with her dark eyes. All it took was a disapproving look from her when he'd done something wrong.

He didn't want those eyes watching him. He grabbed the back of her chair and rotated it to face the wall.

If you don't shut up, I'll throw a sheet over you. Like a bird in a cage.

He didn't like having the woman in his cabin. He could snap her neck and be done with it, and he'd considered that. But none of this was her fault. She had no idea the money had been on her property all these years. She'd let him stay in the shack when she could have turned him in to the law. Besides, he counted on the life force of the Talking Woman—unsettling as it was—to draw the shapeshifter to him.

She struggled against her bindings, squealing like a muffled pig. He decided the sheet was a good idea.

She made a small whimper when the fabric billowed over her head, but in a moment she stopped struggling, her head drooping beneath the pale sheet. He hoped she was unconscious.

He turned away from his captive and went to the bedroom. From the doorless closet he took out his shotgun, broke it open, inserted two long shells from a box on the shelf and snapped the barrels shut. The woman must have heard the sound, because she started struggling again, coughing against the scarf in her mouth.

Bite down on it and it won't gag you, he said, forgetting that she couldn't hear his thoughts. Only Liddy did that.

He wished the shells were a heavier load, but at close range, they would do the job. He went back to the main room and stood by the window that faced the road. The sun was well up now, a fierce yellow globe above the horizon, but the inside of the cabin was still dim and cool. Through a slit between the curtains no wider than a knife blade, he could see anyone who approached.

How long would it take for Liddy to come?

It didn't matter. He was practiced at waiting. If she brought the law with her, as the Talking Woman threatened, he'd wait until the lawman stood on the front step and then blow him away. He wouldn't use the shotgun for Liddy, though. He had other plans for her.

He watched the road and waited.

While he waited, he thought about the foxes, his companions for a short time. Companionship never lasted. He thought of Naomi, too, and wondered how long it had been. He'd lost track of the years. If she was alive, Naomi's ample hips would be heavier now, and she'd be gray-headed like him. Things would have been different if she hadn't left him, hadn't betrayed him and set off his temper. In the Marines he'd been trained to control his temper, to kill without passion. That training had saved Naomi's life. Instead he'd seized her prized white bird from its cage and snapped the neck while Naomi screamed.

Naomi had called him a monster. She'd snatched a kitchen knife and hurled it at his head, nicking his cheek.

Maybe she was right. He was a monster. And Liddy was his punishment. She was his tormentor, a demon who took first one form and then another.

So be it. Today he'd face the demon and take her down.

TWENTY-SEVEN

SKELETONS OF LAST year's sunflowers leaned from the bar ditch along the dirt road, brushing Chantalene's jeans as Whippoorwill clopped along the narrow path. Except for the daily run of Hank Littlejohn's mail truck, the road along the eastern edge of Thelma Patterson's farm likely would have disappeared altogether.

Whip pricked his ears forward as they approached a tumble-down cabin that sat some distance from the road, obscured in the brush. The shack looked deserted except for a set of tire tracks that led around back. Chantalene patted the horse's neck and spoke to him in a low voice. "Creepy, isn't it. We'll get out of here as fast as we can."

North of the cabin, a grove of twisted fruit trees reached up from the pasture with bony fingers. It must have been somebody's prized orchard fifty years ago. Now, a single pear tree bloomed white above the brush.

She halted Whip beside a battered tin mailbox at the roadside. There was no name on its side, just faded black letters, barely readable. *Rt 1, #73.*

One, seventy-three.

On the long ride home from the crime scene, she had worried the numbers in her head like fingered beads, sure they were somehow the key to finding Thelma. After the deputy dropped her off, she paced the floor until, finally, it came to her.

Thelma knew the postal address of every resident for miles around Tetumka. Often, especially if she didn't have much use for particular citizens, she called them by their numbers instead of by name. Thelma's house was Route 1, Box 72. The next mail stop would be the old hermit's shack on the opposite edge of her farm, two miles cross-country from Thelma's house, three miles by road.

On that hunch, Chantalene had saddled Whip and headed out.

Sitting her horse beside the mailbox now, she wondered what this harmless old fart could possibly have to do with Henry Carl Hill. Had somebody taken over his place as a hideout? Maybe he lay dead inside. Any such idea seemed far-fetched—but it was the only clue she had, and Thelma's time could be running out.

Her hand went to Devereau's cell phone in her shirt pocket. Thank God she'd forgotten to return it in the confusion of finding Hill dead. If she saw any sign of Thelma, she would call the sheriff, stat.

But no signs of life or light showed behind the dirt-stained windows of the shack. One of the panes was broken at the corner and taped over with yellowed newspaper. Chantalene had been out here with Thelma once, to check on the old man when his BIA checks were collecting in the mailbox. She'd waited in the car without getting a glimpse of him when Thelma went to the door. Thelma had bought the land where the cabin sat years ago, after it was tied up for ages while some rich man's heirs haggled over more valuable property. Thelma said the old Indian was squatting here then, and she saw no reason to run him off. Maybe Thelma's good deed hadn't gone unpunished.

Chantalene scanned the weedy yard, the abandoned outdoor john that leaned beneath the trees. What kind of mind would it take to live like this? Or what desperation?

She fidgeted in the saddle, wishing for the third time today that Drew was here. She pictured him winging his way toward the Wicked Witch of the East, a fine place for him to be when she needed his help. A cloud passed over the sun. She slipped her jacket on and moved the cell phone to its pocket.

"Let's go, Whip."

She nudged him with her heels and they turned up the track toward the cabin, passing through a gateway of leafless brush at the fence line. Close beneath the eaves stood an old cistern, a relic of the days before rural co-ops brought water to country homes. The metal hand-crank was frozen in rust and the down spout that once collected water from the roof was long gone. Chantalene shivered. She had a bad memory of an old cistern.

In the dooryard lay the remnants of a bonfire, recent enough that no weeds grew from the ashes. A swath of raked coals stretched out to one side, a weird windrow of ashes. She halted her horse a safe distance from the house and dismounted. A scarlet cardinal called urgently from a bare treetop in the orchard.

Whip snuffled and shifted his feet, showing her the whites of his eyes as she looped his reins around a sumac sapling. She turned toward the front door. Through the tall weeds she glimpsed something red and white lying on the concrete blocks that formed a front step to the house. The crickets fell silent as she approached.

On the doorstep lay her missing hairbrush, and beneath it, a folded paper.

Her hands shook as she picked them up. Maybe Hill wasn't the only one who'd broken into her house. Had the old hermit been stalking her, stealing her things?

She pocketed the brush and unfolded the paper. It was the flyer she'd taken from the post office, the defiant face of Lydia Sue Raintree staring up at her. A shudder ran down her back.

How was it all connected? Nothing made sense. Unless he was just freaking nuts.

One thing was sure—somebody was expecting her. He had known she'd come looking for Thelma, probably had watched her approach and was cowering right now behind a dirt-smeared window.

Her face flushed hot, her fists clenching the flyer. *Get your jollies quick, you perverted jerk, because by nightfall your ass will be in jail.* She pulled out the phone and started jabbing numbers.

Whippoorwill whinnied. But the warning came too late.

She never heard him coming, didn't see his face when the iron forearm clamped around her neck from behind and jerked her off her feet.

The phone went flying.

She couldn't scream. She couldn't breathe. Her hands wrenched at the bony arm pressing against her throat and her legs thrashed. The more she struggled, the tighter his grip. God, he was strong! He wrenched her head back and spiked his knee into her spinal column. Her legs buckled.

Blackness closed in. And nauseating, overwhelming pain.

He's going to kill me. Right here.

She went limp and sank.

The grip on her windpipe relaxed just enough for air to reach her lungs. She gagged and coughed. Her body hung slack in his grasp, her legs useless.

He hooked her elbows behind her back and held them, his other arm still pressing against her throat so hard she couldn't swallow. Coarse white hair fell into her line of vision as he hunched over her, smelling of ashes and sweat.

She knew that smell. It had been in her house, and she had ignored the warning. His foul breath was hot against her cheek, his voice dry as paper. "Liddy girl. I've been waiting for you."

What? She tried to yell but could barely choke out a whisper.

"Where's... Thelma?"

He lifted her to her feet like a rag doll. "She's not your problem, Liddy. *I'm* your problem."

"I'm not Liddy!" she rasped. "I don't know anybody named Liddy."

It was the wrong response. He jerked her elbows together and pain ripped her shoulder blades. She clamped her teeth, tasting blood.

His arms were steel. If she kept struggling, he would break her neck for sure. Like Henry Carl Hill. She unclenched her muscles and stopped fighting.

His grip eased. She breathed through her mouth until the fuzziness cleared from her brain.

Who the hell was Liddy?

The girl on the flyer—Lydia Sue Raintree.

Did he think she was someone who'd disappeared twenty-five years ago—about the time she was born? God, he was insane.

What had he done with Thelma?

He shoved her forward, stumbling, toward the side of the house. If she was going to save herself, let alone Thelma, she had to think of something.

"I know who you are." She coughed again, her throat ragged. "You stole the bingo hall money with the Patterson brothers. They called you Songdog."

He didn't answer.

"Listen, I'm not Liddy. She would be much older now. But my partner's a lawyer and we could help you find Liddy. Just tell me where Thelma is."

But he was through talking. He dragged her toward the old cistern at the side of the house and shoved her to the ground, pinning her there with a boot in her back.

A childhood memory rose like a bubble in a muddy pond. They had a cistern at her house when she was small. Her mother pumped the rainwater and heated it to wash their hair. Once her mother had taken the metal lid off the top so Chantalene could see how the water came up in the square metal cups, attached to a looped chain like the seats on a Ferris wheel. The cups slid over the top of the cogwheel and down, spilling cool water into a catch-pan for the spout. Chantalene had watched, fascinated, until a drowned mouse rode up and spilled out into their bucket. Afterward, she had nightmares about falling into the cistern, where the water was neck deep and there was no way to climb out.

The boot ground into her backbone, raking her cheek in the dirt. She heard the sheet-metal top of the square cistern box wrench open and tasted panic in her mouth.

Jesus, no!

The opening was large enough to accommodate a bucket—or a human body. She was living her nightmare.

Was Thelma down there already? She sucked in a breath and screamed. "Thelma!"

He grabbed her hair and jerked her upright, staying out of range of her flying fists until he caught one arm and crooked it up behind her. She screamed again.

He shoved her toward the gaping black square in the top of the cistern and she gathered herself for one desperate lunge. She twisted her body toward him, felt a handful of hair rip loose, and kicked out hard, aiming for his groin.

He saw it coming and stepped back. Her foot slammed into his belly and she heard the surprised, guttural sound as he lost his breath. In that instant she wrenched her arm free and slammed her open hands against his chest, shoving him back with all her strength.

It wasn't enough. He rocked like a bowling pin but didn't go down. She turned to run. His fist struck the side of her head, the pain exploding in her ear. Her feet left the ground and she sprawled.

She couldn't see, couldn't hear. She thought her head had split open. He pulled her limp body up by the arms and she couldn't resist.

Metal scraped against her ribcage when he dumped her headfirst into the hole.

Her last conscious sensation was of falling, falling, into the dark.

TWENTY-EIGHT

DREW LOOKED OUT through the wall of windows facing the tarmac at Will Rogers World Airport. His Delta flight sat ready for boarding, the accordion hood of the jetway clamped over the airplane's door like the mandible of a giant caterpillar. He'd almost forgotten how he hated flying—the used-air smell of the cabin, the compressing and decompressing that made his sinuses ache. But he remembered now, and it didn't help his lousy feeling about this trip.

Beside him, a toddler came to the window and pressed miniature hands on the glass. He wore Oshkosh overalls and blue tennies no longer than Drew's palm. Drew smiled down at him. "Hi. You going for an airplane ride?"

The boy smiled back, pointing at the jet and pounding the window. His mother hustled him back to the row of seats and Drew watched their reflection in the glass. The mom was in jeans and a pony tail, going to see Grandma, she told a traveler next to them in the row. The man was about Drew's age, wearing a suit, with a carry-on beside him. "I have a little girl about that age," he said. Going off on a business trip, leaving his family behind. Drew's smile faded.

Outside on the tarmac, workers wearing ear mufflers loaded luggage and serviced the snack bar at the back of the plane. When things went bad with Emily in New York, he had run to Oklahoma. Today it felt like he was running away again. Everything he cared about was back in Tetumka. What the hell was he doing here?

Going to visit an old friend who's dying. That was the thing that had pulled him toward New York. Not the job offer, and certainly not the prospect of tangling with Emily again. A man he admired and respected had asked him to come. How did you turn down a dying man's request?

He wished he'd explained that to Chantalene, instead of saying something asinine about needing perspective. What bullshit. The truth was that he was angry that she hadn't told him about that internship application. She kept pushing him away, and it hurt.

He turned on his cell phone and tried her number. No answer.

The gate agent's voice crackled through the loudspeaker, summoning pre-boards and first class passengers. His boarding pass had the first-class stamp—nothing but the best for Savolini, Inc.—but he waited a while before he shuffled down the jetway, stuffed his bag into the overhead bin, and settled into an aisle seat. At least in first class he had some leg room.

He drank a Bloody Mary while the rest of the passengers filed through, the young father among them. *Hey, man, I'll be glad to stay home with your wife and baby.* Probably the guy would, too. Maybe he didn't like his job any better than Drew had liked his in New York.

He closed his eyes while the jet hurtled down the runway and lifted off, then slid his seat back and hoped for sleep. It didn't happen. The businessman next to him offered Drew his *USA Today*, then snored from Little Rock to Atlanta. In Atlanta, where Drew changed planes, he tried to call Chantalene again, with no results.

He had a headache by the time the jet touched down at LaGuardia, at 3:45 New York time. A light drizzle was falling. He took a cab to William's mid-town office, still wearing his sport shirt and cotton pants. He would look like a tourist among the black-clad New Yorkers, and that made him smile.

The sidewalk where he stepped from the car rarely emerged from the shadow of tall buildings even on a sunny day. Today it was chilly and dark as a tunnel. Still, he inhaled the familiar diesel smell of the city and couldn't deny a certain excitement. For a moment he saw the City through Chantalene's eyes. She would love this. Why the hell hadn't he asked her to come?

She wouldn't have, though, with Thelma missing. Guilt poked him again. He should have waited until Thelma showed back up before making the trip.

Alone on the elevator to the 34th floor, Drew stared into the polished brass patina of the closed doors and asked the questions he'd been avoiding. Did he miss living in New York? Wouldn't it be nice to have a job that paid well again?

The answer to the second part was a no-brainer. But he still hadn't answered the first question when he stepped into the outer office of the Bratten & Baird law firm.

William's long-time secretary, a petite woman who seemed ageless, lit up when she saw him. "Drew!" Usually the soul of propriety, Sherry surprised him by coming around her desk to give him an efficient hug. "We miss seeing you around here."

"How's it going, Sherry?"

"Not all that well."

He saw the strain of William's illness on her face. Sherry had been William's devoted friend and associate for more years than Drew had known them. A plaque on her desk read, *"I'm nobody's assistant. I'm The Secretary,"* and she was the true Ex-O for the firm of Bratten & Baird. He wondered if Sherry would stay with the firm after William left, but he wouldn't ask.

Sherry straightened the jacket of her dark suit and returned to her post. "He's expecting you," she said, and buzzed Drew in.

William Bratten—nobody called him Bill—met him at the door and shook his hand. "Good to see you, Drew. Thanks for coming."

William's grip wasn't as firm as it once had been, and his skin looked like wax. He was thinner, too, with less hair. But the intelligence in his eyes was undimmed and his smile was warm. "I wish it were under better circumstances," Drew said.

"Me, too. But there it is."

He motioned Drew to a leather wing chair that looked out on a spectacular view of Manhattan. The skyline looked wrong. Drew's eyes found the vacant place where the Twin Towers should have been, and it hit his stomach like a punch. Today the tops of the World Trade Center would have been obscured by low-hanging clouds. He'd talked to William on the phone after watching the tragedy on television and knew that both William and Emily's father had lost friends there. And a lot of business.

Everything had changed since he'd left New York.

"Can I get you something to drink?" William offered.

"No, thanks. In first class, they were very generous."

William laughed. "Sure they were." He poured ice water for himself from the sidebar and sat in the chair beside Drew, his gray eyes attentive. "So how's the country life?"

"Love the country. But farming's riskier than I remembered."

"I'll bet. I see wheat prices have gone to hell, along with most everything else." His eyes narrowed, assessing. "You look good. I believe you've even put on a few pounds."

"I had to learn to cook."

William laughed again. "Never hurts to be self-sufficient. Emily says you're practicing law, too?"

Drew shrugged. "Not exactly. I passed the Oklahoma bar, but my practice right now is ninety percent tax work."

William smiled. "That's your specialty." Then he got down to business. "So what do you think about the offer from Savolini, Inc.?"

"It's a hell of an offer. I'm flattered." He paused. "But that's not why I came to town."

William nodded. "I know. And I appreciate that."

He met Drew's eyes and for a moment Drew saw the pain and regret. And he knew William well enough to know the sadness wasn't for himself, but for the family he'd leave behind.

William cleared his throat. "But as you say, it's a hell of an offer. The board squirmed a little, but they voted for it unanimously. They're worried about the scrutiny the company will go through in the wake of Sam's death. We need a cool head in the financial department, somebody with scruples who's not afraid to make the tough decisions."

"I'm not sure I'm your man."

"You're the right man at the right time. If Sam were here, he'd agree." William sipped his water. "Notwithstanding your value to the company, Drew, this could make your future. If things go well, you'd be in a position to write your own ticket with Savolini or any other top company."

Drew's gaze shifted to the hazy skyline outside the window again. Money and power. Maybe he was crazy not to consider it. But there was another side to money and power—tremendous pressure, long hours, constant stress. He thought of the young father on the plane. Two years ago, he'd opted for a simpler life. He thought he'd found what he wanted in Tetumka.

So how's that working out for you?

Would Chantalene agree to move to New York with him? If she wanted to experience the world, New York was definitely it. He tried to picture the two of them living in a high-rise apartment, or maybe an old brownstone. While he was working nine to nine, what would Chantalene do all day? Shop? He shook his head.

William was watching him. "I get the feeling there are extenuating circumstances."

Drew nodded.

William held the water glass in both hands and rubbed its rim with his thumbs. His voice was quiet when he spoke again.

"Son, I'd love for you to come on board and help me dig this company out of a hole. But you've got to do what feels right. If there's one thing this cancer has taught me, that's it. For me, family and integrity are the things that really count. All the rest is just score-keeping. You've got to decide what counts for you."

Drew was quiet for a moment. "The farm is no utopia," he said finally, "but I was happier this last year than I have been since I was a little kid."

William looked at him thoughtfully. "I wish I had moved to the country when I was your age."

Drew's eyes widened. "Really."

"I grew up on a farm in New Hampshire, you know. Or probably you didn't know. Anyway. I've had a great life and I wouldn't trade it. But it's always been about reaching for something, aiming for something out ahead. I should have learned to enjoy it one moment at a time."

Drew nodded, his throat tight.

William got up and retrieved a folder from his football-field of a desk. He handed it to Drew. "Here's the contract offer in writing, with all the details. Take it home and think it over. We can hold off two weeks, but then we'll have to make a move."

Drew took the maroon folder imprinted with the Savolini logo in gold foil.

William sat down again. "Much as I hope you'll take the job, I'll understand if you don't." He smiled. "The Board won't, but I will."

"Thanks," Drew said.

"One way or another, Sam's company will survive. And so will Emily."

"I appreciate your confidence in me, William, and your friendship. And I'm damned sorry about the cancer."

"I know. It stinks." He smiled and shrugged his thin shoulders.

Drew stood up and extended his hand. William shook it without getting up. "Let me know if there's anything I can do for you, Drew. Anything."

Drew nodded. "Please give my best to Mrs. Bratten."

"I'll do that." His face looked tired. "Be happy, son."

At the door Drew turned to glance back at him. William grinned. "Send Sherry a postcard with cows on it. She'd love that."

Drew closed the door thinking that was the way he wanted to remember William Bratten. Still smiling, his extraordinary mind still alert.

OUTSIDE THE REVOLVING glass doors on ground level, a premature dusk enveloped the misty street. He stood a moment on the sidewalk, hearing the pulse of the city around him. He felt hollowed out, and not only because he'd skipped lunch on the plane.

The Roosevelt Hotel was only a few blocks from here. On a weeknight, he could probably get a room and some early dinner. Maybe he'd phone a guy he used to work with and meet him for a beer. He set out walking, angling his body and his leather duffle through the foot traffic with familiar precision.

He picked up a copy of the Times in the hotel lobby and went into the bar. At this hour the long, narrow room was nearly deserted. The gray daylight of the street didn't enter here, the room's lighting golden and warm. He took a table in a far corner and ordered a beer and a pricey sandwich off the menu. When the waiter left, he opened his newspaper. *The Times* was one thing he really did miss in Oklahoma.

"Buy a girl a drink?"

He knew the voice before he looked up. "Em."

"Good guess." She sat in the only other chair at the round table. The waiter appeared instantly, whereas Drew had waited for five minutes, and took Emily's order for a highball.

"How did you find me?"

"I followed you from William's office."

He pictured her bumping along the sidewalk with an umbrella over her immaculate head, then amended that thought. She would have followed him in a cab. Her black slacks and turtleneck were perfectly dry.

"So you're stalking me."

"I have to. Since you don't let me know when you're coming to town."

Sherry had ratted him out, he bet. So much for her postcard with cows. He folded his newspaper and waited for his beer.

Emily lit a cigarette with a gold lighter and blew smoke toward the ceiling. "Have you checked in?"

"Not yet."

"You can stay at the apartment if you like."

"No thanks."

Their drinks arrived and Drew took a long pull from his beer. The beer at Pete's place in El Rio was colder. And a fourth the price.

At a table across the room, a young couple leaned toward each other, holding hands, their conversation animated. Honeymooners, he bet. The girl's back was toward him, her hair long and dark, but not curly.

If Chantalene had come with him, he could show her the city. They could take the elevator up the Empire State Building, ride the Staten Island Ferry. Or just curl up in a room upstairs and watch it rain.

"Earth to Drew. I said, did you give William an answer?"

"Um, no. Not yet."

She nodded, her eyebrows raised. "That's good. I was afraid you'd just reject the offer without thinking it over."

"I probably will."

His sandwich arrived and he ordered another beer. Her eyes followed his sandwich to his mouth, watched him as he chewed.

She leaned forward. "Come home with me. For old times' sake." She watched him sip the beer. "We can sit up late and talk. I won't molest you unless you want me to."

He met her eyes, and what he saw wasn't lust, it was survival instinct. Emily's life had become uncomfortable and scary. If she manipulated Drew successfully, she thought he could fix that for her.

The light laughter of the young woman across the room drifted to them as the couple left together.

Chantalene wouldn't have come until they found Thelma. He was weary of Thelma's soap opera with Billy Ray Patterson, so he'd refused to worry about her. He had figured whatever enemies Billy Ray Patterson had made in his life, they'd have no reason to harm Thelma. What if he was wrong?

Sheriff Justin had asked him to keep Chantalene from doing something crazy. He glanced at his watch and wondered what she was doing right now. A bad feeling rolled over him.

"I'm a world-class jerk," he mumbled.

"What?"

"Never mind. Nothing you didn't already know."

"Drew." Exasperation edged her voice. "You're not talking to me. You're not even here."

"Emily, dear, you're exactly right."

A waiter appeared beside them. "Can I get you something else, sir?"

"The check, please." Drew reached for his wallet.

"You can sign it to your room if you like."

"I'm not staying. I've got to catch the red-eye."

But there was no overnight flight from New York to Oklahoma City. He spent that night on a bench in Hartsfield Atlanta International.

TWENTY-NINE

CHANTALENE AWOKE TO darkness and the smell of damp earth, the metallic taste of dirt on her tongue. Silence rang in her ears. Her shoulder throbbed and her cheek burned where it pressed against the ground.

Gingerly, she shifted the weight off her shoulder. Something small and fast scuttled out from under her hair. Her head jerked up and shot lightning through her temple. When the pain receded, she rolled onto her back, her groan echoing in the hollow dark. Above her, a small square of light marked the rabbit hole into her nightmare.

She wiped her fingers on her jeans and explored her face. The left cheek felt puffy and sore, her eye swollen. She couldn't move, couldn't think. For a long time she lay still, counting her breaths, listening for sounds from above. She heard nothing except the wind singing through the metal housing of the cistern.

Don't panic. Take stock.

A, you're not dead. B, you're not underwater. C, this hole isn't as deep as you thought.

Gradually her heartbeat slowed. She squinted at the square of light, trying to gain depth perception. Ground level appeared to be about ten feet above her. The sheet-metal cistern box, with the square of light at its top, rose three feet above the ground in the approximate center of the underground chamber. Even if she found a way to climb the wall, she couldn't get to the opening.

At least the cistern was dry. The chilly earth beneath her smelled musty and sour. Images of blind creatures that lurked in the corners webbed her brain.

Don't panic. Breathe.

What did Alice do, when she hit the bottom of the hole?

She couldn't remember. Didn't want to. That story had scared her spitless when she was small.

Shifting the weight off her left side, she pushed up on her elbow. Dizziness enveloped her, then subsided. Her shoulder felt strained and bruised, but nothing seemed to be broken. She sat up and tried to make out the dimensions of her dungeon.

The wall nearest her was vertical, blackened by water and time. She sensed that the chamber was about twice the width of a coat closet and longer, like a large grave. How long she couldn't tell. The far end receded into the dark. A wooden frame formed the roof of the cavern and supported a concrete base for the cistern housing.

She inched forward to sit in the small square of light from the opening above. Wrapping her arms around her bent legs, she rested her forehead on her knees. The light on her back warmed her and held the crawly things at bay. As long as she had that shaft of light, she could manage not to go crazy.

For now she would rest, then try to find a way out.

There is no way out. No way out. No way out.

She swallowed a rising urge to scream. If he heard her, he might put the lid on the cistern. She tried not to imagine the absolute blackness if he covered the opening.

Oh my god—Thelma. Is she down here, too?

Her whisper sounded eerie in the darkness. "Thelma?"

But Thelma wouldn't answer if she was dead.

Her spine rigid, she rolled onto her hands and knees. She put out one hand and felt the rough earth in front of her, then extended the other hand, crawling forward toward blackness.

Don't think about it. Just crawl. Maybe you can find a way out. She hung onto that hope. If the fear overtook her, she'd die screaming.

She shuddered as she put out her hand and slapped the ground to scare away any creatures in her path. Then she waited, screwing up her courage to reach out again, hoping weirdly to find Thelma, dead or alive, so she wouldn't be alone. The ground beneath her sloped and the dampness increased. She held onto each breath, dreading the next intake of musty air.

Minutes ticked past, unmeasurable. She had traveled only a few feet, but it felt like miles.

Her hand struck something long and thin.

Snake!

She recoiled, gasping.

No. It hadn't moved under her touch, didn't feel alive. And it felt too rough for snake scales. She took a shuddering breath and reached out again.

This time her fingers found a different shape—something heavy and coarse, like canvas. She sat up and felt ahead of her with both hands.

The cloth covered a solid mass—but not like human flesh. The edge of the fabric melted into the dirt floor. Whatever this was, it had been here a long time, maybe even in standing water.

Her fingers found the skinny object again. It was stiff and rough—a rope. She followed its length, intermingled with the coarse cloth, and found where the rope had been knotted around it. What she was feeling was a bag, a canvas bag tied with rope. She pressed down on the cloth again, feeling the shape inside. It felt solid and rectangular, and there was more than one—like bricks. But not that heavy.

Bricks of money?

What else would be hidden in a canvas bag down here? If the hermit was the third man from the bingo hall robbery, maybe this was the loot, the money Henry Carl Hill had died for. Would the hermit have kept it all this time without spending it? She wasn't about to stick her hand inside the bag and make sure, but the more her fingers explored the shapes, the more she was convinced of its contents.

The Kingmans' ill-gotten money. If Hill were alive, she could buy her way out of this hole. But Hill was dead.

The money couldn't help her, but the rope might be useful if it wasn't rotted away and if it was long enough. She pulled the rope hand over hand until it came free. Only a few feet long, it was too short to reach the square opening above her. Her hope sank.

She felt something else, half buried in the dirt. Long, hard shapes bigger around than the rope. She reached forward again into the darkness.

And felt hair. Repulsed past terror, she moved her fingers lightly over its surface. Long, soft hair, too long to be an animal's.

It was attached to a human skull.

Her whimper echoed from the walls. She wrapped her arms around her waist, rocked back and forth while her stomach jittered. She was sitting on a woman's grave. Some poor, lost sister who had died here—maybe the girl, Lydia Raintree. She touched the hair again, stroked it, and tears slipped down her face.

A keening rose inside her but she pinched it off. *Quiet!* The dank chill of the cave soaked through her clothes and she shivered. How many years would it be before somebody found *her* bones?

She looked back toward the light. Through blurred vision, she saw something suspended from the ceiling, just beyond the column of light. A chain— the looped chain with metal cups attached that once had brought up water from the bottom of the cistern. It was still hanging from the cogwheel above, adjacent to the square box that opened to the light. She crouched and crawled toward it.

The chain links were caked with rust but apparently intact. She grasped both sides of the loop, careful to avoid the sharp edges of the metal cups which hung on the outside, and pulled hard. It held.

Her pulse rabbited. She placed one foot inside the bottom of the loop, several feet above the floor, and shifted her weight onto it, reaching above her head for a hand-hold in the corroded links. A knife-edged pain shot through her shoulder when she tried to pull herself up. She waited it out, tried again.

The cog gear above her head creaked, but the chain held. She dangled there a moment, her fingers laced into the links, blood pounding in her ears. Above her head, she could barely make out the cogwheel holding the chain. It was mounted in its own housing beside the square opening she'd fallen through. If she could manage to climb to the top, it might be possible to swing her legs up through the opening, catch the lip and somehow pull her body up. If the sheet metal housing didn't crumple under her weight.

She hooked her fingers higher in the loop and pulled herself up. Waited out the stab of pain in her shoulder. Tried again. She wedged her free foot behind one of the metal cups on the outside of the chain and prayed that it held. Pushing hard with her leg and pulling with both arms, she lifted herself a few inches up the chain. She wound her right leg around the chain to hold her place, felt the metal cups cutting into her thigh. Her palms were slick with grime.

Rust sifted into her eyes when she looked up toward the window of light. Only a few more feet. Her head would have to be pressed against the ceiling in order for her feet to reach through the square hole. She repositioned her hands and one foot, took a deep breath, and lifted herself again.

Something cracked, loud in the cavern. The chain jerked. She clamped on and froze, panting. Had he heard?

When nothing happened, she wrapped her right leg around the chain and moved one hand at a time up the links. Replaced her left foot, lifted herself a few inches.

Her head was almost to ground level now, just below the oval housing that held the cog gear and the top of the chain. She couldn't climb much farther. But she also couldn't reach the square opening with her legs. She positioned her hands higher on the chain, reaching into the darkness of the oval housing above her head. Metal scraped her hand. She wrapped her right leg, searched for a foothold with her left, and pushed.

The cup under her left foot tore loose, rattling to the floor. She clung to the chain, her foot flailing, heartbeat slamming her ears. Finally she secured the foot again, took two deep breaths and hoisted herself upward until her neck bent against a rafter beneath the concrete platform of the cistern.

Cobwebs plaited her hair. In this awkward position, she couldn't see her escape route. She wrapped one leg around the chain and reached the other foot toward the light.

It wouldn't work. Her leg wasn't long enough, and there was nothing inside the square metal cylinder for a foothold. She'd have to swing both feet up at once and hope to hang her sneakers over the top.

She pictured how to do this. With her feet hooked at the top, when she turned loose of the chain, she would be hanging upside down. There was a chance the sheet-metal housing would crater beneath her weight. If it didn't, and by some miracle she mustered the strength to torque her shoulders up to her legs, she wasn't sure she could double herself small enough to fit through the opening.

The hell she couldn't. She could be a contortionist to get out of here.

She took a deep breath, firmed her grip on the chain and turned loose with her legs. Her hands burned and her arm muscles strained, but she ignored them. She began to pump her feet, forwards and backwards like a child on a swing. She'd have to get a good arc going before she could aim her legs up into the metal box far enough to catch the opening.

The chain creaked and the cogwheel made an ominous snapping noise. She kept swinging. Backwards, forwards. One more swing.

Backward, forward, and *up*—

The cogwheel sounded like a car wreck as it ripped loose from the housing.

Her hands slipped. She fought to grasp something—anything—with her feet, felt her sneakers slide uselessly inside the box.

Gravity took over. She tucked her head and somersaulted into the fall.

Her shoulders jolted when she hit the ground. Flat on her back, she lay still, head pounding, every sinew on fire. She fought for air, closing her eyes against the cruel square of light that fell across her face.

A shadow crossed the light and she heard a noise. Squinting against the dirt and rust sifting down, she watched the opening above her shrink to a rectangle, then a slit. The lid scraped shut with a final clunk, and all light disappeared.

THIRTY

CHANTALENE LAY STILL on the sour dirt floor of the cistern, eyes closed, her body ringing like an endless echo. Waiting to breathe, she thought of a *Beverly Hillbillies* rerun she'd watched with Drew. Granny Clampett declared that from age 13 to 16, kids ought to be sealed up in a barrel with nothing but the bung hole open for air. Jed asked what happens at 16, and Granny shrieked, "Then you seal up the hole!"

The old hermit son of a bitch had just sealed up the bung hole.

Her skittish laugh sounded eerie in the silence. Tears crawled down her temples and into her hair. She kept her eyes squeezed shut, postponing the moment when she would open them to the blackness of eternity.

Of all the ways to die.

How long will it take, without water? Two days? Three? She felt thirsty already.

She wished she and Drew hadn't argued. It seemed so pointless now. She wondered if he would abandon his farm and move back to New York when she was gone.

Who would feed Whippoorwill and Bones, and take them in? Thelma would if she were alive. Maybe Thelma's misery was already over.

Insects and rodents will pick my bones clean, like the poor soul who shares this grave.

Her body ached. She was beaten. There was no way out of this godforsaken hole.

She took deep breaths and tried removing her mind to a sunny place where the air was clean and fresh. For a few seconds, it worked. The hysteria passed, and she felt nothing but a sucking fatigue that made her groggy. Maybe it was some kind of chemical reaction to the knowledge that she was going to die.

Maybe I can just go to sleep, like freezing, and it will be over.

Instead, she opened her eyes.

The blackness didn't change. She stopped the panic by taking deep breaths. But she couldn't stop the ringing darkness.

Then she saw it—or thought she did—a thread of light. She blinked dirt from her lashes. Yes. A tiny seam of daylight showed around the tin housing where the cogwheel had torn loose. Just enough of a crack for light to show through.

She stared at the seam until her vision blurred. Her eyes closed again and she slipped into a hazy doze, rousing every few minutes to search again for that narrow lifeline, stingy as string.

It was impossible to gauge how much time had passed.

But what did it matter?

Ashes to ashes, dust to dust. She felt her skin migrate as if she were changing shape. Was the crack of light getting dimmer? Maybe her eyesight was giving out.

No—the sun was going down. Night was coming, and the white thread would disappear.

Her shoulders shook, but she kept her eyes open and her sight fastened on the cracked housing, afraid to blink, saving the light. It grew dimmer and dimmer. Her retinal memory retained the tiny streak past the moment it faded into blackness, but finally, even that was gone.

Something awful and heavy weighted her limbs as if her flesh were already melting into the earth. Her hair inched longer from its follicles. The fabric of her jacket settled for sleep. Her heartbeat thundered, pounding the blood through her veins. And behind all that, there was the incessant ringing.

I'm losing my mind. Maybe it's easier that way.

Her arms slid to her sides. She felt a lump in the pocket of her jacket—her hairbrush, a friend. She pulled it out and fingered the familiar shape. She held it to her cheek and a sorrow like love welled in her chest. *The little things that comprise a life, those are the secret. Not all the big things I always worried about.* This new-found knowledge seemed vital—she wanted to tell Drew, and Thelma. But she would never see them again.

The plastic handle of the brush felt hard and real in her palm. She sat up in the darkness and began to brush her hair in slow strokes, listening to the slide of the bristles, the snap of individual hairs. When the back of her hair was free of dirt and tangles, she brushed the left side, and the right.

Above ground, the wind no longer sang through the cracked cistern. The night was still. Probably the stars were out, and the moon.

Something hummed on her skin. A vibration, like the rhythm of human steps.

She stopped brushing and listened. There it was again. Up above, her enemy was afoot. Songdog was prowling the night.

He moved with purpose, crossing and recrossing the same ground. Then the movement stopped. She heard a muffled *whoosh,* and then nothing. She turned her face upward, listening. Silence and darkness pulsed on her skin. She shoved the brush into her pocket.

A metallic *skreak* pierced the cave, so loud she cringed. A square of palest light appeared above her head.

He had opened the cistern.

Something dropped inside. She scuttled away, waiting for the object to hit ground. It never did. She felt his presence move away from the opening and disappear.

Light flickered at the square mouth of the cistern. Firelight?

Of course. That was the whooshing sound she'd heard, the lighting of a fire. In its glow she made out a rope dangling from the hole.

She sat motionless, hearing only the slam of her heartbeat. There was no sound from above, no movement. Had he given her an escape route and gone away?

Not bloody likely.

If she climbed up, he'd be waiting to kill her.

And what did she have to lose? It would be faster than dying down here like a poisoned mole. Above, she might have a fighting chance.

Still she waited. Hope, devoid of reason, crept into her brain. If she got out of this hole, she'd jab out his eyes with the handle of her hairbrush. Tie her jacket over his head and suffocate him. Shove *him* down the cistern....

Crouching, she moved toward the rope. She grasped it with both hands and yanked as hard as she could. It held, apparently fastened to something solid. She tested the rope again and listened. The light flickered, but that was all.

Her hands shook as she tied a knot chest high in the rope, and another at the bottom. She hadn't tried to climb a rope since seventh grade gym class, but by God she would do it now. A memory of her gypsy mother, scaling the side of a barn in the moonlight with her bare feet and hands, gave her courage. She remembered, too, the curse her mother had screamed into the night, and she laid it silently on Songdog Jones. *Gruesome death to you and all your lineage!* If he let her out of this hole, she'd make him regret it.

She grabbed the higher knot, hoisted herself, and braced her feet on the bottom one. And began to climb. Hand over hand, wrapping her leg in the rope as she inched upward. The hemp burned her hands and pain spiked her shoulder. The pain felt good; it meant she was alive.

He was baiting her, no doubt. Waiting in the silence with a shotgun, or an axe. It didn't matter. If she could get one hand or foot over the top of that opening, he'd have hell getting the cat back into the bag. At least she'd die breathing fresh air.

She was almost there. When her head and shoulders entered the squared cylinder that formed the opening, she stopped, smelling the night air just above her head. It was scented with wood smoke.

The top edge of the opening was raw metal. If she grabbed it to pull herself up, it would slice her hands. One arm at a time, she wriggled out of her jacket. The hairbrush clattered against the metal housing as it fell, her only weapon gone. She wrapped her jacket over her right forearm and stopped to listen. Nothing except the flickering light and the crackling of logs. Maybe he'd gone to tend the fire.

She reached her protected arm over the top of the metal frame and pulled herself up. Her biceps quivered and stalled. But she pictured the bones on the cistern floor and adrenaline stiffened her muscles. Hauling her body upward, she slung one arm at a time over the side, expecting an attack.

None came. She hung there panting, metal digging into her armpits, her vision blinded by the bonfire. When her breath returned, she grasped the rope, pulled her torso over the side and somersaulted onto the ground.

Above the bonfire, the old man had constructed a crude platform. What the hell? Did he intend to *roast* her?

Then he attacked.

A blanket smothered her head, the full weight of his body pressing her to the ground. She rolled, kicking and screaming, as he tried to anchor the blanket around her arms. She wrenched one arm out of the blanket, grabbed a handful of horse-like hair and yanked hard. He grunted as his head jerked back, and she scrambled to her feet.

An iron fist caught her arm and twisted, sent her screaming to her knees. His hand smashed across her cheekbone. She sprawled, sparks exploding behind her eyes. Again he lunged and she rolled away, her head ringing, hands searching for a weapon. She came to her knees holding a stick of firewood and swung out blindly.

The stick struck his outstretched arm and broke apart. He yelled and recoiled, and in that instant she was on her feet, running.

Whippoorwill's whinny shredded the night. He was too far away. She'd never make it to him. She ran instead toward the outhouse half hidden in the trees. Crouching behind it in the shadows where the firelight didn't reach, she listened for his steps. A weapon—she had to have a weapon. Her hands searched the weeds around her but found no tree limb, no stray board, nothing. She thought of her shoestring but there wasn't time. He was coming. Then, by the footing of the outhouse, she found a crumbled chunk of concrete the size of an egg. She clutched the rock, her back against the curling boards, and held her breath.

His steps drew nearer, slowly. He knew where she was and was deciding how to approach. *Come this way, you old bastard. Show me your face.* She gripped the rock like a baseball, a sharp edge digging into her palm. As a kid she'd thrown rocks to knock down wasps' nests below the eaves of the shed. She drew back her arm and prayed her aim was still true.

When he sprang, he was too close. She couldn't throw. She gouged at his face but he caught her arm and swung her to the ground. She twisted loose and ran blindly, hearing his rough breath behind her as he stumbled and fell.

She hit the bottom step to the shack and leaped through the open door, slamming it behind her. There was no lock. She pressed her back against the door.

The interior was dark and smelled of urine. In one corner, a light-colored ghost gyrated and squealed. Her breath sucked in. The sound was muffled—but definitely feminine. Chantalene squinted at the shape.

"Thelma?"

She grabbed the sheet and yanked it away. Thelma was tied to a chair, tipped over sideways on the floor. Her eyes were wide with terror, but she was doing her best to yell something past the gag tied around her face. Chantalene jerked the scarf from her mouth.

"His shotgun," Thelma croaked. "By the window!"

Chantalene saw a thin shape propped against the wall. She grabbed it as Songdog burst through the door, waving a flaming branch that illuminated the room.

He lifted the torch—but stopped when he saw she had the shotgun. Ghostlike shadows danced on the walls.

She leveled the double barrel at his chest. "Stop! I'll blow your head off!"

Her fingers found both triggers, no hammer.

Please God, let this thing be loaded.

Firelight carved a horrible mask of Songdog's face. His arm drew back slowly, slowly, madness glittering in his eyes.

He launched the torch like a cannon shot, howling.

Thelma screamed.

Chantalene fired.

THIRTY-ONE

IN THE TWO-room cabin, the explosion of the shotgun hit Chantalene like a fist, knocking her backwards into the wall. In the same instant, she saw her attacker lifted from his feet, his shirtfront splattered red.

Songdog Jones sprawled in the open doorway of the cabin and lay still.

The shotgun fell from her hands, weirdly silent to her stunned ears. She slid to the floor, her eyes fixed on the old man's body. *I killed him. I shot a human being.*

When the echo of the gunshot subsided, she heard Thelma screaming.

"Chantalene! The curtains are on fire!"

Flames from the hermit's torch crawled up the faded curtains and licked at the ceiling above her head. Chantalene rolled away and scrambled toward Thelma, who lay on her side, her hands tied behind the fallen chair, her head pressed awkwardly to the floor. Chantalene tried to right the chair, but Thelma flinched with pain. She gave it up and checked the twine that cut into Thelma's wrists and ankles. No time to untie, and it was too strong to break. She ran to the kitchen sink and grabbed a paring knife from the drainboard.

Smoke snaked across the ceiling as she sawed at the twine. A chunk of fire fell past her head and lit near Thelma's shirt. Chantalene pounded it out with the wadded sheet, but more debris rained around them. She grabbed the knife, slid it between Thelma's swollen wrists and the twine, and pulled up hard.

Finally the thin rope split. Together they slid the ropes off the chair legs, leaving them to hang around her ankles. A beam cracked overhead and they ducked at the sound. Chantalene pulled Thelma to her feet, but when she tried to walk, one of her ankles gave way. Chantalene ducked under Thelma's arm and supported her as they stumbled toward the door, crouching below the thickening smoke.

The flames had spread with amazing speed, engulfing two walls and the ceiling. Heat pressed down like a steam iron.

Songdog's body lay splayed in their path. What if he was still alive?

One look at his chest convinced her otherwise. Chantalene yelled above the hissing of the fire. "Don't look at him. Just go!"

In unison they stepped over his torso and leaned toward the door where fresh air rushed in.

Something jerked them back and Thelma screamed. "My leg!"

Her weight sagged and Chantalene's grip gave way. They staggered and fell in a heap across Songdog's body.

Thelma shrieked. "He has my leg! My leg!"

Through the smoke and sweat in her eyes Chantalene saw his claw-like hand outstretched. But the old Indian's eyes were closed, his jaw slack. "No! The twine on your foot is caught on his hand."

Thelma yanked harder, screeching, jerking his arm and tangling the twine even more.

"Stop it! Hold still so I can get you loose!"

Thelma obeyed. Her scream faded to a wail while Chantalene knelt to untangle the rope from the dead fingers.

"You're loose! Go!"

On hands and knees they crawled out the door and down the concrete-block step.

Cool air washed their faces. The night was alive with flickering firelight, Songdog's bonfire dwarfed by the burning cabin. Chantalene pulled Thelma away from the house, where they sank to the ground, coughing.

Flames shot through the doorway of the shack and licked through the dry timber of the roof. In minutes, the whole structure foamed like a roasting marshmallow.

Chantalene could still see the hermit lying in the doorway. Could they ever prove who he was? She got to her knees, debating.

Thelma laid a firm hand on her arm. "Don't try it. Let him burn."

It was a good decision. Within seconds the cabin imploded. Sparks shot into the night sky, but no one else was likely to see the fire's light. They were miles from town.

If not for the recent rains, the whole pasture might have burned. They watched in silence, mesmerized like aboriginal tribesmen at their first sight of fire, until the smell of burning flesh drove them farther into the darkness. Slowly the volume of flames began to shrink and Chantalene remembered the cell phone she'd dropped in the front yard.

She found it in the dust, still turned on, the battery dead.

From the shadows of the orchard, Whippoorwill whinnied. She walked into the cool night, stepping over fallen branches, and found Whip jittering beside a pear tree in full bloom. She spoke to him softly.

"Good horse. I can't believe you aren't miles away and still running." She approached the spooked horse slowly, caught his reins and stroked his smooth muzzle. Whip snuffled and tossed his head, still wary of the fire. "It's over now. Easy does it." She secured his reins around a branch.

A battered pickup truck hunched in the weedy shadows behind the house. She circled towards it, giving a wide berth to the wall of heat still emanating from the dying fire. The truck was dented and spotted with rust, the passenger-side window devoid of glass. Inside the musty smelling cab, a rabbit's foot key chain dangled from the ignition.

Chantalene walked the tire-track path around the cabin, back to where she'd left Thelma. She sat cross-legged on the ground beside her, facing the fire. Low flames crawled along fallen beams that cross-hatched the glowing mound of debris.

Thelma sat with her back straight, her eyes focused on the burned-out cabin. Mulberry-colored bruises stained her cheekbone and jaw, and firelight aureoled the thin hair frizzed out around her head. With her face draped in shadows, Thelma looked twice her age, a crone from a fairy tale.

"You okay?" Chantalene said.

"I am now."

"Can you drive a stick shift?"

"I could drive a Sherman tank if it would get us home."

Chantalene rode in the cab beside Thelma with her arm out the glassless window, holding Whippoorwill's reins. Pre-dawn light streaked the sky with magenta as the trio rolled the three miles toward Thelma's house at funeral-procession pace. They didn't talk. The countryside was silent except for the slow crunch of tires on shale, and a chorus of crickets in the roadside grass.

A split in the plastic seat cover pinched Chantalene's leg. Beyond the bug-spattered windshield, she saw the old man's body flying backwards, a blossom of red imprinted on his chest. Over and over, like a radar loop. She closed her eyes but it didn't stop.

She had killed a man.

And she didn't even regret it.

Everything inside of her had gone numb. *Don't over-think it. If you hadn't shot him, he'd have killed you and Thelma, too.*

Thelma's farmhouse appeared from the semi-darkness, and Chantalene saw a cluster of vehicles beneath the sentry light near the barn. Thelma saw them, too—three police cars, a rescue unit and an unmarked pickup, nosed together like marble-shooters in a schoolyard. Thelma turned the old truck slowly into the driveway, with the dappled gelding clopping alongside, just as the sun breached the horizon and the sentry light winked off.

The lawmen standing near the cars looked up in open-mouthed silence at the weird tableau appearing out of the dawn. Even the crickets were silent as they rolled to a stop and Thelma cut the engine.

One of the men was wearing red suspenders. Chantalene heard a familiar, gravelly voice.

"Holy jalapeños. Will you look at this."

Retired Chief Watson Wilson swept off his wide-brimmed hat and held it over his heart.

THIRTY-TWO

SUNNY RAY PATTERSON Diehl sat at Thelma's kitchen table and took her coffee black. She lit her cigarette with a see-through lighter filled with tiny, plastic seahorses.

"You were right," she told Thelma through a stream of smoke. "He wasn't your husband. But he was Billy Ray. You were married to Donnie Ray."

Chantalene saw Sunny's eyes shift again toward the brass urn that sat on the sideboard along with Sheriff Justin's ten-gallon hat. The funeral home had presented Billy Ray's ashes to Thelma, as the deceased's wife, but Thelma agreed to release his remains to the surviving sister.

Sunny nodded toward Watson Wilson, seated beside Thelma at the table. "The Chief here had it figured out by the time he located me."

"The print on Thelma's letter didn't match the ones from San Juan prison," Watson said. He tactfully didn't mention the bloody prints Chantalene had taken from the cowboy. Sheriff Justin would never have to know. But those prints did prove the cowboy's prison time and also convinced Watson that the brothers had switched identities.

"So I was married to an imposter from the beginning," Thelma said. Her freckled hands lay motionless on the table beside her coffee mug, red rope burns braceleting her wrists.

Sunny Ray's eyes looked as if they'd seen everything humans could do and forgiven it. "Only in name, honey. Donnie Ray really loved you. That's why he lit out so fast and never told you about the bingo hall money. He was scared the Kingman family would come after you if they found out there was any connection."

Sunny Ray's face was thin and weathered, the resemblance to her handsome brothers faded by the years. She worked as a hair stylist in Tulsa, and her honey-blonde color concealed most of the gray. Chantalene handed her a saucer for an ash tray and opened the kitchen door for ventilation. Nobody here was going to deny the surviving sister her smokes.

Sunlight and the scent of lilacs drifted through the screen. Chantalene sat at the table with her tea bag and mug of hot water and listened to Sunny Ray's low-pitched, sandy voice. The kind of voice with stories to tell.

"The summer you met Donnie," Sunny Ray said, "he'd run off and joined that combine crew to avoid a scrape with the law. And he lifted Billy Ray's ID to take with him, just in case. It was no big deal to Billy. They used to trade ID's all the time, just for a prank. But once Donnie told you he was Billy Ray and married you under that name, he didn't see how he could change his story without getting in a bunch more trouble." She shook her head. "Donnie was a sweet kid, but he was a little short on logic."

Chantalene dangled her tea bag in the hot water and watched its color deepen. Late yesterday, she had watched while a crime scene team recovered the charred body of Oswald "Songdog" Jones. They'd also removed the bones of Lydia Sue Raintree from the cistern, and a canvas bag filled with bricks of dirty money. Her senses—along with her muscles, her eyeballs, her skin—felt strafed.

She glanced at Thelma, whose chin was lifted, her eyes clear behind the bruises. Watson Wilson was watching her, too, with open admiration.

"Donnie was killed in that car wreck in New Mexico," Sheriff Justin said.

Sunny Ray nodded. "I didn't find out about it for a long time. Finally Billy Ray called me from California, and he was really messed up about Donnie's death. But prison sobered him up and he came out changed. When he took to cowboying, he'd send me a card every so often to let me know where he was. So when somebody started asking around Tulsa for him, I let him know."

She took another long drag on the cigarette and tactfully aimed her exhale at the ceiling. "The day before he came here, he stopped by my house and we sat up half the night talking. Those lonely months on the range, Billy spent a lot of time remembering the stories Donnie had told him about Thelma and the farm, and their life together in Tetumka." She smiled, smoke trailing up from her fingers. "Donnie had described everything in Tetumka to the finest detail. Every neighbor and all the livestock. Billy said he liked the happiness in Donnie's voice when he talked. Pretty soon Billy'd memorized all those people and places as if he'd been there himself. All over Nevada, Montana and Wyoming, he thought about that farm in Tetumka that had his name on the deed as joint owner. But he never intended to come here. Not until I wrote that Thelma's lawyer had been looking for him."

Chantalene thought of Billy Ray's lonely years on the range dreaming somebody else's dream and of Thelma's lost hopes for a family. A sudden image of lazy, pajamaed mornings spent with Drew at his kitchen table popped up in her mind. She wondered if he was having breakfast with Emily in New York today, and her breath caught in her chest.

Maybe she was destined to be alone, like Thelma and Billy Ray.

Sunny touched the lipstick stain on her cup with a white fingernail. "I wish now I'd never told him. We both thought Thelma might have passed away and left him the farm. He never even thought about the bingo money. He figured Songdog had got that and spent it years ago."

"Until Henry Carl Hill showed up," Watson said.

"Right. The last time Billy Ray phoned me, he said somebody was still looking for the money, and he thought it might be hidden on Thelma's farm. He knew Donnie and Songdog had buried it under a pear tree somewhere. He hadn't located it yet, but I think he was looking."

"Songdog must have recognized him before he figured it out," Chantalene said.

Sheriff Justin shook his head. "It was Hill that killed Patterson, not Jones."

"It was Hill, all right." Thelma's face turned hard. "He bragged about it. But he made the mistake of going out for cigarettes, and the old hermit was waiting outside the door. He grabbed Hill from behind and dragged him back into the room and snapped his neck like a matchstick. Never said a word. I didn't know if he was going to rescue me or kill me."

Watson Wilson patted Thelma's hand on the table.

"But who was Lydia Sue Raintree?" Chantalene asked. "And how did she end up in that cistern?" All night long she had dreamed the smell of stale earth and wrestled dark fingers that squeezed the air from her lungs. She hoped Liddy was already dead when she was dumped in there.

"Lydia Sue was the gal who hooked up with Songdog Jones after the bingo robbery," Sheriff Justin said. "Her mother posted those flyers about ten years ago when her common-law husband left and she got a guilty conscience about her runaway daughter. She had heard the girl was around here somewhere. Apparently the two of them lived with Songdog when Lydia was small, but he wasn't her father."

Sunny Ray lit up again, the tiny seahorses rocking in their combustible sea. She expelled smoke and turned the lighter end over end in her hand. "I'll bet she didn't show up at that El Paso truck stop by accident, and she was in on the robbery from the beginning."

"We'll never know that for sure," Watson said. "But I'd lay odds she got tired of her older man and planned to take off with the money. That's what got her killed and pitched in the cistern."

Sheriff Justin nodded. "The mother died a couple years ago, so at least she won't have to know what happened to her daughter."

"So," Thelma said, and heaved a sigh. "My husband wasn't who I thought he was, there was no oil company interested in leasing my land, and the old hermit I felt sorry for was a murderer. I feel like the world's biggest jughead."

"Good-hearted people have a hard time predicting the bad motives of others," Chief Wilson said, his leathery brow creasing. "You don't have a thing to regret."

Thelma looked wistful. "Anybody our age has some regrets, I imagine. But if I had to live it over, I'd probably do the same darned things."

Chief Wilson grinned. "Good for you."

That was all the warm-fuzzy Sheriff Justin could stand. His chair scraped backwards. "Ms. Diehl, are we ready to go?" The sheriff had brought her out from El Rio, where Sunny had left her car.

"Almost." Sunny took a last swallow of coffee and pushed the mug away. "There's one more thing. Out in California, Billy got a young woman pregnant, a waitress at one of the clubs where he drank and shot pool. About a year after he got sent up, the gal showed up at my house with a baby in her arms. She was crying, said she couldn't look after a baby, that she wasn't a fit mother. Before I knew it, I was holding the baby and she was gone."

Thelma's mouth dropped open. "You raised his child?"

"I had a little boy and girl of my own, so I just raised them all together." Sunny stubbed out her cigarette. "I never told Billy Ray that Anna was his daughter. It was selfish, maybe, but I figured they were both better off. I'd been cleaning up after my brothers for twenty years, and I was sick of it. Anna Lee thinks she's adopted."

"Anna Lee," Thelma said.

"She's twenty-six now. Fine young woman. She got married a few years ago, and she's expecting a baby in July. Maybe you'd like to meet her."

"Good heavens," Thelma said, and wiped her eyes. "I'm going to need some more yarn."

Sunny Ray dug in a faux reptile handbag and came out with a slightly worn business card and a pen. She wrote something on the back and placed the card on the table in front of Thelma. "My home number's on the back. You come up to Tulsa any time and I'll do your hair for free."

"I just might take you up on that. I'll bring Chantalene with me."

Sunny Ray winked at Thelma. "Please do. I'd love to get my hands on that head of hair."

"Hey!" Chantalene said. "This look scares the vandals away from my house on Halloween."

Sunny and the sheriff stood up but Chief Wilson motioned Thelma to stay seated. "You better stay off that sprained ankle," he said. "I'll see them out."

Sunny Ray picked up the urn that held her brother's ashes and cradled it in both arms as they filed through the living room to Thelma's front door. Chantalene followed, trying to imagine what it would be like to have a brother, let alone lose two of them to violent death. It had to feel damned lonely.

She stood with Chief Wilson on the porch while the sheriff's car drove away, Sunny Ray riding shotgun with Billy Ray on her lap. The blue morning was cloudless with just enough breeze to stir Thelma's collection of windchimes suspended from the porch beams. They watched the county car recede toward the horizon, thinking their own long thoughts. In the hours since she'd escaped from the certain knowledge of death, the world had changed, in ways both larger and smaller than the simple advent of spring.

"I guess you'll be heading back to New Mexico," Chantalene said.

"Probably so." Watson studied the white chickens scattered around the farmyard looking for bugs. "Unless I could be of some use in helping Thelma clear things up around here."

Chantalene smiled. Maybe one good thing would come out of all this yet.

An approaching vehicle slowed and turned into Thelma's driveway. Chantalene made an involuntary sound that caused Watson to look at her, then at the red pickup as it parked by the gate.

"Is something wrong?"

"It's Drew," she whispered, her eyes riveted to the truck. "I thought he was in New York."

Watson glanced at her face again. "I'll go inside and check on Thelma," he said, but she was already off the porch.

THIRTY-THREE

SHE DIDN'T ASK questions. Not now.

Drew flinched when he saw her swollen eye and bruised cheek, but she didn't give him time for questions, either. She hugged him until her sore shoulder hurt, unashamed of the moisture that came to her eyes when she felt him hugging back.

"Drive me home?"

"Your place or mine?"

Thelma and Watson came out of the house, Thelma leaning on Watson's arm while she hobbled to the porch swing.

"Hey, Drew," Thelma called. "About time my lawyer showed up."

Chantalene made introductions, and Watson eyed Drew with an assessing look worthy of any grandfather. Then they said goodbye, leaving Whippoorwill to graze contentedly on fresh rye grass in Thelma's barnyard. Chantalene could ride him home tomorrow.

Drew rolled down the windows and let the April morning whip around them. He rested his hand over hers on the seat.

Bones hopped and wagged at first sight of them. It felt so normal, driving up with Drew to the house where she was born, where the rooms held familiar things and her dog was glad to see her. The simple good fortune of it nearly blinded her.

Drew helped her out on his side of the cab and left the door standing open and the seat-belt bell pinging. He held her, stroked her hair, touched the bruise on her cheek. Beneath the gentleness she felt something fierce in the set of his spine. A lump the size of Dallas massed in her chest, partly relief that Drew was home, partly fatigue, partly gratitude for being safe again.

His voice by her ear made her shiver. "I'm sorry I left. I should have been here."

Yes, you should have.

But she didn't say it, because nobody could have predicted her encounter with a madman. Not her, and certainly not Drew. On the phone, she hadn't told him about Hill's note or his threatening call. She hadn't even told him about the missing items from her house, or her suspicion that she was being stalked. The many ways she had shut him out illuminated in her mind like tiny explosions. She began to understand how much that had hurt him. Except for his farm, it was a wonder he'd come back from New York at all.

She didn't say that either, just enjoyed the comfort of his familiar body against her. *That's the problem, you dummy. You're not saying any of it. You're shutting him out again.*

"Come inside," she said. "Let's get something to drink, and I'll tell you about it—" though the prospect of describing her ordeal scared the hell out of her, resurrecting the panic of those awful hours, "—and you tell me about New York."

She made coffee and poured two mugs. Drew accepted his cup and frowned at hers. "You don't like coffee."

"I'm going to learn."

They sat in the wooden rocking chairs on her front porch with Bones between them. Chantalene massaged the dog's neck and savored the feel of smooth fur slipping through her fingers.

She started from the beginning. She told him about the stalking incidents, waking to the strange odor in the house, how she'd thought she might be imagining things and had simply lost the missing items until she found the window left open in the spare bedroom. She told him about Billy Ray and Donnie Ray switching identities, some of which he already knew because he'd called Deputy Bobby Ethridge when he couldn't reach her by phone. She told him about Sunny Ray Patterson Diehl coming for her brother's ashes.

Then she told him about Songdog Jones, his madness, how he'd cast her into the cistern and let her climb back out again and how she'd fought him, about the cabin fire and Thelma's bruised face and finding the bones of Lydia Sue Raintree and the money.

She could talk about those things, because they were past.

What wasn't past was her abject terror in that earthen grave, when she knew for certain she was going to die and she had wept and wet herself and felt the fist of her sanity releasing its grip one finger at a time. The terror and humiliation of those hours was a living thing that loomed huge and dark at the edge of consciousness, breaking loose from its fragile tethers when she slept. She had no words to explain that terror, or the ways it had changed her. It would be a long time before she could talk about that if she ever could.

Drew listened, his gaze narrowed and far away. He let her talk without asking questions, though she could sense the tension in his body. Perhaps he understood something of the things she couldn't say.

The sun arched westward and the shadow of the porch roof slowly reached out and covered their feet. Chantalene blew her nose and shifted her thoughts to safer ground.

"I don't envy Sheriff Justin when he notifies the Kingman family about Henry Carl Hill."

"Hill seemed to be the black sheep. Maybe they won't care," Drew said.

"Will the sheriff have to give the stolen money back to them?"

Drew shrugged. "How could they prove it was theirs? It'll probably end up in the indigent defense fund."

A good place for it. In memory of lost souls like Lydia Sue.

They rocked slowly, their heads leaned back against the chairs. Bones had melted into a heap on the porch floor, snoring softly with each breath. Chantalene melted, too, fatigue heavy in her limbs. Maybe she'd just sit here forever, never move, never make another decision.

Fat chance.

"Your turn," she said finally. "Are you moving back to New York?"

He turned his face toward her and held her gaze for several beats before he answered. "I will if you want to go."

"*Me?*"

"William Bratten—he's chairman of the board for Emily's dad's company—made me an unbelievable job offer. We could get a nice apartment and live quite comfortably. See everything there is to see in the Big Apple."

She stopped rocking and frowned at him. "Do you want this job?"

He shrugged, looking out across the spiky asparagus field and Whippoorwill's empty corral. "I could live with it. I told William no, but then I got to thinking maybe this is the answer for us. At least for a year or two."

"But do you *want* this job? Do you really want to live back in New York?"

"I asked you first."

She shook her head and went back to rocking. "What about Emily?"

"What about her?"

"Is she the real reason you made the trip?"

He pulled an envelope from his shirt pocket and handed it to her. "I went for two reasons, and neither of them was Emily."

She opened the letter from William Bratten and read it silently. "Wow," she said softly. "That is quite an offer."

"What he doesn't say is that he's dying of cancer. Emily told me that. I have a lot of respect for William, even when we don't agree on things. I consider him a friend. And I don't have many."

Chantalene had thought about that before. She wasn't the only one with no friends her age except for Drew. Very few young people lived in Tetumka.

"What was your other reason?"

"That application you'd filled out for a museum internship in New Mexico this fall."

She'd forgotten about the internship. It was another of those things she had put off talking to Drew about.

"If you're moving on without me, I don't know that I could stay here."

"What about your farm?"

"There's not much to do now until the first of June when the wheat's ready to harvest, and I'll hire custom cutters. Next season I could rent the land. I can't picture selling the place, but as I told William, farming's not as noble as I remembered it. And it's a hell of a lot less profitable."

He'd never expressed any doubts about his farming operation before, and she found this unsettling. Drew was supposed to be unchanging. She counted on his constancy while her own ideas bounced all over the place.

"All things being equal," she said, "which means leaving other people out of the picture, would you be happier here, farming and practicing small-time law, or in the City with a challenging job and plenty of money?"

He rolled his head against the chair back. "Flawed question. All things are not equal, other people being you."

Chantalene closed her eyes and pictured the two of them in a Manhattan apartment, among the sights and sounds and smells of the fabled city. All she knew of New York was what she'd read in travel magazines or seen on Drew's TV—the Statue of Liberty, Central Park, Ground Zero. All that water, all those people. She'd love to see it in person. But whenever she'd yearned to live somewhere else, she always had pictured going west, where there was lots of space and she understood the people.

The job would undoubtedly require long hours for Drew. She tried to picture herself negotiating the crowded streets alone, attending the theater, maybe, or shopping on Fifth Avenue. What in the world would she wear?

She felt a canyon of buildings rise around her, the sky no more than a window of light above her head, and her chest tightened. How could she breathe? What if somebody covered the window?

She realized she was sweating.

Calm down. A city is not a dungeon with no way out.

"Anyway, you turned down the job." *No decisions, please. Not right now.*

"Not exactly. He gave me two weeks to think it over," Drew said.

Could she pull the fragments of herself together in two weeks? There was the internship, which she hadn't really considered or explored, and her college degree, so close to completion. There was the trip to see Gamma Rose. And what about Whippoorwill and Bones?

She'd said she wanted out of Tetumka. Was it just a bluff?

Stop.

In the pit of that cistern she'd learned some things, and chief among them was the absurdity of worrying about the future.

She closed her eyes and extended her bare toes into the sunlight, inhaling and exhaling until her pulse slowed. Right now she was sitting on her porch in the fragrance of spring, with her lazy dog at her feet and her best friend beside her, a man that she loved. Her heart expanded with the rightness of it.

This is it. Just today.

She smiled, her eyes still closed. "I can't think about that today, Rhett," she said in her best southern drawl. "Let's think about it tomorrow."

Drew's hand found hers and he resumed his rocking.

"No problem."

MARCIA PRESTON writes mysteries and women's literary fiction. Her second mystery, *Song of the Bones,* won the Mary Higgins Clark Award for suspense fiction and the Oklahoma Book Award. She lives beside a creek in central Oklahoma, where she feeds the birds and dodges tornadoes.

Printed in the USA
CPSIA information can be obtained
at www.ICGtesting.com
JSHW082337210823
46965JS00001B/43